ANIMAL ASSASSIN

The strange, bittern-like bird was there again, its beak thrusting into the shadows above its head, its small eyes, like beads of sparkling ebony, blinking in the morning light. Its course carried the creature low over the lawn, so close that Emily could feel small gusts of breeze from its heavy, straining wings. Again the bird circled. Alarmed, she moved to one side. The bird's orbit shifted to remain centered on her—and then, with a raucous shriek, it dove straight for Emily, its beak an out-thrust dagger. . . .

SPARROWHAWK

"SPARROWHAWK moves right along as a twisty police-procedural mystery. Characters have breadth and depth; you care about them."

—*OtherRealms*

SPARROWHAWK

THOMAS A. EASTON

ACE BOOKS, NEW YORK

A shorter version of this book was serialized in *Analog*,
October–December 1989, copyright © 1989 by *Analog*.

SPARROWHAWK

An Ace Book/published by arrangement with
the author

PRINTING HISTORY
Ace edition/October 1990

ISBN: 0-441-77778-3

Ace Books are published by the Berkley Publishing Group,
200 Madison Avenue, New York, New York 10016.
The name "ACE" and the "A" logo
are trademarks belonging to Charter Communications, Inc.

PRINTED IN THE UNITED STATES OF AMERICA

10 9 8 7 6 5 4 3 2 1

For Larry Haley and
the Lantana Gang

SPARROWHAWK

Chapter
One

FIVE-YEAR-OLD ANDY GILMAN, towheaded and gap-toothed, was kneeling on a chair by the kitchen window. Half a dozen plastic Warbirds were scattered on the floor beneath him. With the tip of one finger, he was writing his name in the large smudge his nose had left on the glass. Suddenly he stiffened and pointed beyond the pane. "Look, Daddy!" he cried. "See the bird! By the feeder! A big one!"

Nick Gilman grinned and crossed the room in a stride. He looked, and the kid was right. A Chickadee, the size of an old-fashioned Piper Cub, was on the lawn beside the back porch. It wasn't wearing its two-seater passenger or engine pods. As Nick watched, it cocked its head to one side, inserted its beak between the shelf and the overhanging roof of the feeder, and seized a mouthful of seeds. Then, shaking its head as if the treat had been more effort than it was worth, it stepped back a pace.

As it did so, nongineered birds of more normal size approached to try to reach the seeds remaining in the feeder. Few succeeded, for as they fluttered past the Chickadee, they fell prey instead to its darting beak. Nick shuddered, remembering when all chickadees had been vegetarians. "C'mon, Andy. We're in a rush. Gotta go get Mommy."

"But, Daddy! I wanna watch!"

Nick had no time for nonsense. Emily's jet would be late, of course, but it was due in an hour, and he had to be there just in case she was on time or—God forbid!—early. He should have left ten minutes before, but the casserole had needed its finishing touches and he had had to adjust the oven

and he had had to run a comb through his hair and he had
had to straighten the throw rug that had slid beneath his feet
and . . . It wasn't easy being a househusband.

The radio began to mutter that, on this hot and muggy
Tuesday in July of 2044, terrorist attacks were becoming more
frequent, but he had no time to listen. Nor did he care to
think of what such a thing might mean for Emily, or him, or
their towheaded son. He turned it off and grabbed his jacket.
Then he picked the boy up in his arms, wiped the snot from
his nose with a handkerchief, and rushed from the room.

Emily was a high-bracket gengineer, she would be back
soon from her trip—she had flown to Washington on Sunday
to testify before a patent board on Monday—he loved her
dearly, and he didn't want to leave her waiting. Sometimes
he wished their roles were reversed, with him the one wandering the world on high adventures and she the one at home
in their small, old-fashioned brick house. But his doctorate
had been in Romantic Poets, there were fewer new college
students than ever, few colleges were hiring young faculty,
and his attempts at selling his own poems and short stories
had earned him the grand total of $79.85. He could have
bought a pair of shoes. Cheap ones.

Nick had opened the garage door that morning and led the
Tortoise out for relief from the heat. Now the family vehicle
was waiting in the drive, shaded by nearby trees. Nick had
bought it when he was in college and single. It had been
young then, with the passenger compartment in the shell just
big enough, in a squeeze, for two. And he had squeezed more
than one girl in it, he had, until he had found Emily and
grown up a bit. As advertised, the Tortoise had grown too,
maturing from the sportscar stage to coupe. Eventually, timed
by gengineers like Emily to match a family's growth, it would
gain the capacity of a station wagon.

The Tortoise didn't look like a tortoise. Its chief ancestor
had been a lean, low terrapin. The gengineers had given it
size and speed, and a cavity beneath the shell. The General
Bodies shops had fitted a windshield, side windows, and
doors, installed plush seats, added headlights and taillights,
and wired the controls into the Tortoise's nervous system. At

periodic checkups, they added new fittings and enlarged or refitted the old to keep pace with the creature's growth.

Roachsters, half cockroach and half lobster; Hoppers, derived from grasshoppers; and other Buggies could keep pace with a family's needs just as well. But Nick preferred the more classic lines of the Tortoise. Its shape reminded him of the gas-burners his parents had driven when he had been a child, when the Machine Age had still been vigorous. The oil that had made that Age possible had been on the verge of exhaustion, and most liquid fuels were being produced—expensively—from coal. But people had not yet recognized that new forms of technology were essential if civilization were to continue, nor that the replacement technology was already taking shape. The Biological Revolution had by then been fermenting in the world's laboratories for decades, and the gengineers had been on the verge of long-sought success.

As Nick and Andy left the house, the Tortoise's barrellike head turned toward them. The legs on the side facing the house flexed, Nick stepped onto the offered lip of shell, resembling an old-time running board, and opened the door. Andy scooted across the bucket seats to let his father take his position behind the tiller.

Even before the door clicked into its frame, the Tortoise's knees were rising and falling, pistonlike, in Nick's peripheral vision. He steered it onto the greenway that had long since replaced paved streets in his suburb, guided it toward the expressway on-ramp, and accelerated. The Tortoise's knees became a blur, its breathing an audible gale of wind.

The expressway itself was still paved. The Public Works Department kept promising to have it grassed, for almost all vehicles were now bioforms, or genimals. But public money was as short as ever, and the Biological Revolution was still new. Many residential neighborhoods, unlike Nick's, also still had paved streets. Only a few neighborhoods had yet gone to modern bioform houses, gengineered from pumpkins, squash, beanstalks, eggplants, and even more exotic stock.

Air transportation was somewhat more advanced. As Nick and Andy neared the airport, they passed a zone of bedraggled hangars and paved runways. Airplanes—Comanches, Beechcrafts, Boeings—stood about in varying states of deshabille. A few showed the faded, painted-over logos of major airlines. Most wore nothing but their serial numbers.

"What's that, Daddy? Jets?" To him, the gengineered birds were the normal technology. These were strange variants, stiff and featherless, emblems of a realm set askew from the world he knew, but oddly reminiscent of it.

"Obsolete junkers, Andy." The traffic had been light, they would be there in plenty of time, and Nick had relaxed. He spared a glance for the display beside the expressway. "Real airplanes. They used to carry people. Now it's just cargo." Many, the papers said, carried contraband—guns, illegal immigrants, fugitives from the law, laundered money—across the border. Many more carried banned bioforms such as cannibal grass, or cheap bootleg copies of glow-in-the-dark philodendrons and goldfish bushes.

Their Tortoise sped them past another airport zone. The runways were still paved, but the hangars were in better shape and the planes wore shiny coats of paint. "Hobbyists," said Nick. "Weekend flyers." One of the planes was a bulb-nosed giant, towering above all the others. On its tail was a stylized rabbit head.

"How do they fly?"

"They have engines, just like the jets. On the wings." He pointed. "And propeller engines, in the nose. And see the windows up front?" When Andy nodded, Nick added, "People drive them, like the old-time cars." He paused. "I took a few lessons once. On a small one."

The terminal loomed ahead, all glass and steel and concrete, with mown grass beyond. The control tower held a faceted ball above everything. Nick fantasized some Paul Bunyan of a golfer poised to send that ball down the green runways. He pointed and said, "Fore!" Andy giggled.

There was a parking barn whose attendants would feed and water vehicles for weeks at a time, while, the rumors went, breeding strange, illicit hybrids. Nick avoided it, searching for and finding a space in an open lot nearer their destination. Once in the air-conditioned terminal, he checked a board to find that Emily's flight would, as he had expected, be a few minutes late. Then, at Andy's insistence, they took the escalator to the observation deck.

He let Andy lead him, running, to the edge of the deck. He braced himself against the warm wind, wished that they had stayed inside and cool, peered into the sky looking for his wife, and listened to the airport noises. The boy chinned himself on the railing, imitated his father's searching gaze, and pointed into the distance.

A flight was coming in above the ranks of trees that filled in the middle distance beyond the runways. The trees had been gengineered from a tropical species to stand more northern climates. Their diesel-fuellike sap provided the fuel needed for the engines of jets and the few other powered vehicles civilization still used.

The approaching jet was still too far away to show any detail, but they could make out the distinctive curve of the extended wings, the elevated, horizontal tail without an upright, the rounded bulge of the forepart. It came closer, and they could see the two engines mounted just in front of the tail, the fuel tanks, the passenger pod strapped to the back. Still closer, and the slate-grey upper surfaces separated from the lighter underside.

Andy cried, "That's a Junco 47!" He had a plastic model of the huge genimal hanging from the ceiling of his room at home. Perhaps inevitably, the model had a more mechanical appearance than the real thing. So had the models of bombers and airliners and space shuttles that had decorated Nick's childhood bedroom.

The Junco extended its feet and cupped its wings. Now Nick could make out the China Airlines logo on the side of one fuel tank. The gengineers had triumphed with the airliners, he thought. Birds, ordinary birds, had been redesigned to such extremes of size that they could no longer fly on their own. The biggest, like the Junco, even needed metal-composite implants to strengthen their skeletons. Only the smallest, like that Chickadee at home, could get into the air without their jet engines and fuel tanks, and even they needed help when they were carrying passengers or freight. Still,

Nick knew, larger creatures had once flown entirely under their own power. Periodically, the press reminded the public that millions of years ago, in the age of dinosaurs, there had been a pteranodon the size of an Air Force fighter.

Emily had told him why the gengineers had bothered. Jets like the Junco needed much less in the way of the metals that cost so much to mine and process. They were more efficient and safer as well. Though they could not normally fly on their own, in emergencies they could manage a few flaps of their wings. They could control their machine-powered flight, and they needed very short runways. They were also self-building, once the gengineers were done with the design work, and self-repairing.

The landing was smooth. Nick followed Andy's pointing finger to the side, where an Alitalia Cardinal, free for the moment of its passenger pod and engines, preened its plumage. Bright red feathers littered the grass around it, most of them too big to blow in the wind.

Nearby were an American Bald Eagle, a Canadian Pacific Snow Goose, and a British Caledonian Chimney Swift, its morning-coat tails recalling the formalities of another age. A fat-bodied Wild Turkey bore the Delta logo, and Nick remembered that that was the complimentary bourbon they served on board. He and Emily had flown Delta on their honeymoon. United, with its Lovebirds, had seemed too cute to appeal to them.

"What's that, Daddy?"

"That" was a metal box much like the trailer of an eighteen-wheel semi. As the Junco 47 approached the terminal, it converged on the same destination, drawn by a squat, heavy-muscled, squash-faced creature whose rootstock had clearly been a bulldog. Its top was covered by pleats of heavy fabric, and liquid dripped from its base onto the ground.

"Watch," said Nick. The Junco was in position. As the passenger tunnel snugged its mouth, lampreylike, against the jet's pod, the trailer drew under its nose. The ground crew turned cranks mounted on the trailer's ends, and the fabric rose on an internal frame to surround the Junco's head. The motions that promptly began to shake the fabric could not be misinterpreted. The jet's—the bird's—refueling was under way.

"What kind of seeds is it eating?" asked Andy. He had seen ordinary juncos on the ground beneath the bird feeder at home. He had even thrown out the sunflower seeds for them.

Nick shook his head. "Uh-uh," he said. "It's like the Chickadee. When they're this big, they have to eat meat." It was cheaper than any alternative, for it was obtained from worms and slugs gengineered to thrive on human wastes and garbage. They had been among the first of the large-scale bioforms to be developed when the gengineers had stepped beyond single-gene changes in bacteria, viruses, and plants.

"See the litterbugs?" he added. The rattle of cloven hooves reached them even on the observation deck as a trio of strange-looking creatures raced toward the liner's other end from the service bay that had disgorged the feed trailer. They vaguely resembled pigs, but their limbs were longer and their snouts were distorted into broad scoops. Smaller versions patrolled city streets, seeking out and devouring the leavings of other genimals. They did not neglect banana peels, paper scraps, and beverage containers.

They did not interest Andy. The boy glanced at them briefly, dismissed them as common, and looked skyward again. Nick chuckled quietly, thinking that someday the boy might see some small, wild bird release its wastes in flight. Perhaps he would wonder, then, about the airliners. They had, Nick knew, been gengineered to discharge their wastes while feeding. Many mammals—even humans—did it without the gengineering. It was, Emily had told him once, a simple "make-room" reflex.

Andy shouted. He was pointing toward the horizon once more. In a moment, they could identify a Northwest Albatross. Once the jet was on the ground, Nick took Andy by the hand and they headed for the gate.

Emily was the third person to come striding up the ramp from the plane, grinning, eyes scanning the small crowd for her family. A slender, dark-haired woman whose wide mouth often showed its teeth in a smile that would have done justice

to a veedo evangelist, she exuded alertness and energy. One
hand held in place on a shoulder a garment bag and a purse.
The other clutched a briefcase and a plastic bag from whose
top protruded a few green leaves.

Nick, grinning as broadly as she, took the garment bag.
She knelt then, to wrap her free arm around their son. "Ah,
Andy," she said. "You need to blow. And look what I've got
right here."

She opened the bag she carried to reveal a plant whose
dark green leaves alternated with white oblongs. One of the
latter she picked and held to Andy's nose. "Blow!" The boy
obliged, laughed, and cried, "A hanky bush!"

"Right!" She looked at her husband. "Something new.
They're working on more productive models for the bathroom
and kitchen."

"That should save a few trees," he said.

Her mouth twisted into a rueful grin, and she shook her
head. "It won't help the paper industry. But . . ."

She didn't need to tell him more. The technology was
changing. The gengineers had already changed the sewage
treatment, aircraft, highway, housing, and automobile indus-
tries beyond recognition. Now it was the turn of the pulp and
paper industry. Yet, in the nature of things, as old jobs vanished, new ones appeared. He did not believe what some
claimed, that the Biological Revolution would in time free
people entirely of the need to labor. He did believe that,
eventually, the labor market would stabilize and the unem-
ployment rate would fall. Then their taxes need not be so
high, and more of Emily's income could be theirs.

"Let's go," said Emily. "I want to put my feet up."

"How'd it go?" The patent hearing had concerned what
she hoped would be her company's latest product, a jellyfish
modified to inflate itself with hydrogen. It was the size of a
blimp, and its tentacles gave it a built-in cargo-handling system.

She shook her head as she stood. Andy seized her hand.
"I got some heavy interest from a van company. But no patent."

They were nearing a souvenir kiosk, and Andy was pointing at the jet feathers on display. "I wanta red one!"

Emily shrugged. "The Pentagon said they'd already grown some. Very few details."

Nick snorted and reached for his wallet. A moment later, Andy had his feather—longer than his father was tall—and their Tortoise was in sight.

The expressway never seemed so crowded as when they were on their way home. While Emily cuddled Andy and listened to him chatter about his two days alone with Daddy, Nick swore at the Roachsters and other Buggies that dawdled in front of their Tortoise, the Mack trucks that strained to keep their heavy trailers up to speed, the Hoppers that plunged past them into whatever gaps opened up in the flow of traffic, the occasional old-style automobile whose noise made the Tortoise lurch aside. It occurred to him that if he were just a little paranoid, it would be very easy to believe in some vast conspiracy of other drivers: They *knew* he was in a rush to get home, and every slowcoach, every lane-jumper, every flare of brake lights, was one more deliberate, intended effort to drive him nuts!

"Can I have a soda? Please?"

A small cooler was built into the dashboard, beside the map compartment. Emily unlatched its door and peered inside. "Ginger ale or root beer, honey. Take your pick."

"Root beer." She passed the can into the back seat, and there was silence except for the small noises that went with opening and draining a can of soda. The odor of root beer drifted toward the front seat, and in a moment there was a loud burp and a giggle. "That was a good one," she said.

Fortunately, for all the apparent crowd, the expressway journey never seemed so short either. Even as Nick swore and Andy drank, while the tip of his feather fluttered in the wind outside his window, Emily talked of what had gone on in Washington—the general who had wanted to classify both the patent application and the Bioblimp it described, the vice president of Mayflower Van Lines who had asked whether Emily's lab could give the Bioblimp built-in cargo pockets, the official from the Bioform Regulatory Administration who had wanted a more detailed Environmental Impact Statement, the . . . It seemed impossible that their journey from the airport could give her the time she needed to tell it all.

She was talking about the sort of environmental impacts a giant jellyfish could have when a gust of wind sent the Hopper before them staggering and a shadow fell across the road. She craned her neck to look out her window and up. "It's a Sparrow!"

The sound of the Sparrow's jet engine swelled until it dominated the air. The shadow swept past the Tortoise, and the airliner was plainly visible. Long and sleek, the size of an old Boeing 707, its extended feet as large and stark as elm trees, stripped by death of all but major branches and turned upside down, it did not much resemble its rootstock. But its eye had the perky ancestral gleam and the feathers that showed on the wings and below the passenger pod were the proper streaky brown. Written along the side of the passenger pod, in both English and Arabic, was the Palestine Airways motto: "No Sparrow Falls."

The Sparrow sideslipped, swung broadside to their view, and landed in the road ahead. Its body spread across all six traffic lanes, its feet squashing a Roachster and a Hopper.

"What the . . . ?" The brake pedal was in the traditional place, and Nick stepped on it, hard. As the Tortoise stiffened its legs and skidded toward a halt, the man's voice rose to a shout: "What are those idiots doing?"

Emily's broad mouth hung open. She shook her head, both in disbelief and in admission that she too knew nothing about the motivations of idiots. The Tortoise slowed and stopped, as did the traffic around it. A cacophony of Buggy voices arose as traffic began to pile up and drivers leaned on their horns.

The Sparrow cocked its head, first one way, then the other, casting its eyes by turns upon the chaos it had created. Its beak thrust, and a Hopper went down its throat, in pieces, one by one. A Roachster quickly followed.

Nick swore more genuinely as he reached for the panel hiding a control he had never dreamed he would have to use.

Drops of sweat appeared on his forehead. "Where . . . ? Ah."

The panel stuck, gave way to the bang of Nick's fist, and opened. He pushed the switch behind it, and the Tortoise lowered its belly-plate, or plastron, to the pavement. Then it drew its head and legs as far into its shell as possible. Unfortunately, it was not a box turtle and it could not protect itself entirely. Its nose and feet remained exposed.

The doors locked, and the windows slid smoothly all the way up, sealing the Tortoise's passengers into as safe a redoubt as foresighted engineers could manage to provide. As a side effect, the severed tip of Andy's jet feather fell to the pavement outside.

"Wow!" said Andy. He ignored what on any other day would have been a major disaster. His nose was plastered to the window, just as it had been at home when Nick had collared him for this trip.

The day's heat wasted no time in making itself felt. The Tortoise had no air-conditioning, and its interior quickly became intolerable despite the best efforts of the ventilation system. But they dared not leave their shelter or open its windows. Nor did they want to. Nick thought that the ventilator admitted quite enough of the metallic scent of fresh blood.

Fortunately, the carnage and the chaos outside the Tortoise was more than enough to keep their minds off their suffering inside it. Buggies struggled to reverse in the middle of the road. But the traffic jam was now too thick. A few, luckily near the shoulder, tried to use the embankment to make the turn or as a route to off-road freedom. But soon that lane too was blocked. Drivers and passengers fled their grid-locked vehicles. But nothing helped.

As soon as anyone left their Buggy, the Sparrow's eye turned their way. Split seconds later, the beak thrust, clamped down on wildly struggling limbs, and choked off screams. Few who were within the Sparrow's reach escaped successfully.

Even those who cowered within their Buggies were not safe. When the Sparrow saw no prey fleeing, it accepted the vehicles with every appearance of relish. Its ancestors had been opportunists, dining on seeds, crumbs, and insects as they found them. Now it faced a wealth of insectile creatures, all of a size proportionate to itself. Its satisfaction was obvious.

Only the few Tortoises on the road, each one pulled as much as possible into its shell; the old-style automobiles, even more hard-shelled; and the trucks, too huge, seemed immune to the terrifying attack.

"Jesus!" Nick knew they were as safe as possible, given the circumstances, but that did not comfort him. When a limb—it might have been a Buggy's—bounced off the Tortoise's shell below the windshield, he clutched the tiller with a grip that death alone would slacken.

"They probably still want the Israelis out of Tehran."

"The Palestinians?"

"Whoever." Emily shrugged and pointed at the logo on the airliner's flank. "We should never have let Palestine Airways into the country. Once a terrorist, always a . . ."

"Look!" cried Andy. "Here come the cops!"

As the sound of sirens split the air, Nick peered upward through the windshield. Three Sparrowhawks were just coming out of their dives and sweeping into tight turns above the expressway.

Chapter
Two

THE LAND SPREAD out below, wheeling, turning, pivoting now on some skyscraper near the city's core, now on the crossing of two major roadways, now on the airport control tower. Small white clouds swung above. Broad, steel-grey wings swept through the peripheries of the pilot's vision, immense feathers twitching from time to time in response to the flow of air or to the muscles that controlled his path through the sky.

The pilot's name was Bernie, Bernie Fischer, and he was letting his Hawk soar at will while he bathed morosely in the whirling views. His hands rested lightly on the control yoke as he stared out over the sheet-metal cabinets, round-cornered, grey-enameled, of the vehicle's console. Behind one of the panels, he knew, was the computer that translated his bendings of the yoke, his treadings of the pedals, and his twistings of knobs into landings, liftoffs, and smoothly sweeping turns to left and right.

His seat was enclosed by a broad bubble or pod of clear plastic, marked only by an oval door frame, and, within that, a small porthole. The porthole seemed superfluous, unnecessary for vision when the door itself was transparent. It was there, he guessed, because the door's manufacturer used the pattern for all its doors, clear or not.

Bernie's field of view was interrupted only beneath his feet, for only there did his vehicle turn opaque. There was the bird itself and, behind him, the engines and fuel tanks strapped near the base of its tail. There were the metal fittings that bore the Hawk's serial number and to which attached the heavy straps that held the pod to the bird's back. There was no need for metal structural members in the pod itself, or for rotor-mountings, as in the helicopters that still were used at times.

Bernie was seeking comfort in the clean peace of the sky, reluctant to return to Earth, even though his shift was nearly over, even though he could soon go home to his small apartment and pour a drink or two and try to forget what he had seen this day. He wished he had someone waiting for him, someone he could talk to, someone whose touch could ease him when things went so badly awry in the world with which he must deal each day.

He had had chances, yes, he had. He had loved and been loved. He had come close to proposing. He had been proposed to. But he had held back, said no, temporized. He didn't dare, he told them all, to impose his life on anyone. They had tried to talk him out of his refusal to run the risk of hurting, but he had insisted. It wouldn't be fair, he had told them, for one day he might not come home.

Bernie Fischer was a cop. At times, he wished he wasn't, for only as a cop, or a physician or a paramedic, could he possibly encounter horrors such as the one that preoccupied his mind at the moment. Unless he or his should become a victim. He shuddered at the thought. Today's horror was too much for sanity.

His father had been a professional soldier. A peacetime soldier until the Venezuelan Crisis, when he and ten thousand others had parachuted in to help a presidente and his cronies escape their thoroughly justified slaughter. He hadn't come back, and Bernie had seen the effects of the pain of his loss on his mother. She had lived only five years more.

There had been Bernie's own pain too. He had learned to handle it, yes. He had survived. But every time he encountered atrocities like today's, he felt it anew.

Someone had enticed a young black girl into a newly grown house in the suburb of Greenacres. There he had taped her mouth shut and put tourniquets on both her arms. He had removed the arms, just below the elbows, with an axe. He had raped her, fore and aft, with the amputated limbs. And finally, he had removed the tourniquets and left her to bleed to death. She had.

Bernie had heard of such things. There were people who were turned on by amputees. There were even people who were turned on by *being* amputees—to the extent that they would try to persuade surgeons to remove a leg, a foot, "At least a finger, please!" But this?

Her name had been Jasmine. Jasmine Willison. An old family name, her mother had said, again and again in those moments when she could talk half sensibly. Her grandmother's name, as Bernie's had been his grandfather's. She had been pretty, a good student, going steady, thinking of college. And some monster . . . Bernie couldn't help it. It was unprofessional, he knew. But the bastard *was* a monster. He was even worse a monster because he had left no clues. No fingerprints. Not even any semen.

What other horrors were happening below him even now? He watched the concrete cityscape as it wheeled across his gaze. He stared at the greener suburbs, and the green, crisscross strips of the airport, with the big birds, big enough to dwarf his Hawk, landing and taking off in the distance.

His mouth began to water, his throat to tighten. He sniffed, suddenly aware of the rankness of his sweat. He needed, he thought, a shower. Then he opened the small port in the door beside him, knowing for the first time what it was there for, glad that it was there, leaned, and vomited into space.

He always did that. Whenever the world turned especially nasty, whenever he could stomach it no longer, he puked his guts out. But he had never done it before while in the air.

The call came while he was rinsing his mouth from the thermos he always carried with him: "CODE NINER NINER. ALL OFFICERS TO REAGAN EXPRESSWAY, MILE THREE EIGHT. REPEAT: CODE NINER NINER. ALL OFFICERS TO REAGAN EXPRESSWAY, MILE THREE EIGHT, MILE THREE EIGHT."

Pausing only long enough to spit and close the port, he turned off the autopilot, seized the control yoke, and kicked the Hawk into a power dive toward Mile 38 on the old Reagan Expressway. Code 99 was a rare one. It meant a military or paramilitary attack. In this country, this age of the world, it had to be terrorists.

His destination was not far away. As his Hawk cupped its wings to slow its dive, he saw two other Hawks arriving from nearer the city, diving like his own, converging on a scene of chaos. Traffic was backed up in both directions, six lanes of pavement covered with automobiles, Tortoises, Roachsters, Hoppers, and other Buggies. Only the zone immediately surrounding the Sparrow airliner was clear of vehicles, and the reason was obvious: The bare pavement was coated with blood and other body fluids and littered with the scraps of the Sparrow's meal.

Bernie was not surprised to see the logo on the Sparrow's side. The Palestinians—along with the Iranian Shi'ites, Lebanese Christians and Moslems, Irish Nationalists, Afrikaaners, and a hundred other factions—had long since broadened their battles to encompass all the world.

The three arriving Hawks began their siren calls together. The ululating rising-falling screams were as unlike a natural hawk's screech as they could be, for the gengineers had labored hard to mimic the sound of traditional police cars. They had succeeded, and now, as the three Hawks swept, screaming, into a tight circle above the carnage, the Sparrow stopped its feeding and lowered itself on its legs. Then it cocked its head, half spread its wings, and, beak agape, lunged at its threateners.

But the Hawks were still too high aloft. Bernie eyed his fellows. One—he recognized Connie Skoglund—held a microphone and was gesturing. When Bernie waved his acquiescence, the other's voice boomed out of the police radio: "YOU ARE UNDER ARREST! TAKE OFF IMMEDIATELY AND FOLLOW US. YOU ARE UNDER ARREST! COME QUIETLY, OR WE WILL BE FORCED TO STOOP!"

Bernie wished the rapist he had sought earlier were beneath him now. Hawks had replaced helicopters for most police purposes because their built-in weaponry, by its nature—beaks and talons as sharp as scythe blades, and larger—had more deterrent effect on evil-doers than machine guns or rockets.

The Hawks were also quite effective at catching those who fled the scenes of their crimes.

The Sparrow—or its crew—ignored the threat. It sidled a few steps down the road, and its beak dipped once more into the grid-locked traffic. Years ago, Bernie reflected, that Sparrow and its crew and passengers would have been safe. Terrorists routinely once had taken hostages as guarantees of their own safety. But those days were gone. The world could not afford them. Governments had accepted that the only way to handle terrorists was to destroy them promptly—hostages, if necessary, and all—in hope of convincing other terrorists, and would-be terrorists, that they had nothing to gain by their actions. Sadly, some terrorists continued to believe that publicity was enough of a reward. It had been proposed that government bar the press from covering terrorist attacks, but such proposals had never been implemented. If they had, they would not have worked. No government could ever muzzle the press for long.

The Hawks folded their wings and dived. The Sparrow sidestepped and its engines roared, their exhaust sweeping a number of Buggies across the pavement behind it, tumbling into one another and the ditch. To Bernie, one tiny detail stood out: A Roachster's antennae crumpling in the gust of hot exhaust; he could almost smell the scorching chitin.

The Sparrow spread its wings and lurched into the air. The Hawks lunged, trying to force it toward the airport.

It refused. Even though its stubby beak was no match for the predatory hooks and talons of the Hawks, it was larger. It slashed at its tormentors and, steadily gaining altitude, tried to push past their lunges.

The Hawks attacked. Their beaks slashed. Their talons seized and tore, and impacts jolted Bernie in his harness. The straps that held the Sparrow's engines and passenger pod in place gave way, and the Sparrow, too large to fly unaided, even without its burden of passengers, fell to the highway. Its engines fell too, smashing into the packed traffic. The passenger pod, when it too hit the pavement, broke open, spilling bodies among the wreckage already there.

* * *

The road was blocked as badly as ever, but now the end and a resumption of journeys was in sight. Long-legged, police-model Roachsters and wrecker Crabs, waving massive claws above their cabs, were picking their ways down the embankments of the highway. Ambulances—gengineered from pigeons not only for the value of the symbolism, but also for their vertical takeoff-and-landing abilities and for their broad, compact bodies that could support multigurney cargo pods—were descending on the road.

The Hawks perched on the Sparrow's carcass. The Hawks' red-brown tails jerked as they eyed their kill, and their hooked beaks opened and closed. Their talons dug possessively into the cooling flesh. Gouts of blood were visible as new spots on their plumage, especially against the dark-splashed cream of their undersides, the white of their throats and cheeks. They cocked their heads, each one marked, as if it wore an ancient warrior's helm, with dark guard-pieces jutting downward past the eyes and ears. A reddish crest, resembling a tonsure, suggested that those warriors might have been monks as well.

Bernie had never before seen a Hawk on the prey for which its ancestors had been named. Now he reflected that a Sparrowhawk, or Kestrel, had to be the perfect bird for police work. There were larger natural hawks, but that mattered little to gengineers who could resize a sparrow into a Sparrow. There was one Hawk, the Duck-Hawk, that had a single-barred helm and no tonsure, but it had been claimed by the Air Force. Other, less aptly marked raptors had gone to the other armed services—the Osprey to the Navy, the Broad-Winged Hawk, with its chevroned tail, to the Army, Harlan's Hawk to the Marines.

He knew that, if he left his Hawk to its own devices, it would feed. The instincts were there, after all; they were, in fact, a large part of what made a Hawk so effective for police work. But they had to be suppressed at times, especially when the public had already seen more than enough raw meat. He lifted a small, bright green hatch in the control panel to reveal a recessed toggle. The switch was wired to the Hawk's sleep center. When he flicked it, the bird would tuck its head be-

neath one wing and go dormant. It would wake only when
he touched the switch again.

A puff of breeze ruffled the feathers at the crest of his
Hawk's head. He flicked the switch. So did his fellow Hawk-
ers, for even as his Hawk lifted one wing and bent its neck,
so did theirs. In a moment, he joined his fellows on the
ground. Connie was a thin brunette, as wiry and tough as
the Hawk she flew; Bernie had dated her more than once,
and he knew both the appeal of her soul and the strength of
her body. The third Hawker was less familiar, though Bernie
knew him—Larry Randecker, softer in appearance, almost
chubby. Yet he was tough enough; Bernie thought his had
been the Hawk that had sliced the Sparrow's engine straps.
There had been no hesitation; to all appearances, Randecker
had embraced the possibility that he would not be able to
dodge the blades of incandescent gas erupting from the tumbling, still blasting jets.

The cleanup crews were already removing the wreckage
from the roadway, loading the remains of vehicles into trailers
and those of their drivers into body bags and gurneys. The
wreckers avoided the Sparrow and its pod, for they would
have to be moved to the airport for examination. Proper
emergency procedure allowed them only to open the liner's
stomach to retrieve its victims. The genimal's body would
have to wait for a Crane.

The medics working over the wreckage of the Sparrow's
passenger pod kept the few survivors of the jet's fall separate,
for they would have to be interrogated. The dead were trucked
away to morgues, though first a single officer recorded their
features with a computer-compatible electronic camera. Later,
he would record the living as well. Then the electronic images would be routed through the police department's computers for comparison with their extensive files of known
terrorists, and then through the worldwide computer net for
a broader search. If any of the Sparrow's passengers and crew
members—alive or dead—had any past association at all with
terrorism, the local authorities would soon know the details.

Bernie, Connie, and Larry now were traffic cops. They
waded through the chaos of the scene, guiding vehicles that

had, in their efforts to escape, gotten tangled in the ditches or on the embankments, or even in the roadway, back into position on the road. Using pocket recorders, they took names, addresses, and phone numbers of witnesses for later interviewing. And in due time, the road began to resemble nothing so much as a vast parking lot, covered with serried ranks of vehicles awaiting some signal to move. Behind the congested zone, traffic had been diverted and no longer accumulated. To the rear of the jam, other cops were getting some of the stopped vehicles turned around and headed toward the nearest exit ramps.

One of the last vehicles that Bernie checked was a Tortoise in full withdrawal. In front, only its nose poked out of the crack between its shell and plastron. Its eyes were safely hidden away from pecking beaks; the headlights mounted on the lip of the shell served as giant surrogates. To the sides, only the stub-clawed toes showed. Inside the passenger compartment, a man, a woman, and a child, holding a bob-tailed Cardinal feather, watched his approach. All were sweating heavily, although the vehicle's windows were open. He guessed they had waited to unseal the Tortoise until the Sparrow was dead.

He held their gaze with his own—the woman was attractive, but she was clearly unavailable, married—while he gestured for their attention. But then he let his eyes drop to the running board and the severed arm that lay upon it. It was a small arm, with a yellow plastic watchband around the wrist.

He vomited again.

When he looked up once more, the Tortoise's head and legs had emerged from the shell. The door was open, and the driver was holding out a can of soda. "It's cold," he said. "We have a small fridge on board."

"Thanks." Bernie rinsed the foulness from his mouth, spat, and drank the remaining ginger ale. He handed back the can. Then he bent, picked up the arm, and waved it overhead. His stomach remained still, though he was grateful that the limb, its shoulder end all torn and ragged, did not drip. From the corner of one eye, he noticed that the kid in the Tortoise's back seat stared, wide-eyed. His parents paled, and his father covered his mouth with one hand as if he too had a rebellious stomach.

In a moment, one of the medics, pale herself and shaking her head over the carnage, retrieved the arm. Only then did he turn on his recorder. "I'm collecting information on the witnesses," he said. "Your names?"

"Nick Gilman," said the driver. He pointed at the woman unnecessarily. "My wife, Emily."

"I'm Andy," said the kid. He waved his feather. "Boy, you really hit that Sparrow! Pow! It was eating everybody up!"

Bernie hoped Andy would never meet worse, as Jasmine had. The kid was too young to truly appreciate horror such as he had just witnessed, though it would surely sink in eventually. He might even have nightmares tonight, as Bernie expected for himself.

"Reason for being here?"

"I was picking Emily up at the airport."

"I was flying in from Washington. I work for Neoform."

He collected their home and work addresses and numbers before saying to the woman, "You're a gengineer, then?" When she nodded, he added, "Did you have anything to do with the Hawks?" Neoform, he knew, held the design patents.

"That was before my time," she said.

He snorted. "Whoever it was, tell 'em they're great. I love 'em." He turned then to survey the road ahead of the Tortoise. A Starling short-hauler was unloading a crew of litterbugs to clean up the final, small scraps and the piles of dung left by both the Sparrow and its victims. Irrelevantly, the thought crossed his mind that some people called the cleanup genimals "shit-pickers." Most people preferred the less offensive label, but there was a strong tendency for people to call a spade a spade, almost despite themselves. "Litter" was now just another synonym for manure.

From the corner of his eye, he glimpsed an angular skeleton, like a tipsy rocket gantry against the sky, lurching toward them. It was the Crane from the airport's repair yard, all stiltlike legs and reaching neck, its beak fitted out with metal hooks and pulleys. It was already coming for the Sparrow's carcass.

There seemed to be a clear lane past the beak of the Sparrow. Connie and Larry were already guiding traffic in that direction. He pointed, ''Through there. We'll be in touch for your statements.''

Chapter
Three

WHEN THE CLOCK radio came on, Emily wanted to ignore it. Andy had awakened screaming at three in the morning. When he had refused to go back to bed alone, Emily and Nick had taken him into their bed between them. He had then dropped off immediately. They had taken longer to return to sleep, and now she felt distinctly shortchanged.

Nick pushed at her with the arm on which Andy's head was pillowed—where her head ought to be—as if to remind her that she had to go to work. She pushed back, throwing one bare calf over his own; she could get no closer, with their son between them. She was asleep, cozy, safe, and she wanted to stay that way, all three. But then the news began, and it was all a repeat of the nightmare of the day before. She growled softly and rolled out of bed. By the time she had turned the electronic voice off, she was awake.

She had not forgotten the carnage on the expressway, but every time she tried to think of it, or every time someone, or something—the radio—brought the subject up, her mind veered away to other thoughts. Right now, it reminded her that she and Nick had long ago decided that the best place for the radio was on a bureau several steps away from the bed. Mundane thoughts were a refuge to which she clung as if against her will.

She dressed. She watered the hanky bush on the bathroom windowsill. She ate. By then Nick and Andy were up and bickering amicably over the profound question of whether doughnuts or toast would make a more satisfying breakfast. That settled, Andy went to the window to look at the bird feeder. "Mommy," he said. "See the Chickadee?" She did. "It was there yesterday." They watched it devouring the other smaller birds. After a moment, he added wistfully, "Can you make it go away?"

"We'll call the airport later, kid," said Nick. "We'll tell them to come and get it."

"That's the only thing to do," said Emily. "We don't need that sort of reminder." Then she kissed both her men goodbye, broke a chunk from one of the doughnuts on the table, and left the house, first touching the garage-door control by the front door. By the time she reached the garage, the Tortoise was already emerging. When it saw her, it cocked its head and lowered its shell for her just as it had for Nick and Andy the day before. When it saw the food in her hand, it also opened its cavernous mouth and uttered a soft "Whonk." She tossed the bite of cake between its jaws and patted its nose before she boarded.

She always took the Tortoise to work. She felt guilty, for the genimal was Nick's, yes, but hers, like her father's before her, was the need for daily transportation. She was fully and painfully aware that the Tortoise was the family's only car, and that Nick often had shopping to do and errands to run. She was even more painfully aware that her father had been much less sensitive to her mother's needs.

She told herself that there was a mini-mall just a few blocks away, and that both he and Andy needed the exercise. Next year, when the boy entered school, might be another story. From time to time, Nick said something about looking for a job then. If she reminded him that he hadn't had the skills for a decent job before Andy had come along, he said that, just maybe, he would go back to school.

So they would need a second vehicle. She wondered what it would be. A Beetle? A Roachster? Some other Buggy? Those had been awfully vulnerable on the expressway the day before. Another Tortoise? They had been safe, after all. How about something that could fly away from that sort of trouble? A Chickadee like the one on the lawn? But they needed airports.

Perhaps she could alter the design of the jellyfish-based

Bioblimp she was working on. It didn't have to be the size of a moving van. If she could just halt its growth at some earlier stage, the result might be just right for a commuter. She would have to think about it.

Like the airport, Neoform Laboratories was surrounded by green. Once a visitor had passed the security guard's gate, there was a parking lot shaded by trees, with the lines of vehicles separated by concrete troughs through which ran fresh water. There were paddocks marked off by white board fences, as at a Kentucky horse farm. There was a track for testing the vehicular genimals. There were flower beds near every building, and the smell of flowers, and of hay, and of many kinds of litter.

Most of the outbuildings were red-painted, white-trimmed barns that housed the experimental stock and prototypes. One was an inflated fabric dome, its triangular panels alternating blue and gold. Jutting high above everything else and stabilized by guy wires, it had been erected for Emily's prototype Bioblimps. Later, she hoped, it would be the nursery for the first commercial models.

A concrete walk led from the parking lot to the entrance of the main building, a classic structure of contoured ledges and artful setbacks, all white concrete and tinted glass. The metal ductwork of the air-conditioning system showed on the roof, and though the day was so far very nice, Emily knew that that system would be essential later on.

Someday, she reflected, a bioform might replace the metal, pumping cooled air through the building with the bellows of its breath. Someday there might be bioform appliances in kitchens and toys in nurseries. There might even be broad-leaved philodendrons whose every leaf was a veedo screen, or bioform computers, or . . .

There were people in Neoform's labs, she knew, who were working on such things. At a recent seminar, she had seen how flat surfaces—leaves or skins—could generate high-resolution images, their pixels nothing more than single cells that emitted bioluminescence, like fireflies or ocean algae or deep-sea fish, on command. Neural logics and signal processors were also under development, and she could foresee the day when bioform vehicles and other devices would have their controlling computers built in, not plugged in. Houses and offices would be grown not as mere shells to be dried and painted and furnished, but complete, with furniture, appliances, communications, and computers as part of their flesh. Never again would humanity need to build mechanical or electronic devices. If she doubted that industry would give way entirely to a new version of agriculture, and that all the environmental problems that the world had learned accompanied mines and factories and machinery would disappear, well, she had been called a cynic.

The Biological Revolution was young. Just as that earlier revolution marked by the internal combustion engine had begun with automobiles and aircraft, it had begun with their equivalents. Only much later had the internal combustion engine spawned power lawn mowers and weed-whackers. That bioform air conditioner might be decades away, though already she could glimpse how it would have to be designed: part tree, for the cooling power of transpiration, the same thing that made a tree's shade so pleasant on a hot day; part beast, for the lungs that could make the cooled air move. Perhaps she could work on it, once the Bioblimp project was out of the way.

There were advantages to being in on the ground floor of a technology and an industry. Later, it would become difficult to think of new things to gengineer. The bioform houses and hanky bushes, now just beginning to appear, would all have been invented. Now, there was plenty of room for creativity and fame and wealth. The future was limited only by the imaginations of gengineers like herself, working for companies like Neoform. And there were jobs in plenty for all the nongengineers who sold and serviced their products or worked at adjusting society to the impacts of the Biological Revolution, even in such simple ways as replacing pavement with turf.

She stood before the Neoform building. Here were the offices of the company's administrators, the conference rooms, the laboratories of half a dozen gengineers like Emily. But before Emily could proceed to her lab, she had to confront the grey-haired receptionist who insisted on being called "Miss Carol."

From her throne behind a low barricade just within the building's door, Miss Carol presided over four things: a small switchboard, a computer terminal, an electronic pad on which each person entering or leaving the premises was obliged to sign his or her name, and the control for the turnstile that blocked all passage. When she spoke, she displayed a deep southern accent.

Emily opened her thin briefcase for inspection, signed in, said she was glad to be back and yes-Miss-Carol she'd heard of the awful thing that had happened on the expressway and yes-Miss-Carol she expected that the memo on the meeting later on would be in her box. Finally, she squeezed through the turnstile and escaped. As soon as she was around the corner, she sighed with relief. When someone laughed, she started guiltily.

The odor of pipe tobacco told her who the laugher was before she turned. Frank Janifer, one of the company's few smokers, was standing in the doorway to the company library. "You didn't give her much of an opening, did you?"

Emily smiled. Frank was in marketing, and he knew everyone. "She'll go for half an hour."

"But only if you encourage her."

She snorted. "All you have to do is stand still! If you have any dirt to give her . . ."

There was nothing slow about Frank. "So you were there?" He stepped into the hallway to walk beside her while she said as little as she could about the day before. As always, he made her feel small when he began to move. He wasn't tall, but he had the kind of bulk that came only with weight lifting, and that was indeed Frank's hobby. He wore his blond hair past his ears, and Emily had heard the single women in his department remark that it was a pity that he was gay. "Will you be giving us something to market soon?"

She shrugged. "We don't have a patent, if that's what you mean. But we do have a contract possibility." When he raised his eyebrows, she added, "It'll all come out at the meeting."

They parted at the door to her lab, where her technician, Alan Bryant, offered her the mug of coffee in his hand. "Thanks, Al." Her nostrils flared as she inhaled the welcome scent. "Anything new?"

He had a doctorate as good as hers, but he was younger, still new to the world of research. His position was the equivalent of the postdoc of the previous century. He took her briefcase and led the way toward her office cubby at the rear of the lab, in the corner by the window. "There's that meeting . . ." They both ignored the computer workstation on the other side of the room. Its screen was running a simulation of the growth of a Bioblimp, from a hydrogen-filled egg floating in air to an adult blimp, its muscular tentacles unloading a ship.

She rummaged through the pile of mail that had accumulated in the past two days and found the memo. The first item on the agenda was her report on the patent hearing. Second was . . .

"And Chowdhury is pushing those armadilloes of his." Bryant's tone was not approving. The man he had mentioned was abrasive toward everyone, but he seemed to take a special pleasure in his sneers at blacks. Grudgingly, Bryant added, "He's got a prototype."

"He's wasting his time. General Bodies has that market locked up with their Roachsters." She paused, sipping at the coffee. Then she looked for her briefcase, found it on a chair, lifted it onto the desk, atop the litter of mail, and opened it. The sheaf of papers she wanted was on top of the stack. "Do we have any kangaroo DNA on hand?"

Bryant shrugged. "I don't think so. But we can get it overnight."

She pointed at a computer-generated sketch. "While I was gone, I talked to a VP for Mayflower Van Lines. He was at the hearing. He liked the blimp's cargo-handling and thought it could make a good moving van. But only if it had built-in cargo holds." The sketch showed a blimp hovering above a house. Tentacles were stuffing furniture into openmouthed pouches on either side of the blimp.

"Gotcha." He turned and stepped to the computer workstation. A touch of his finger canceled the growth-simulation program, and a genebank's long list of genetic stock began to scroll up the oversize screen. The genebanks were accustomed to hurry-up orders. "I'll get right on it."

The meeting was scheduled for ten. That gave Emily barely enough time to sort through the rest of her mail and pull her notes together. The company would want a formal, written report eventually. Right now, it wanted whatever she could give, in whatever form she could manage.

When she and Alan walked into the conference room, the research head, Sean Gelarean, was already there, marking the air with a touch of lime aftershave. Come to the States with the last gurgle of the British Brain Drain, he had found that his Mediterranean coloring could, for a change, make life easier. He told the story often: In England, he had been just another wog, his Palestinian ancestry weighing more than three generations of loyalty to the Crown. Here, he had blended in among hybridized Italians, Greeks, Spanish, Portuguese, Afghanis, Lebanese, and more. The old Italian-American family, the Campanas, into which he had, in time, married had barely noticed that he was not one of their particular group. Rumor had it that he had never converted to their Catholicism, that, in fact, he kept a prayer rug in his office closet and unrolled it five times a day to pray to Mecca in the east.

With the Campana money, he had become one of Neoform's founders. Not long after that, though still long before Emily's tenure with the company had begun, he had been the gengineer behind the Hawks that cop had appreciated so much. If further rumor were right, the fact that the Campana money had gone into making police vehicles might make him feel even better. Most of their investments leaned toward the other side of the fence.

Also present were Frank Janifer and two aides from marketing, an anonymous VP from financial, and two of the firm's other gengineers, Ralph Chowdhury and Wilma Atkinson. A sharp edge of sweat overlaid the lime, Frank's tobacco, Wilma's floral perfume, and all the other less-distinctive scents.

Emily supposed the sweat belonged to Ralph, for that odor seemed to accompany him everywhere. He was dark of both hue and temperament, a half Indian whose parents had escaped from South Africa after it went black. He wore flat-lensed spectacles that reflected the room's lights and hid his eyes.

Wilma was an asthenic blonde who specialized in decorative plant-animal hybrids. One of her products occupied a pot on a pedestal near the conference room's one window. Its form was as natural, yet as abstract, as branching coral, it swayed gracefully, and from time to time it emitted a soft, tuneful moan. Her work provided Neoform with one of its most successful and profitable product lines.

Everyone waited quietly while Emily straightened her notes to one side of the small keyboard and flat screen set flush in the table before her. She stalled a moment longer to plug her graphics disk into the drive slot next to the screen. When she was done at last, and her hands were folded atop her papers, Sean said, "I wish you had called last night, Emily. I wanted to know immediately."

Emily shrugged and opened her mouth. But before she could say anything, Frank interrupted: "I don't believe she was thinking of anything to do with work, Sean. She was on the expressway when . . ."

"Ah." The other nodded his greying head. The beginnings of the bulldog jowls he would wear not much later in his life wobbled. He hadn't known, he said, though he did not look surprised. He turned back to Emily. "But that's over and done with. You're safe, and we're glad of it." When the others had murmured their agreement, he added, "It would have been difficult, finding someone to take over your Bio-blimp project." He sighed. "I probably would have had to do it myself."

Emily thought that he did not look displeased at the thought. She knew that he had accepted such chores in the past, and somehow, his name had always wound up the only one on the project.

"Do you feel up to giving us a report?" he said.

"Of course." She looked down at her papers, though she

had little need to refresh her memory again. Then she told them what had gone on in Washington, adding some detail to what she had told her husband. The patent examiners had agreed that the Bioblimp indeed seemed original and patentable. But then had come the reason why the patent had not simply been issued, and a hearing had been called instead. A Pentagon general had appeared to claim that the Defense Department had already produced similar carriers for troops and cargo. To support the claim, he displayed a single sketch. Then he said that his office wished to classify both the patent application and Neoform's Bioblimp.

Wilma's artwork softly echoed her audience groan. "Fortunately," she went on, "the Hearing Board shot that down. They pointed out that the application had already been published, and besides, the press was present. And then we—I and our lawyers—pointed out that according to the general's sketch . . ." She paused to touch the keyboard, and a screen at the end of the room lit up with a lifelike diagram. "According to the general's sketch, the rootstock was a very different species of cnidarian and the result lacked our cargo-handling tentacles. It had only a rudimentary fringe." A split-screen diagram emphasized the comparison. She shrugged as if to say that she had done her best. "The Board took everything 'under advisement,' and we'll know their decision in a few days."

"Tell them about Mayflower," said Alan Bryant. Ralph Chowdhury scowled, as if offended by the temerity of a mere technician—or a black—who dared to speak, but he said nothing.

Emily looked at her boss, Sean, and activated her third computer graphic. "Alan is referring to a conversation I had with the Vice President for Purchasing of Mayflower Van Lines. He was at the hearing, and he thought the Bioblimps, especially with their tentacles, might make good moving vans. *If* we can equip them with cargo holds. He didn't want strap-ons, he said, because the straps might break." Someone snorted. "I know," she added. "The airlines have no trouble. But we've already begun to look into marsupial genes."

Frank muttered to one of his aides, who produced a disk, inserted it in the drive before her, and copied the graphic.

Sean held a single piece of paper in front of his bifocals. "I understand the Bioform Regulatory Administration posed an obstacle?"

"BRA just wants a more extensive Environmental Impact Statement. But we can't prepare it until we know who our customers will be."

"Hah!" Chowdhury was scowling at her now. "You won't have any! Not if I know the military!" He didn't, Emily thought. But he had never let the truth keep him from attacking everyone within reach, as if he hated them all. His colleagues put up with him because they sympathized with his history, and because, for all his abrasiveness, he was a more than competent gengineer. He was, in fact, one of the best in the industry. Even Emily had to admit that he could do things with a genome that she could never attempt.

"If the decision goes against us," Emily replied, "I think we'll be able to get a military procurement contract. I have a feeling the general thought our design rather better than the one he had. The built-in cargo holds should only help."

Wilma changed the subject. "Have you heard the news, Emily?" When Emily shook her head, she went on, "They didn't find any terrorists at all on that Sparrow. It just stopped responding to its controls."

Frank began to look worried. "Do you think there's a defect in the gengineering? That could hurt sales."

"The station said the PLO, the Free Venezuelans, and the Boer Front have all called to claim the credit."

Frank laughed. So did Emily. The same thing happened every time there was a disaster that might have been caused by terrorists. Some of the more extreme groups had even been known to claim credit for earthquakes and tornadoes.

The research head rapped a pencil on the table. When he had their attention, he said, "I don't think that is our problem."

"But, Sean . . ."

"Wait until they say there's a defect. Or that the terrorists sabotaged the Sparrow in some way, which I think is more likely. Now we have a report from Dr. Chowdhury.''

Chowdhury's motions, as he shoved a disk into his own drive slot with a loud click, were aggressive. He glared at everyone impartially, though his gaze seemed to avoid Sean and to linger just a little on Emily and Alan. "Such problems," he finally said, "certainly won't affect the Bioblimp. That is a dead end. The true future of this company must lie with the armadillo-based vehicles I have been working on." He gestured, and the screen showed his own first diagram.

"The problem is the wheels," said Chowdhury. "When General Bodies designed their Roachster, they had an immense advantage. An arthropod's shell is laid down by an underlying membrane and is periodically replaced or molted. Once they had gengineered their hybrid to grow bumps in suitable places, beneath the legs . . ." Most of them knew what he was talking about with the speech and the diagram he displayed, but review was an essential part of the ritual of presentation. In most people's hands, it was also a comforting rite; in his, it grated.

He continued: "Then they could have the membrane secrete a second layer of shell inside those bumps, just within the first. It does this anyway at molting time. The difference comes in the shaping of the layers where the bumps neck down to join the body, so that the end result is a wheel mounted on a central hub. The genimal's legs run backward on top of the wheels." Another diagram. "And when the wheel wears out, a molt replaces it.

"Unfortunately . . ." A photo replaced the computer graphic. It showed Chowdhury standing beside an armadillo whose back bulged well above his head. Emily thought that the world had seen nothing like it since the South American glyptodont had died out millennia before, if then. The size was comparable. The glyptodont had even had a tail, as did armadilloes. But the glyptodont's shell had not swelled out beneath its legs in four rounded bosses that looked exactly like the wheels of a Roachster. He went on, "An armadillo's shell is really a system of bony plates embedded in the skin.

The plates are covered with horny scales, but the bone is what gives the shell its strength. That's a more internal tissue, and it is never molted. It was therefore difficult, but I did succeed in producing an armadillo with wheels. However, once those wheels wear out, replacing them is a much more time-consuming process. We may have to fit them with rubber tires.''

''Why bother?'' asked Frank. ''With their Roachster, General Bodies has a lock on the wheeled genimal market.''

''Sure,'' said Emily. ''Why can't your 'Dillo Dillies' run on legs, like a Tortoise?''

Chowdhury, his voice taut with anger, said, ''I prefer to call them . . .'' but the group's laughter drowned him out.

In a moment, when quiet reigned once more, Emily said, ''But seriously, have you considered the main drawback to using armadilloes as your rootstock?''

Chowdhury's voice grew tight, and Emily thought she could detect a change in the odor of his sweat. ''There are no problems with my armadilloes!''

Emily showed her teeth in an apparent smile. It was hard to keep her mouth from shifting the little bit that would make the expression an unabashed snarl. ''I've lived in Texas, Ralph, where the roads are splattered with dead armadilloes. The reason is simple: When they are startled, they leap straight upward, just to bumper height. It's a reflex, as such it's wired into their nervous systems, and into their genes, and it would be just wonderful for the reputation of your Dillies if the same reflex showed up under a highway overpass. Have you done anything about it?''

There was a moment's silence. Chowdhury scribbled quickly on one of the papers before him. Then he said smugly, ''That is not necessary.'' He tapped his keyboard, and the room's screen wrote an equation beneath the photo. ''Square-cube scaling turns the wild armadillo's leap into the merest of hops for my 'Armadons.' ''

Frank raised a hand, one finger jutting toward the screen: ''How can it even hop, with the legs on top of the wheels like that? Wouldn't it tear its wheels off?''

Alan laughed out loud. Emily was delighted. Chowdhury

was far less so. His face darkened, and his fingers mashed his keyboard murderously. The screen blinked out. He said, "That is *not* a problem. I will be ready to demonstrate my prototype soon, and then you will see. I hope that you will even applaud."

No one had a chance to say anything more. A discreet beep sounded from their chief's, Sean Gelarean's, place. He leaned over his screen to read some message, and then he said, "Emily? Miss Carol says there's a police officer in the entry. She wants to interview you about the incident yesterday." He grinned, and the flesh around his eyes wrinkled. "She says she's disappointed that you didn't say anything this morning."

Emily snorted and rose from her seat. "I was in a rush." As she backed away from the table, she glimpsed Gelarean's feet—almost as small as her own—in the shadows beneath. He had kicked off one shoe so he could use the toes to scratch the other ankle.

Chapter
Four

BERNIE FISCHER'S PERSONAL vehicle was nothing so satisfying as a Hawk. That was an official police vehicle that must, at the end of each day, be put to bed in the official police Aerie. Despite its name, that structure was on ground level, a huge barn, a stable for all the department genimals. There official police handlers fed the Hawks and Roachsters and flicked their dormancy toggles to put them to bed for the night.

Bernie didn't even own a genimal. He had no Tortoise, no Roachster, no Hopper. And the reason was not expense. He could afford one, and there were public stables where he could keep it. But he didn't need it, for his small apartment was not far from police headquarters. It was so close that sometimes he actually walked to work. Other times, he rode a bicycle and parked it in the Aerie's broad yard. He chained it only elsewhere in the city; where he worked, it was safe.

Despite a grey sky and the promise of rain to combat the summer heat, today was a bicycle day. He hadn't, as he had expected, slept very well. He craved peace, and quiet, and the soft, floating sensation of a Hawk on the wing. The bicycle, when the streets were smooth, as they were by spells, and the litterbugs had been doing their duty, as they generally had, came as close, he was sure, as he would get today. There would be paperwork on both the rape-mutilation and the terrorist attack on the expressway. There might be some legwork to do. He would probably not need the Hawk's speed or weaponry. They would instead delight some other member of the force.

He could at least look in on the Aerie before he had to face his desk. He grinned as he pedaled, dodging traffic and pedestrians. If, he told himself, he could get there early enough, he could spend a little time staring at the sleek forms of the Hawks. Perhaps, if the Aerie's grooms had not done their work as perfectly as usual, he could run a hand down a neck to straighten feathers.

But he never had the chance. As he pulled into the Aerie's yard and swung his right leg back and over the seat, standing on the left pedal while he coasted toward the bike rack, Connie Skoglund hailed him. She shouted, one arm upraised, her uniform blouse stretched tight across her torso, and once again he admired her. He changed course and stopped in front of her. Her scent, of soap and perfume, stood out against the earthier odors of the Aerie and made him think of other days, and nights.

"The Count wants you," she told him. "Right away." Above them, a Hawk noisily departed one of the Aerie's three launch platforms, small, circular decks set against the slanting roof. An elevator within the building carried the birds and their pilots up to what, in a barn, would have been the hayloft. From there, ramps led to arched doorways, each on a different level, stepping upward from the front of the building toward the back. The arches, their tops filled in with stained glass salvaged from some ancient mansion of the city, opened onto the platforms. The platforms themselves pivoted on central hubs, so that the blast shields erected along one edge would always be behind the Hawks when they took off into the wind. They reminded Bernie of the rotating gun platforms on naval warships in old movies.

He grimaced to show his disappointment. The Hawks would have to wait, while he straightened feathers of another sort. "The Count" was Lieutenant Alexander, the chief of the department's detectives, and the nickname was appropriate. His parents, presumably suffering from pretensions to glory, had given him the first name of Napoleon.

"Any idea what for?"

Connie shrugged. "Something to do with that airliner. All

I know is, I'm on witness duty. I've got about twenty of 'em to interview today."

"See you later?"

She looked at him appraisingly. "Dinner?" When he nodded, she added, "Come over to my place, then."

Historians know that Napoleon Bonaparte was short and suspect that Alexander the Great was not much taller. The Count did better on that score, for he and his immediate ancestors had enjoyed the benefits of better nutrition. His more distant ancestors had been of taller stock, and he was as blond as only a Scandinavian, or one sprung from that region, can be.

He also had strikingly red lips. Though one might think that a Napoleon Alexander would be called "General" or "Emperor," and though he was fair, not dark, and was not given to long black capes, that feature was the one that had dictated the form of his nickname. If it failed to capture the flavor of his temper, no one seemed to mind.

"Fischer! How did those goddam terrorists get away?"

Bernie, standing in front of his superior's desk, gave a deliberately sloppy imitation of a military salute. He had been in the army, and he wasn't about to give the SOB the real thing. "Sir?" The Count insisted on the word.

"The night shift checked the passengers. Three quarters of them dead, and every one of them absolutely innocent. Passports in order, no guns in their briefcases or purses. Nothing!" The Count slapped a hand on his desktop in emphasis.

"The crew, sir?"

"Dead, every one of them. No one's talking. But their papers are in order, and . . ." He snarled. "They had to get away!"

"I didn't see anyone leave the Sparrow after it fell, sir."

The Count spun in his swivel chair to stare out his office window at the front of the Aerie. A rack of bicycles, including Bernie's, was visible in the yard below. He sighed gustily. Finally, he admitted, "We have the cockpit voice recorder. It actually looks like there *weren't* any terrorists. That Sparrow simply stopped responding to the controls. It just went berserk.''

"Sir? But how . . . ?" Bernie didn't own a genimal, but he knew they weren't supposed to act independently. They were supposed to be totally obedient to their masters, except when left to their own devices. That was why he had had to switch off his Hawk on the expressway. Left alone, it might well have eaten the Sparrow, or some of it. But as long as he was at the controls, it had to obey him. That was the way the gengineers had designed them.

"I have no idea," muttered Lieutenant Alexander. More loudly, he added, "But they've got that thing in a hangar out at the airport, and they're taking it apart. If they find anything, they'll let us know. And then—even if they find litter!—you can get to work. I want the son of a bitch responsible!"

So did Bernie.

"While you're waiting on them, I want reports. On that rape thing, and on just what you did see yesterday."

Later that morning, after the overcast had burned off and the heat had returned, Bernie's phone rang, echoing around the carrel that served him as an office. He grinned as he lifted his hands from the keyboard of his official municipal antique, an electronic typewriter with a mere half page of memory. Now, maybe, he could escape. Maybe he could get out of the building. Maybe he could even fly a . . .

It was the Count, and his message was simple: "They've found something out at the airport, and they want someone to come see. So go. And take a camera."

"Yes, sir!"

Delightedly, he launched the Hawk from the Aerie's uppermost platform, the jets thrusting the bird into the air, the wings snapping into place, the ground dropping abruptly away beneath him. He burned fuel with a prodigal hand, setting a direct course for the airport, wasting no time in soaring to gain altitude, certainly not to mesmerize himself with whirling landscapes as he had the day before.

Mere minutes later, he was descending on the hangar

apron. Dust flew as he parked the Hawk, this time without the dormancy switch, for here there was nothing to make the bird misbehave. He dismounted, stroked his vehicle's neck feathers with one hand, and strode toward the small door set like a sally port in the hangar's gate. The electronic camera he had brought bumped against his chest, swinging on the strap around his neck. It would record anything, in any light, that he could see with his eyes.

A balding man in a grey suit stood beside the door. Bernie introduced himself and held out a hand. The other took it, said, "Alan Praeger, Air Board," and opened the door. As it closed behind him, Bernie stopped, frozen in place by the scene before him.

The hangar was, of course, large enough for an airliner. A distant air-compressor labored inadequately to fight off the sun that beat down on the metal roof; the cavernous room stank of sweat and dust and spoiling meat. The Sparrow sprawled across the concrete floor and was dwarfed by the walls around it, and by the human mind's insistence on interpreting walls on a more human scale. Yet it was recognizably a sparrow, a small—a tiny—bird, and it paradoxically shrank the hangar to the point that the white-coated technicians laboring over the spotlit chest, neck, and head seemed to have escaped from some tale of munchkins or brownies.

The Sparrow's abdomen was open, the exposed flesh already dark and dry; that was, Bernie thought, where the rescue crews had cut to retrieve the bird's victims. Great gashes, still shining wet, had clearly only recently been opened by the technicians' laser scalpels. "We've been dissecting the thing," said Praeger with a gesture.

"I hear you found something?"

"Over there." Praeger pointed to the other side of the hangar's cavernous space, where more spotlights illuminated the Sparrow's passenger pod. More technicians labored there, their efforts concentrated on the cockpit area. Praeger started walking, and Bernie followed.

A bench had been set up to one side of the work area. Most of it was covered with the workers' tools and test instruments. One end was clear, except for a padded case that stood

open like a casket awaiting a shipment of crown jewels. Their
course, Bernie realized, would end at that casket, and he
wondered what they had found.

Praeger pointed at the casket. The padding was creased in
the center, like that in a jeweler's ring box. In the crease
rested a black plastic oblong with numerous metallic legs.
"A chip," said Bernie.

Praeger nodded. "It had been added to the controller's
motherboard. We have no idea what it does yet." He drew a
pen from his shirt pocket and pointed at a line of identifying
numbers on the chip's casing. "We do know it's a PROM—
programmable read-only memory—chip. With the right
equipment, someone could have stored a program in this
thing."

And if that program could have taken over the Sparrow . . .
"The perfect sabotage," said Bernie. "Like a virus program." The police had been dealing with those for decades.
Invented for laughs when computers were new, soon adopted
by saboteurs and vandals, now they were a favorite weapon
in battles for corporate control. They were also used by political terrorists.

Praeger nodded again. "Long-distance. Remote control.
And untraceable."

Bernie could already visualize other possibilities. A crook
could make an armored car deliver its cargo wherever he
wished. Or send a murder victim's vehicle over a cliff. Or
separate a kidnap target from its guards. Or . . . He reached
for the casket.

Praeger stopped him. "No, Officer. This is a federal case."
Bernie agreed reluctantly. The man was right on two counts:
Anything to do with terrorism was inevitably and promptly
yanked out of local hands, as was anything that interfered
with interstate commerce. But the feds did know that the
local yokels could help. That was why they had summoned
him, and . . . "It stays with us. We'll let you know when
we've analyzed the program."

Bernie had to settle for what his camera could record.

* * *

Aloft once more, Bernie set his Hawk to soaring in circles, but this time he paid little attention to the whirling landscape. He was thinking: It would be weeks before the feds had any results to share, and there was no reason to expect that the chip would reveal a thing about who had set it to subvert the Sparrow. He needed a different approach, an alternative way to seek the villain responsible.

Could he dismiss the idea that terrorists had done the deed? Too many groups had tried to claim the credit, but he could not rule out the possibility. He preferred it, in fact, to the thought that the villain was some nut bent on random destruction. Either might be the case, though he would rather hunt a rational foe—if rational was a word that could possibly fit with such a crime—one with a reason for his act, for through that reason, he might be able to track the man.

Bernie reflected on what any detective had to look for when he sought to solve a mystery. Modus operandi? That was unique, and therefore no help. There would be no clues in the department's records of the past. Did anyone gain from the Sparrow's attack? There must be dozens of insurance beneficiaries, heirs, disgruntled spouses. The sort of pedestrian gruntwork checking all of them out would need could safely be called a last resort. Who had had the opportunity to install the chip? Just every maintenance worker and pilot who had ever been in the Sparrow's cockpit, in every airport it had ever landed in. Even, for that matter, in the factory that had built and installed the control unit.

What was left? Nothing. It was indeed the perfect crime, untrackable until the villain—terrorist or whatever—said or did something to arouse suspicion. Perhaps, however, he could study that modus operandi. He could find out, even before the feds reported, just how a nonspec chip like the one they had found would have to work. How could a tiny thing like that possibly take over something as huge as an airliner? How could it possibly make the airliner do things so far outside its normal range of behaviors?

He needed a gengineer. Fortunately, he remembered, he knew one. He had met her just the day before. She had even been on the expressway, in the midst of the disaster, and she should therefore have some interest in the case. Now all he had to do was remember her name, and where she worked. Unfortunately, all the papers he had filled out, with all the information he needed, were back in the office.

But . . . Neoform was the company. That much he recalled. And he knew where that was located. He tipped the Hawk's soaring from its endless circles into a straight-line course. As he flew, he struggled to recall the name. The kid, the kid with the feather, his name had been Andy. Hers . . . ? The Neoform complex grew visible in the distance, and it came to him: Emily.

When he reached the Neoform headquarters, he was surprised to find another departmental Hawk in the parking lot. It had been toggled into dormancy, presumably because of the Buggies that surrounded it. If it had not been shut down, it might not have been able to resist temptation.

He took an empty space across the aisle, positioning his Hawk so that it faced the other, and put it as well to sleep. Who else was here? Was their business related at all to his own? He supposed he would find out soon enough.

As he walked toward the building entrance, he noticed a Tortoise drinking from the trough before it. Its shell bore splatters of something that had once been liquid. He supposed that most who noticed would have no idea of what the liquid might have been. To him, the splatters said that this was indeed the right place, and Emily—Emily Gilman, that was it—was here.

As he approached the glass doorway, he thought he recognized the figure standing before the receptionist's barrier. Connie, here? She had said she would be interviewing witnesses, and the computer would have parceled out the lists. Had it been alphabetic? Or random? His hand hovered over the door handle, and he decided it didn't matter. It was just coincidence that their paths had crossed here and now.

When he entered, the receptionist's eyebrows rose dramatically, as if to say that one cop on the premises was unusual enough, but two? He ignored her. "Hi, Connie. Mrs. Gilman?"

"She was in a meeting. She's on the way down now."

She had hardly finished speaking when a slim, dark-haired woman rounded the corner. Her dress was tailored both for an appearance of professional competence and for utility—one breast pocket, loaded with pens, had obviously been stiffened to resist sagging; two side pockets, just forward of her hips, supported folded papers.

As Emily approached, her gaze swung back and forth between them. "Yes?"

Connie spoke first: "Dr. Gilman? We're interviewing as many witnesses to yesterday's incident as we can."

"An incident, is it now?" She looked at Bernie, and her eyes widened with recognition.

He couldn't help but blush. "I'm investigating the Sparrow from another angle," he said. "I need some background on how genimals are controlled, and I thought of you."

She smiled at him. "I'll be delighted to help. But I'm afraid I can only oblige one of you today. I've been out of town . . ."

"You were here first, Connie." He turned back to Emily. "Tomorrow?"

They made the appointment. When they had shaken hands, he gave Connie a mock salute and left.

Bernie's quarters were stark and bare, less from some austerity of design than simply because he had never felt the need for pretty tables, pictures for the walls, or draperies. A bed, a bureau, an easy chair, a worn dinette set, one small bookcase, and a sagging couch had all come with the apartment. His own possessions consisted of the clothes in the closet, the dishes in the kitchen cupboard, a few books, some photos of his favorite genimals, all of them raptors, scattered on a bookcase shelf. And, of course, his bicycle.

Connie had an apartment in the same near-work neighborhood as Bernie, and she too was a single police officer, but that was where the resemblance ended. The furniture was her own, all of it, polished wood, fabrics whose roughness was meant to suggest handweaving, soft cushions. The floors wore braided rugs. The walls bore art photos printed in metallic inks on glass.

Now he lay supine on her bed. She sat erect beside him. One of his hands lay on her thigh. One of hers was flat on his bare chest. He circled his index finger in the sweat on her skin. She pretended to coil the same finger in the scant hair between his nipples. He let his eyes wander over her: so slender that she might have seemed anorexic if her muscles weren't so clearly, cleanly drawn beneath the skin, small breasts like plums, hard and sweet, corded neck, fine-drawn features. She surveyed him as well: as strong as she in the male way that needs less work to maintain the muscles, the early signs of later paunch—she pinched his belly flesh—square hands, blocky features, rugged.

If he had gone home when he got off work, he would have fried a couple of hot dogs, or a pork chop, and opened a beer. Connie had stuck lasagna from the freezer in her microwave and opened a bottle of wine. Then she had actually made a salad, and he got a dose of the greens his mother had always told him never to forget to eat.

He closed his eyes while Connie fingered his chest hair. He squeezed her thigh, and he thought that she was good for him. Just what he needed. Maybe . . .

"Hey, Bernie." She tweaked a hair. "Think you'll ever get close to her?" She reached downward with her other hand. "Close like this?"

"Huh? Who you talkin' about?" He opened his eyes. She was smiling.

"Mrs. Gilman. That good-lookin' Emily. She was lookin' at you, Bernie."

"Aaahh, you're full of it, Skoglund." She had looked at him, there in the Neoform entrance lobby, just as she had looked at Connie, just as she would look at any vaguely familiar stranger. There had been no sign of any deeper interest, and he thought that surely he could have told.

"No, I mean it. I think you turned her on when you threw up all over her running board. Showed her how sensitive you are, you know?"

He felt himself turning red. Connie had pumped her for everything, hadn't she?

"Oh, my," she said. "I never knew a man could blush like that!" She laughed. Her hand left his chest and touched the side of his face. "From here . . ." It slid down his neck, over his shoulder, and back to his chest. "To here."

"Come on, Connie!" His voice plaintive, he tried to sit up.

She pushed him back. "Uh-uh. Don't run away. I've always known you were sensitive, Bernie. It's why I like you. Why you're here now."

He glared up at her. "So why push my buttons?"

She giggled. "There's only one button I want to push. The same one she does, I bet. Think it'll work again?"

There was a pause, another giggle, a rustling of sheets as they changed their positions. Then, "Go for it, fella."

Chapter
Five

RALPH CHOWDHURY'S LAB might have seemed strange to another scientist, even to another gengineer. The computer workstations, screens aglow with graphic simulations and columns of figures, were normal enough. So were the scattered aquaria, shelves of reagents, enameled freezers, stainless steel incubators, and LED-illuminated DNA splicers. But Chowdhury's desk, carefully centered before the greenboard at the head of the room, looked much more like a schoolmaster's podium than like a researcher's work space. The desk was a high, slant-topped affair at which he sat on a high stool, his feet wrapped around the rungs. The other desks and workbenches in his lab were less extreme in their idiosyncrasy, but they too were higher than normal, and Chowdhury expected his aides to use the stools he had provided for them.

It might have seemed even stranger to visitors from Neoform's financial or marketing departments. They too favored more conventional furniture, but they would have found most alarming precisely what no gengineer would blink at: the strange things floating in the aquaria, the *particular* subjects of the graphic simulations, the dried puffer hanging above Adam Chand's workstation. They promised new products for the company, but they also gave Chowdhury's lab something of the air of an alchemist's workshop. There was missing only a suitable array of alembics and a grimoire or two, though that absence had never struck Chowdhury. His lab was as it was because, quite simply, he had once seen an old photo of a Bombay accounting shop, with rows of bookkeepers perched on stools and leaning over heavy ledgers set on slant-topped lecterns. He knew perfectly well that modern Indians, like accountants and bookkeepers throughout the world, now used desktop computers, but he had inescapably identified that photo with his ethnic heritage. And as soon as he had earned the right to dictate the design of his own lab, he had exercised that right.

Adam Chand was one of Chowdhury's three technicians. He had found the puffer in an antique shop the summer before, its bleached and empty body inflated like a balloon, but stiff, all spines and prickles. The storekeeper had told him that they were also called blowfish, that they inflated themselves with air to foil predators, that they had been at times used as lanterns, housing candles, and that in Japan, as *fugu*, they were considered delicacies, if only the chef were successful in removing the toxic inner organs.

Now, beneath the puffer's dry benison, Chand labored, exploring the puffer's genome. He had long since, in his spare moments, confirmed the dealer's tales through the data bases. Then he had wondered if the fish could be enlarged and its air cavity turned into a compartment for passengers, cargo, and engines. Gengineers had tried, he knew, to turn porpoises and whales into bioform submarines, but so far they had failed. If he could be the first to succeed . . . Once, he had admitted to his boss that at night he dreamed of promotion to a lab of his own. Chowdhury presumed he still did, though he no longer dared to speak of it.

Chowdhury's other two technicians were busy too. Micaela Potonegra, at another terminal, was working on production schedules for the Armadons. Zhang Dong—everyone but Chowdhury called him Sam—was using the DNA splicer to make certain changes Chowdhury had ordered in several genes taken from a coral snake. Chowdhury, not having told him what genes he was working on, had watched expressionlessly as Dong had consulted the genebanks and learned that they controlled venom production. He had not tried to learn what effects his changes would have.

The door to the lab slammed. Chowdhury had returned

from the meeting at which Emily Gilman had presented the results of her Washington trip and then had ridiculed his Armadons. His technicians stared at him. He stared back. His mouth was a line, his eyes hidden behind his spectacles, his arms stiff at his sides. Chand was the only one who dared to speak: "Dr. Chowdhury? There's an interesting gene complex in these puffers . . ."

He turned toward Chand. He spoke quietly: "Those *verdammt* puffers are none of our business, *Dr.* Chand. Work on them on your own time. And now . . ." Suddenly he screamed, "Out!"

The three were used to being banished. Without a word, Chand and Potonegra closed down their terminals. Dong touched a button, and the splicer spat out a cassette containing the material he had been working on and the reagents he had been using. He would take it to the alternate lab they had set up in the prototype barn. There they could continue their work.

The banishments were frequent. Chowdhury rarely passed a day without a temper tantrum and an "Out!" Sometimes the moment came after a meeting of the company's researchers, as it had today. Sometimes it came after a phone call. Sometimes it seemed to come out of the blue, or swim up out of his first morning cup of tea, or rumble out of his bowels. Sometimes he called his people back in just an hour. Sometimes he let them work in the barn all day.

The barn was isolated from Neoform's main building and other workers, and it could be noisy, for many genimals, like their unmodified ancestors, had voices and used them. Yet, in some ways, the technicians preferred the place. Despite the noise, and sometimes the stink, it was peaceful. It was also comfortable, for the barn lab's desks and benches were all of standard height, unlike the furniture Chowdhury preferred, and the seats were padded swivel chairs.

Now Chowdhury hunched on his high stool, facing his high podium, and stared at nothing. His phone occupied a shelf beneath his desktop. His computer terminal rested on a table, flat-topped but of a height to match his desk, to his right. To his left, another table bore a saltwater aquarium.

"Dillo Dillies!" His head twitched, and a vagrant sun-beam glanced off the flat planes of his spectacles to put a cursor on the wall. His Armadons would outdo those Roach-sters! He knew it! They were warm-blooded, after all, and he would prove to the world what an immense advantage that could be as soon as he got an Armadon and a Roachster head-to-head on the track. Armadons would need more food for fuel, but that should be no problem. Roachsters had been the first bioform vehicles, designed to eat hay, grass clippings, household garbage, whatever was available. The waste dis-posal genimals had not at the time been widespread. Now there were the airliners, they had prodigious appetites, and the gengineers had taken seriously an old adage of the envi-ronmental scientists—"A waste is simply a resource that is out of place." They had redefined waste disposal as fuel pro-duction, and there was no shortage.

The company was wasting its money on Emily Gilman's Bioblimps. He turned to stare at his aquarium. It had been handy having a source of jellyfish on the premises. But there was no need for new cargo vehicles, and no money in them.

They refused to see the truth. They even ridiculed him. And now the police were here. Here!

His phone rang. He picked it up, listened, and was glad that he had thrown his technicians out. He could feel the beads of sweat upon his brow, knew that he was cringing, shrinking upon his stool.

He said, "I know what I owe them. I know what I prom-ised. And part of the package is ready now. The rest is almost ready." There was a pause while he listened. Then he hung up and dropped his forehead into his hands, his fingers grip-ping his scalp. Years before, he had taken a vacation in Las Vegas. He had gambled. He had won. And when he had come home, there had been an invitation to a local club, a back room in a restaurant in an ordinary middle-class neighbor-hood. He had gambled again. And he had lost. They had offered him credit. And he had lost that.

And then . . .

He was perversely glad that the phone call had come from

that particular caller. He knew the man, and though he had
asked Chowdhury to do things of which he had never
dreamed, and though he had uttered words that promised that
Chowdhury would do far more hateful deeds, deeds he could
never conceive of dreaming . . . He sighed. It would be still
worse to be owned by some outsider.

He knew why he had fallen into the trap. He had been born
in this country. But his parents had been South African "coloureds." His father had been a hybrid of Boer and African,
his mother a sari-wearing descendant of Indian merchants.
Both had been physicians and well off compared to other
members of their underclass. But they *had* belonged to an
underclass, and he had been weaned on the bitter tales of
how neither had ever been allowed into such precincts of
privilege and wealth as the local casinos. He had seized his
opportunity with the eagerness of the culturally deprived.
    And then—the man before him had had the well-fed beef-
iness of the Boers who had tyrannized his parents. He sat at
a broad desk, polished until his inverted reflection doubled
the stares aimed Chowdhury's way. One hand rested on a
stack of yellow slips, the credit markers that measured
Chowdhury's foolishness. The other held a small glass vial.
A pair of bodyguards flanked the door behind Chowdhury. A
safe stood open in the paneled wall to the left.
    "We have let you get much too far into us, Dr. Chowd-
hury."
    He stared at the large diamond that held the other's black
tie flat against his shirtfront.
    "You don't seem to have wondered why." A sigh. "They
never do. But now it's time to pay."
    "I can't."
    "You can. You even have a choice of methods." The other
held up the vial and shook it to make the tiny capsule within
it rattle. The glass sparkled in the light. "One way is to take
this pill."
    Chowdhury shrank within. He had heard. He knew. The
Biological Revolution had put an end to drug smuggling, but

not to addiction. Someone, early on, had fitted tapeworms and other parasites with the genes for heroin, cannabinol, cocaine, mescaline, and other substances. There were even parasites for alcoholics. The parasites' eggs could be washed from an addict's wastes and given to anyone who wished infection; some addicts carried a dozen different parasites, and their brains were a chemical stew unmatched since the drug-happy days of the 1960s.

For the first time in history, addicts never had to come down, or worry about how to pay for their next hit. Overdoses were inevitable, for as the parasites grew, they secreted more and more of their drugs, but the addicts never thought of the death awaiting them.

Nor did they think of how their convenience had hurt the drug trade. The man before Chowdhury had. "Take this," he said. "And you will be a very happy man."

It would cost him his job, his career, his very wish to do the gengineering he loved. "And a dead one," whispered Chowdhury. He could not take his eyes off the vial.

The other shrugged. "Eventually. Or . . ."

Did Chowdhury sense a possible reprieve? He looked up, from the vial to the diamond again, to the soft chin, the unblinking eyes.

Another sigh. "These hedonic parasites cost us a very profitable line of business. But they do have a drawback—once one is infected, one is never again free of the drug, even if one should wish to be so. We have wondered whether it would be possible to gengineer an animal, or a plant, that would administer a drug only on command?"

"A snake? A nettle?"

The other's smile showed teeth but did not touch his eyes. "Ah, you understand. And as soon as you bring us something along those lines, something *marketable* you understand, we'll tear these up." He held the credit markers up. One of the bodyguards stepped past Chowdhury to take them, and the vial, and return them to the safe.

"Shall we say—cocaine? Until then, I'm afraid, we can't allow you to gamble any more of our money."

* * *

The cocaine nettle had been easy. Nettle leaves and stalks are covered with tiny, sharp-tipped, hollow hairs. Normally the hairs are filled with venom; when a person brushes against the plant, the hair tips break off and the hairs inject their venom into the skin; the result is an intense itching, burning sensation. All he had had to do was change the venom genes so that the hairs were filled with a strong cocaine solution.

He had known what he was doing. He had known that he was developing a new way, a new variation, really, on an old way, for people to kill themselves. He had done it anyway, telling himself that it was inevitable. New technology first went to major uses, such as Roachsters, Sparrows, and Armadons, even Bioblimps. Soon thereafter, even before it spread widely in legitimate industry, it began to affect crime, and the underworld use of the technology might even find its way to influencing the legitimate. Prohibition, he thought, had spurred automotive technology because liquor smugglers and moonshiners had devised ways to enhance the speed and power of their vehicles. Later, those same techniques had appeared in Detroit, and when Prohibition ended, racing had strengthened to provide a new impetus to the technology.

He had delivered the cocaine nettle within a month, and he had done so proudly, if warily. Now its scions grew in pots all across the country, while those with the money to buy them, and their guests . . .

The head of Neoform's legal department had thrown a party for the company's upper-level staff. He had gone, and in the man's apartment he had seen his creation. A large nettle sat atop the baby grand piano, a second as a centerpiece amid the buffet, a third on the wet bar. The man had called it something new, something expensive, something marvelous, Neoform should have come up with it, see, just pet it, and feel great!

Someone had tried it, and then another. Someone else had said, "That feels like cocaine!" and tried to explain how millions once had snorted white powder through narrow tubes, rolled dollar bills, rolled . . . Governments had been powerless as drug money fueled a criminal empire that stretched from South America around the world. But then the parasites had killed almost all the market. There were very few left who preferred their coke the old-fashioned way. Fortunately, she had once dated one of them.

"Let's try a leaf!" She had plucked one, rolled it, inserted it into her nose, and gasped. Her current boyfriend had made a hit when he suggested that the leaves might be applied elsewhere to good effect, and it had not been long before the lawyer's three plants were reduced to stumps. Chowdhury had had to reassure him that they would quickly regrow from their roots, though he had not confessed his role in the plant's creation.

But his markers had not been destroyed. Someone else had called. A new master who would hold them as a club, while doling out money enough to buy a new Roachster, and talk of fame and wealth, if only he would produce a hedonic pet or two. They wanted genimals, this time. Something cute, perhaps. Something that only he, gengineer par excellence, could possibly create.

He looked at his aquarium again. In it floated a small jellyfish. If it were wild, its tentacles would be studded with cnidoblasts. Some cnidoblasts, when touched, would expel minute threads to entangle prey. Others would expel sticky tubes. Still others would discharge barbed needles loaded with paralyzing toxin. His jellyfish had only the third type of cnidoblast. Its needles he had smoothed of barbs and filled with heroin. If he petted it . . .

He didn't think his masters from the underworld—did anyone still call it the Mafia? the Cosa Nostra?—would like the jellyfish. He would show it to them, but he expected they would prefer his tiny asp, its venom sacs loaded with drugs, the snake just of a size to coil around a lady's throat and, on command, bite her pretty earlobe. Soon he would have a rattlesnake, a coral snake, a mamba. Drugs to be worn. Drugs as fashion. Perhaps he would try a bee, or a spider.

If only his masters were Indian, or half Indian, like himself. Whites reminded him of the *verdammt* Boers, while blacks . . .

Ah! The stories he had grown up on! His parents, young then, shoulder to shoulder with all the oppressed blacks and coloureds, resisting the Boers, giving *them* the Cape Town necklaces of flaming rubber tires, expelling them, those that survived, from the country. And then, with help from America, Europe, Russia, China, everywhere, rebuilding the nation's shattered economy.

His parents had not been there to see success. Through all of Africa, the merchants derived from India, China, and Southeast Asia were hated only a little less than the whites. And with the whites gone, the blacks had turned on their allies. The Chowdhurys had been among the few to escape the pogroms.

He had chosen his technicians carefully. None were white. None were kaffirs, schwartzers. One, Chand, was of Indian ancestry. Potonegra was from Guatemala. Dong was Chinese. They were safe. He could work with them, unlike Emily Gilman, or her technician, Alan Bryant, the black.

He became aware of a thread of music. One of his technicians—there, where Potonegra had been sitting—had left her radio on when she had obeyed his banishment order. He rose from his stool to turn it off. He preferred silence.

When he returned to his desk, he activated the computer terminal. He called up the appropriate data base, and he found that Emily had been quite right. Armadilloes did indeed jump straight upward when startled, and on highways that reflex did indeed lead to many deaths.

He had his own copy of the armadillo genome, with every gene labeled. He called it up, found the genes that specified the neural circuits behind the reflex. Then he checked the Armadon genome. He shook his head when he found the same genes there. It must have the same circuitry, the same reflex. A quick simulation confirmed that an Armadon did not have the strength to jump, but, yes, it could tear its own wheels off. Just what the customer would want in an emergency. He chuckled.

With the simulator, he explored the effects of modifying or deleting various genes and bits of circuitry. One change left the Armadon unable to move its legs at all. Another limited its speed. Still another . . . Finally, he found the change that removed only the startle reflex. He would have Micaela implement it immediately. Then they could grow another prototype, and he would have his fame and fortune without the underworld.

Chapter
Six

SOME THINGS NEVER change. Emily Gilman's grandmother would have been bewildered by what now passed for airplanes and automobiles. But she would have felt quite at home in her granddaughter's kitchen. The sink was stainless steel, and on the shelf above it sat a plastic bottle of lemon-scented detergent and a potted plant, a crown of thorns with two tiny blossoms the size, shape, and color of drops of blood. The table was wood, bright curtains flanked the windows, and the refrigerator, its top a repository for paper napkins and books and old gloves, was covered with kiddy art, notes, coupons, and lists, all held in place by magnetic fruit, lambs, and clowns. The rest of the appliances were all as recognizable— the dishwasher that roared its indigestion every evening, the blender, the coffee maker, the mixer, the range, the microwave, the toaster oven. The only changes that had come over the decades were in size and shape and placement of the knobs.

That wasn't fair, thought Emily. There were other changes as well. For one thing, it had been her grandmother who ruled her kitchen. Here and now, it was Nick, and this kitchen was far more his than hers. Almost the only thing she did in there was make bread. And she didn't do that often enough, for it was less a way to feed her family than to sublimate aggression and work off frustration.

Her grandmother would have thought the arrangement strange, even though in her time househusbands were not all that uncommon. Perhaps it was. Emily felt at times that their

roles were far too reversed. She should be the nurturer, he
the bread-winner. When they had met, in college, they had
both been sure that that would be their pattern, as soon as
his poems, perhaps as songs, or his fiction—would he wind
up writing for the veedo?—made him rich and famous. It
hadn't worked out that way.

And how about the computerized voice synthesizer in the
toaster oven? She had sliced a bagel, laid it on the rack, and
set the knobs for "Dark." Now it chimed gently and announced in a warmly maternal tone, "I'm getting close." In
a moment, it would say, "I'm ready? Aren't you? I'll keep it
warm." If she did not respond, it would do just that, automatically adjusting its temperature to keep the bagel from
burning.

Too many of them talked like that. And it could drive you
nuts. Of course, the voices could be turned off, but when you
had a small child around the house, you let the gadgets talk.
He loved it so. And it could save a parent so much nagging,
as when the toilet said, "Don't forget to wash your hands."

The bagel turned brown behind the toaster's tiny, oblong
window. The appliance spoke its piece, she pressed the latch
bar, and it delivered up her breakfast. She spread cream
cheese, poured coffee, and began to eat.

Moments later, Andy ran into the kitchen, still in his pajamas, eyes still gummed with sleep, breath smelling of
toothpaste, and yelled, "Mommy!" She hugged him with the
arm whose hand did not hold half a bagel and offered him a
bite.

Nick appeared, hair uncombed, and said, "C'mon, kiddo.
You've brushed, but you haven't washed."

"Unh-unhhh!" Andy twisted away from his mother and
threw himself across the room into the chair by the window.
He knelt there and peered toward the bird feeder, his nose
reinforcing the smudge on the glass. Emily took another bite
of her bagel. Nick stepped toward their son, his hand out-
stretched.

Andy pointed. "Look at that, Daddy! That's a funny one!"
Nick bent until his head was beside his son's and he too

could see out the window. "You're right," he said. Emily could see his attention withdraw from all thought of getting the boy washed up. "I've never seen one like that before. Look, dear."

Emily didn't want to look at any goddam birds. She had seen enough of them lately. She checked the gold-framed digital on her wrist. "I'm running late. Gotta rush." She sipped her coffee, but then she discovered it was still too hot to drink rapidly.

"Stop and smell the flowers, sweetheart. It's got long legs and a beak like a dagger. Like a small heron or egret. But grey with orange streaks." She winced and thought that, yes, he did know how to pause and appreciate the small accidents of life, flowers by the wayside, birds upon the lawn. Once she had been able to do the same. "Where's the Peterson?" he asked.

He found the bird guide on top of the refrigerator and flipped through the plates. He hesitated, flipped again, turned back, and held the page for her to see. "It's not here," he said. "But it looks kind of like a bittern." The picture by his finger was of a drab brown bird, beady eyes framing a beak held straight upward to aid its camouflage among the reeds of a swamp.

What, she wondered, would a bittern be doing in a suburban backyard? Surely, every swamp in the county had been drained and filled a century ago, or more. Was there some sort of race memory that sent bitterns back to the swamps of their ancestors? Had there once been a swamp beneath their yard? Or was it not really a bittern?

A shadow wheeled across the window, and both the room and the yard outside darkened momentarily. "The Chickadee's back!" cried Andy's delighted voice.

Nick turned back to the window. "Hey! It's grabbin' for it, Emily! The stranger's dodgin', flappin' its wings, trying to take off!"

"It made it!" Andy crowed. He had a Warbird in his hand, red plastic in the shape of an Eagle bearing a pod bedecked with futuristic weaponry. Now he waved the toy in the air and shrilled a war cry.

"Please!" Finally Emily set down her cup and crossed to the window to see what all the fuss was about. The strange bird was no longer in sight, though a few brown and orange feathers were just sashaying down through the air, settling to the ground. The Chickadee was staring into the sky, cocking its black-capped head toward the house, peering toward the nearest tree, and spinning with amazing lightness to seize a robin that only wanted to find a worm for its own breakfast. Then it proved once more that it was not a pure carnivore by stepping ponderously to the feeder on its post to clean it of its seeds.

Emily felt her gorge beginning to rise. The incident on the expressway had been more than enough to wipe from her mind any tendency she had ever had to find overgrown, jet-assisted carnivores charming, with or without their jets. She swallowed convulsively and sipped coffee to clear the taste from her mouth. Then she tipped her mug to the ceiling and finished the last of it. "I thought you were going to call the airport?"

Nick shrugged. "I did. And they came and got it."

She glared at him. "Obviously, it got loose again."

"You're not going to call them again, are you, Daddy?"

Emily put just a hint of steel in her voice. "You'd better."

Her husband waved one hand toward the ceiling, palm upward, fingers spread as if he were throwing a handful of bird seed into the air. He made a face that suggested, she supposed, resigned confusion. "But why bother? Andy loves it."

"Yeah!"

She nodded. "I'd like strange birds to hang around long enough for me to see them."

He sighed. Yes, that was why they had installed the feeder in the first place, so they could watch the birds that came to dine on their offerings. They had always felt an extra thrill when a new kind of bird joined the feathered throng. "If you'd . . ."

Yes, if she had gotten off her duff and looked when he had first invited her, if she weren't turned off birds for now, if she hadn't told herself she had to rush, if . . . She wasn't being fair, and she knew it. Still, her voice rang with that stiffer gauge of steel she sometimes used when technicians, especially those who held doctorates as certificates of competence, made a royal mess of something critical: "I want that goddam Chickadee gone. What normal birds it doesn't eat, it scares away." Andy stared at her, his eyes wide; this was a side of his mother he did not often see. She shook her head sharply, her hair swirling around her ears, and turned away. On the job, she could be pure boss, a tyrant on occasion as nasty as even Ralph Chowdhury at his worst. Here, at home, the situation was contaminated by emotions that never arose in the lab. She felt a tremor in her throat and a moistness—tears—hovering behind her eyes.

She checked her watch again. It was time to go. If she lingered to argue, she would be late. "Just call."

"Watch," said Alan Bryant. "We can get the kangaroo sequence from San Diego." The only marsupial whose genes the commercial genebanks had proved to carry had been the common opossum; their stock was drawn almost exclusively from plants and animals common in the northern hemisphere. He had had to turn to the zoo's more specialized bank, which supplied gengineers around the world with the basic components of more exotic species.

He was sitting at the computer workstation in the lab. Emily was leaning over his shoulder, staring at the depiction of the Bioblimp's genome on the screen. Several lines, each one coiled upon itself to avoid tangling, represented the genimal's several chromosomes. Individual genes were identified by labels. Alan pointed. "It fits in right here. That puts it under the same control sequences as the tentacles, and then . . ."

He wore on his right hand a mouse, a glove patterned in swirling arabesques meant to suggest the intricate array of circuitry and accelerometers embedded in the thin fabric. The glove was the lineal descendant of the ancient computer control device that had first borne its name. Now he pointed, used his thumb to press a switch set against the side of his

index finger, and pointed again. A line segment, marked
"Pouch," moved into position beside the chromosome he
had indicated. The chromosome broke, the "Pouch" gene
moved into the gap, and the break resealed. He tapped the
keyboard, used the mouse to choose the "Simulation" option
on the menu that popped into view, and leaned back in his
chair.

An egg divided, and divided again. As the borders of the
growing embryo approached the edges of the screen, the
computer reset the scale, reducing the image once more to a
glowing icon. It enlarged again, reset once more, grew and
hollowed, added a dozen tentacles, and began to show grooves
in the side of the gasbag above each tentacle's base. The
grooves became slits, and then pouches, and the genimal was
complete. A new menu appeared, Alan chose "Animate,"
and the tentacles began to flex and twine. A simple cube
sprang into existence on the screen. A tentacle picked it up
and stuffed it into a pouch.

"We still need sphincters," he said. "To seal the pouches
when they're full."

Emily straightened, one hand on the small of her back.
"Very pretty," she said.

Alan rolled his chair back from the terminal to face her.
"But," he said. "I can hear it in your voice."

She nodded. "You've done some real good work. But there
are just too many pouches. They're too small to work for a
moving van. Give it just two, one on each side."

"That'll violate the symmetry," he said. As the new design now stood, the Bioblimp's growth-regulating genes would
make it grow a pouch every time it grew a tentacle. Getting
around that would be tricky, for it was difficult to mix radial
and bilateral symmetries in a single organism.

"You can do it. Give the gene a new control sequence. Let
the first two openings set up a gradient that inhibits other
openings and breaks down the walls between pouches. Or we
can cut the walls later."

He was nodding when the phone rang. It was Miss Carol
at the desk downstairs. Detective Bernie Fischer was there to
see Dr. Gilman. Was she available?

* * *

By the time Emily led the police officer back into the lab, Alan Bryant was intent on his screen. A glance let her see one hand moving sporadically over the keyboard, the other, the one wearing the mouse, twitching back and forth. He was clearly struggling with the task she had set him, but from the small, satisfied grunts that issued periodically from his lips, he was making progress rapidly enough to please him. She expected it would please her as well.

She was silent as she led the cop to her corner of the lab, pointed him at the seat by the window, and poured coffee. Then, as he set his briefcase on the corner of her desk and began to undo its latches, she said, "You wanted to know about how we control our genimals, Detective Fischer?"

"Call me Bernie, Dr. Gilman." If voices could be seen and not heard, she thought, his would be a soft and mellow brown. Nick's, by contrast, would be orange, touched with red, a higher pitch, more brassy.

"Then I'm Emily. But . . ."

He withdrew from his briefcase a single glossy photo. She took it from his hand, and stared. "It's a chip," he said. "A PROM chip. A computer can read it but not write to it, though it is programmable with the right equipment. We have no idea what it does."

"From the Sparrow?" Her voice shook. She knew, too well, what the Sparrow itself had done.

"That's right."

"Where was it?"

"Plugged into the main board—the motherboard—in the cockpit computer. The federal people, from the Air Board, have the original."

"What does it . . . ?"

He shook his head. "They haven't analyzed it yet. I was hoping . . ."

She stared at him. Nick was so slender, nonmuscular, almost as willowy as convention would have a poet. This Bernie was a sturdier soul, clearly of an age with her husband and her but thicker in the middle, stronger, more . . . more *masculine.* She had only just met him, really, though she knew she had seen him at the expressway and, briefly, the day before. But when he gestured with one of his large, square hands, she imagined his touch on her, on her breasts, her thighs, her . . . Her skin felt warm. Yet his appeal was not solely physical.

She too shook her head, though more abruptly, and her hair flew around her ears. "I can't tell you much from a photograph," she said. "But I can tell you what it might have done, what the possibilities are."

"Please," he said, smiling. He sipped his coffee. "That's all I want."

She touched a switch and the screen of her own desktop workstation lit up. Her fingers rattled briefly over the keyboard. A schematic diagram appeared. "This is a Hawk," she said. "Like yours." She pointed. "There's the brain, the spinal cord, the motor centers. There's the passenger pod, the driver's console, the controller. A cable, here, from the controller to the interface plug under the forward lip of the pod. Wires from that to the brain." She explained how the controller, a computer, translated movements of the tiller or control yoke and the throttle and brake pedals into electrical signals and routed them as appropriate to the jets or the genimal's motor centers, triggering the genimal's own nervous system into commanding its muscles to serve its driver. All the necessary programming was built into the hardware, burned into PROM chips like the one pictured in his glossy.

"It's only a little different," she added, "in a genimal whose passenger compartment is built in, like a Tortoise. There the controller cable could go directly to the brain, without an interface plug, though there is one to make maintenance easier. A Roachster's plug is installed beneath the shell-secreting membrane, so molting will not affect it. To get at it, the techs have to cut through the shell."

He had nodded periodically as she talked, as if he understood it all. Perhaps he did. Now he said, "But the chip?"

She felt her face grow warm. She had forgotten the point. "Anywhere in this pathway," she said, pointing again at the circuitry of the controller. "Insert it, and it can lock out the driver. Then it can cancel legitimate commands and substitute its own. And its own commands might be very simple. That Sparrow—I think a block on the pilot's commands, plus a trigger to the jet's hunger center, might be enough. Especially if there were a timer on the chip, so it turned on only at a specific time, or when a source of food such as the expressway was in view.''

She paused reflectively. ''You could try to prevent this sort of hijacking by putting feedback circuits in the controller. They would check that the proper signals were getting through, but a chip could fake those too. There really isn't any way to block such a thing.''

He leaned forward, so close that she could smell the maleness of his body, studying the screen. ''Couldn't you make the beast smarter?''

She shook her head. ''Uh-uh. Intelligence just isn't that easy to produce. They've been trying for a century to produce it in computers, and we haven't made any better progress with the genimals.''

''But what about transplanting human genes?''

''That's the other reason why we don't have smart genimals. There are sixty different humane societies out there, and when they got together, they had very little trouble persuading Washington to ban transplanting human genes to genimals. They said it would be reinventing slavery. So, for that matter, would be gengineering a nonhuman intelligence.'' She hesitated before adding, ''They're probably right. At least, if we're talking human-level intelligence.''

He grunted as if to say he was listening, but his attention had turned back to the computer screen. With one blunt finger, he was tracing the circuitry she had tried to explain to him. Finally, he shook his head. ''I can't picture it.''

''Then I'll show you.'' She sighed, reached out a hand, and pulled him to his feet. As they crossed the lab, she said, ''Alan, we're going out to Ralph's prototype barn.''

Emily and Bernie heard the flat cracks—one, a pause, another, a pause, a third—as they approached the barn. Bernie immediately identified the sounds as gunshots, drew his pistol from beneath his uniform jacket, and ran to the door. Emily followed so closely that she clearly heard him yell "Freeze!" and something clatter as it hit the floor.

When she entered the cavernous room that housed the Armadon, she saw Chowdhury, legs spread, arms above his head, facing into the corrugated, scaly flank of his genimal. He was standing between its two waist-high left wheels, his arms straddling a doorway set into the bulge of the beast's side and back. Stubby legs twitched beside his shoulders. The geminal's long snout was bent back toward him, audibly sniffing, eyes blinking, tongue flicking. The long tail switched back and forth, stirring the hay that littered the barn floor. Above Chowdhury's head, ample windows set into the beast's side revealed an empty interior. Chowdhury was sweating, and his muscles trembled visibly.

"What were you trying to do?" Bernie's voice was an outraged bellow, as if he found personally offensive whatever he had seen Chowdhury doing.

"Startle it." Chowdhury's voice was weak, but it strengthened as he glared at Emily. "I wanted to see whether I really would have to take the time to grow a new prototype."

Emily spoke to the policeman's back. "We warned him that it might kick its legs off." She briefly described the armadillo's startle reflex.

Bernie laughed. "Look," he said, turning toward Emily for the first time since she had entered the room. "It's just a .22. A popgun." He retrieved it from the floor near his feet, aimed it at a bale of hay near the wall, and pulled the trigger. The noise was unimpressive. "My magnum, now . . ." He grasped his pistol in both hands, aimed, and fired.

The Armadon convulsed. Chowdhury flew across the floor to land on his back, spectacles askew, eyes wide. There was a loud crackle, as of breaking wood or bone.

Emily helped Chowdhury to his feet. "I'm sorry." She did not say, "I told you so." The point was far too obvious, for now the Armadon rested on its belly, its feet unable to reach the floor. Its tail quivered, its snout twitched, and a soft, panting whine crept from its throat. One of its wheels had rolled across the barn to fetch up against a wall, looking much like a wagon wheel decorating the set of a western movie. The other three splayed from the Armadon's bulk, still attached by shreds of bone and skin, but useless.

Bernie stared sympathetically at the genimal. It had feelings, he knew, but . . . When he looked at the people in the room with him, his expression grew sheepish. "You needed something louder," he said.

The other man straightened his glasses. He stared at the damage. He trembled harder. Then he took a deep breath, clenched his fists, and screamed at them: "What are you doing here?"

Emily laid a hand on his rigid arm as if to calm him. He shook it off. She said, "I wanted to show him how a genimal's controller works. He's investigating the Sparrow attack on the expressway."

Chowdhury spun around to stare at the cop. In a moment, he said, "So show him. Then get out of here." He turned his back on both of them. The Armadon whined again. He stepped to its side and laid a hand on its flank. After a moment he stalked toward the door into the lab that shared the barn building, leaving them alone with the crippled genimal.

Bernie returned his gun to its holster. "Touchy, isn't he?"

"Almost always." Emily patted the still-whining Armadon's flank, opened its metal door, and waved him in. The door remained open behind them, and the windows in the genimal's sides gave them a clear view of the outside room. The cabinet that held the control computer, obviously not fastened down, stood askew. Emily presumed it had been jolted out of position when Bernie had startled the Armadon. A control tiller jutted from the cabinet, and a single seat, a cylindrical hassock, lay on its side nearby.

Emily stood the hassock upright, sat down, and removed the front panel from the computer cabinet. Then she repeated the lesson she had begun indoors. Now he nodded repeatedly, understanding what she said as long as he could see and touch a three-dimensional reality rather than some baffling, lifeless diagram.

Absorbed in their work of instruction and absorption, they

nevertheless heard the door to the lab open and close and noticed when Chowdhury came to stand, listening, by the Armadon's doorway. Emily felt his presence as a weight upon her back. Eventually, she turned to include him in the conversation and noticed the syringe in his hand. It held at least a pint of clear yellow fluid. "Bernie says they found a foreign chip in the Sparrow, Ralph," she said. "I've been showing him how such a thing might work. It probably had some sort of internal timer."

"It's like a virus program," said Bernie. "It sits there in the computer, just waiting for its moment, and then it takes over."

Chowdhury snorted, scowled, and shook his head. "It wouldn't work," he said. "There are too many redundant pathways between the controller and the genimal. No chip could possibly block them all. And anyway, it couldn't hold a program for anything as complex as what that Sparrow was doing."

Why, wondered Emily, should redundant pathways make any difference? It should be electronic child's play to program the chip to intercept them all. She said nothing about that objection, however. "It wouldn't have to," she put in. "The controller doesn't control a genimal move by move anyway. It activates coordinative structures in the nervous system, hierarchies of reflexes and instincts that make it do what we want it to do. So why couldn't this chip simply activate a different set of instincts? Or even a single drive, such as hunger? Instincts and drives we normally want suppressed?"

Chowdhury opened his mouth and aimed the reflections from his spectacles at her alone, but before he could speak, Bernie said, "A chip like this would be lovely for criminals and terrorists—for hijackings, murders and assassinations, robberies . . ."

"Bah!" Chowdhury held his syringe up as if to be sure they saw it. His open hand slapped the side of the door. The Armadon twitched beneath them, sensitized to such noises by its recent painful experience. "You are talking nonsense. Criminals don't have the facilities! And I will thank you to leave my Armadon now. Out! It is suffering."

Emily waited until he had stepped aside before she descended from the Armadon, Bernie close behind her. While they maneuvered through the doorway, Chowdhury was silent. But as they moved away, she thought she heard him murmur, "And I must destroy it."

Chapter
Seven

As soon as Andy had eaten his breakfast, he had returned to the window to watch the Chickadee. Nick watched him with a smile, while he finished his coffee. The gengineered birds were as familiar to the boy as metal airplanes had been to Nick as a child, or as wood and fabric biplanes had been to an earlier generation. Andy had seen the big ones at the airport, on the veedo, flying high overhead. He had one hanging from his bedroom ceiling. But this one was in his own backyard, and it was real.

Nick could hear the voice clearly, so much deeper than a wild chickadee's that the normal "dee-dee-dee" became a "doo-doo-doo." He knew Andy could see the details—the scale-covered legs, the chunky, conical beak, the plumage, white below, grey above, the alertly gleaming eye beneath the black skullcap, shaggy instead of velvety, as it was on normal, small chickadees. He could hear his son muttering— "Zoom! Whee!"—and knew that he was fantasizing about hopping onto its back and flying off to high adventures. He could be Sinbad, the Little Prince, Aladdin, Superman, any hero, every hero he had ever seen flying on the veedo shows or in books.

Nick left the boy to his dreams. He brushed crumbs from the breakfast table into his cupped hand, washed the breakfast dishes, and checked the refrigerator and freezer to see what he had in stock that might make a decent dinner that night. He added to the grocery list and checked his wallet to be sure he had the cash he needed. Then, with a glance at Andy—he was still absorbed in the Chickadee—he went to the small room he called his office and turned on his word processor.

It had been secondhand, or maybe third, when he had bought it in college. It had already been obsolete for decades, so obsolete in fact that its mouse was a little box, equipped with push-buttons and a roller ball, at the end of a cable that plugged into the back of the computer. But the dealer had made sense when he said that obsolescence was a relative thing. If a computer did what you wanted it to, it did not matter whether it was state-of-the-art technology. And five megabytes of memory, with half a gigabyte of hard disk storage, had been more than enough for a would-be writer with no wish to run scientific or business simulations. It had been cheap too. And in the years he had owned it, it had indeed done all he had wished of it.

He had been reading *Hey, Mabel!*, Jennie Bone's recent book on the tabloids and the magazines that followed in their tracks. Bone—years before, in school, she had been one of his professors—had quoted a long-dead tabloid editor to show why those rags never seemed to die: Any story, true or not, that could make a husband cry, "Hey, Mabel! Dja see this?" would sell papers. Nick had appreciated her pungent views of the tabloid-readers' minds, and he had come in time to the poem now on the screen before him:

You say good wine is fragrant, pure, and clean?
It takes a gritty wine to suit my friend.
He thinks pyramids can sharpen razors
And his wife lusts for exercise machines.

He believes easy chairs can spread the plague,
Living in closets makes the brain leak blood,
Soft water is disaster for the back,
And tabloids never fail to shout the truth.

He is a bubblehead who hopes the grit
Of wine that you reject as cheapest cheat
Will fill up his emptiness with wisdom.
Instead, we think, it only makes him thick.

Now he needed a title, at least, and then he could try to find it a home. "Vintage Wisdom"? "Wine of Wisdom"?

It had taken him a month to get this far. Andy was a distraction, as were all the chores of running a home, but those were by no means all the reason for his slow progress. He sighed. He simply did not have the drive to be a successful writer.

He flicked off the machine. Speaking of chores, and of drive, or driving . . . He checked the kitchen; Andy was still at the window. "I'll be in the garage," he called.

"Sure, Daddy."

The garage. The Tortoise's stable. There was the food bin, there the water, there the tools for mucking out. Some families had larger garages, with two—or more—vehicles, and their own litterbugs to keep the floor clean. Someday, he and Emily would have as much. Right now, even if they could afford a litterbug, one Tortoise was not enough to keep it fed. They would have to supplement its diet, and that would cost more money. Emily's pay was ample, but so much of it went for taxes and insurance and to repay the loans that had put them both through school. He wished he had had the sense to study something more employable.

He replaced his shoes with rubber boots from a wall-mounted cupboard, positioned the wheelbarrow near the pile of grey-streaked paste, and muttered to himself that a reptile's crap didn't look much like a mammal's. Like a bird, the Tortoise had a single exit, a cloaca, for all its wastes, and the product looked it.

He fleered, raising his upper lip and exhaling gustily like an animal confronting some awful stink. Then he laughed at himself—he *was* an animal, and the mess *did* stink—and began his labors. To escape the smell as best he could, he breathed through his mouth.

Thankfully, he reflected that the task was not really so bad. The Hercules of ancient myth, drafted by a king without the sense to hire enough stablehands to do the job, or to tell the ones he had to muck out the barn more often, had had to divert a river to cleanse the Augean stables. His job might feel that great at times, but a Tortoise excreted fairly small amounts of manure. What it did excrete was rich in nitrogen and other nutrients. It would, as always, make excellent fertilizer for their flower beds and shrubbery. If they didn't have the Tortoise, they would have to buy manure.

When he returned inside, Andy cried, "Daddy! It's looking right at me!" And indeed it was. He stood behind his son and watched the Chickadee, a foot away, separated only by the glass of the window, twitch its head back and forth, first one eye trained on the boy, then the other. What was it thinking?

"Get away from the window, kiddo." Window "glass" had been replaced by a harder, tougher polycarbonate plastic in the days of his grandparents, but the word and the image persisted in people's minds. Besides, the Chickadee's beak was the size of a kitchen wastebasket. Its tip and edges looked quite sharp enough to smash even plastic "glass," and then to do far more damage than he could stand to contemplate. He laid a hand on his son's shoulder and tugged.

Andy looked up at his father with all the scorn a five-year-old can muster for a too-protective parent. "Oh, Daddy! It's not going to eat me!" To his mind, the incident on the expressway had no bearing on the rest of life. Besides, that incident had not really touched them. Nick, like Emily, felt differently.

"Come on. I'm going to call the airport." He drew the boy away from the window. As he did so, the Chickadee stepped back itself, as if it could have heard and understood his words. When he picked up the phone, it launched itself heavily into the air, its wings straining. It was clearly, even to Nick's untrained eye, just about at the limit for unassisted flight.

The Chickadee didn't go far, for Nick could hear its feet scrabble on the roof. With nothing to watch, Andy wandered into the living room, turned on the veedo, and sat down on the thickest of the several throw rugs scattered over the polished hardwood floor. He lay down on his belly and stretched an arm under the couch to retrieve a toy, a small metal truck that had somehow survived Nick's own childhood.

The airport Nick called was not the regional jetport he had

visited to pick up Emily. It was just a few miles away, a much
more local affair that catered to the owners of private one-
and two-passenger jets. He had driven past it several times,
remembering the few lessons he had once had on mechanical
airplanes and wondering if they could afford a few lessons on
these modern aircraft. He had seen that the airport was small
and shabby, but not so derelict that most of its planes could
not be kept in small hangars. A few jets were tethered in the
open. He would have thought the Chickadee one of the latter,
except that there was no broken tether cord around its neck.
Perhaps it was kept in a hangar, but its owner carelessly failed
to latch the door.

The airport clerk sighed with audible impatience. "You
called us yesterday, didn't you?"

"That's right. And you came and got the thing. Now it's
back. On the roof."

The clerk sighed again. Jets weren't supposed to take off
on their own, but sometimes they did. Or the small ones did.
The big ones couldn't, and Nick should be thankful he didn't
have a Sparrow on the roof.

When Nick grunted, the clerk said hurriedly, "I didn't
mean . . . If you were . . ."

"I was."

"So was my sister, and she won't even go in the park now.
The pigeons." The clerk's tone was instantly more sympathetic. "We'll get someone right out there. It might be an
hour or so, but we'll get that jet off your roof. Yes, we will."

From the walk in front of their house, Nick and Andy could
see a streak of birdlime running down the slope of the roof.
A glob of the stuff had beaded there, while the rest had fallen,
some of it hitting the brick side of the house beside the bedroom window, all of it spattering over the rhododendrons
below. He would, Nick thought, have to hose it off later, or
it would burn the shrubs, or even kill them. Fertilizer belonged in the soil, not on the leaves.

The Chickadee was still on the roof. Its head jerked this
way, that way. Its tail pumped at the air, compensating for
the head movements that might have thrown it off balance.

Swallows swirled around its head, trying to drive it from their nesting territory. Occasionally, it seized and ate one.

"Yuck," said Andy, and as if noticing his disapproval, the Chickadee spread its wings and hopped into the air, flapping, gliding to another rooftop down the block. Nick hoped that it would remain in the neighborhood until the airport crew could get there.

"C'mon," he said. "Let's go get those groceries."

"I'll get it!" Nick smiled as Andy dashed into the garage to lift their folding wire cart from its nail. Without it, they would need a cab to bring the groceries home. With it, the walk home would be only a little more labor than that to the store. It would be much less if Andy would not insist on helping him to pull it along the walk. He would have to walk with his knees half bent, and by the time they reached home, his back would be in agony.

But before they left . . . A large oak tree overhung one corner of the front yard, its branches drooping with the weight of leaves. For some reason, Nick turned to stare at it, his eyes scanning the limbs revealed in shadows by the shifting of the foliage. There, the streaks of orange in its plumage spoiling the camouflage that might have worked quite well in a swamp, was the strange bird of breakfast time. It held a bittern's posture, tapered body still, beak upthrust, eyes blinking. As he watched, it twisted on its feet as if to let its gaze sweep over the front of the house.

Nick shuddered. "Let's go, kiddo."

Nick was in the kitchen, in the back of the house, when he heard the garage door close. Footsteps sounded on the walk, the front door's latch clicked, hinges squeaked, and the footsteps vanished as they touched the throw rug in the front hall. A clunk announced that Andy had dropped his toy, and there was a glad cry of "Mommy!" Emily's briefcase struck the floor with a soft thud. Nick could tell when she bent to kiss their son, for there was a soft creak as the fabric of her skirt stretched across her butt.

He sliced the last potato half, arranged the slices in the pan—they would have scalloped potatoes tonight, with fried tofu and salad—and set down the knife. He blinked away the odor of the onions he had sliced first and rinsed his hands. He opened the refrigerator, took out a carton of white wine, and poured two glasses. Then he stepped into the living room and saw: Just as he had imagined, his wife was scooching, one knee on the floor and the fabric of her skirt drawn tightly over one haunch. She was hugging Andy, and her dark hair fell forward to curtain her face, and the boy's, from his view.

"Hi, honey." He held one wine glass out to her.

She looked up, her eyes narrowing, her mouth as hard and tight as if there had been no hiatus between this moment and the morning. "Did you call?"

"Sure. It's gone, and I saw that strange bird again. You'll get to see it. Good day?"

Her mouth finally softened. She accepted the wine. She smiled at him, and he remembered when he had first seen those wide, expressive lips. He had been with another girl, at a party in a dorm, when a gust of laughter had drawn his attention to the other side of the room. There she had been, enjoying the joke, her mouth all teeth and tongue and happy noise, and her date—Nick had seen it—had slid a hand over the seat of her jeans. Her face had closed in, turned dark, erupted with her fury. There had been a slap, a curse, a stalking away. And when he noticed her again, in some un-remembered class, he had asked her out. He had long forgotten the name of his date at that party.

Why had she appealed to him? Had he seen her fury as a challenge? Had he thought, someplace within his mind, out of reach of any conscious intent, that he might be able to please her more? If so . . . He smiled back at her now. He lived for those sunny moments, fully aware that she could get mad with little notice and over what he, at least, thought were only minor slights. What's worse, her anger could last for hours and days, until the world—or he—finally bent to her will. Though, to be fair, she really seemed to react that way only when whatever offended her might be judged to have some component of personal animus. She accepted imper-sonal events such as power outages and traffic jams and terrorist attacks on the expressway with more equanimity than he.

"I'll know for sure when Alan gets those kangaroo genes installed in the blimp."

Nick laughed. "The cargo pockets?"

She nodded. "It looks like they'll work." She paused, ruffled Andy's hair, and stood up. Then she added, "We had a cop at the lab today."

"I hope he wasn't suspecting you of anything." Nick led the way into the kitchen.

"Can I have a sip?" Andy, toy truck in his hands, was staring at his mother's glass. It was something of a family ritual: Whenever they had drinks—beer, wine, scotch, whatever—he could have one small sip from each of their glasses. They believed it could do no harm and might do good, if he grew up with the idea that alcohol was acceptable in small amounts.

As he busied himself with getting their dinner onto the stove, she said, "They found a chip in that Sparrow's control computer." She had, she said, explained to the detective how such a chip might preempt control. She did not give the cop a name, or say that Nick had met him on the expressway.

"I took him out to Ralph's lab," she said, and laughed. When Nick turned toward her, face poised in inquiry, she was sitting at the kitchen table, drink in one hand, her gaze aimed toward some vague place beyond the walls of the room. Yet she noticed his expression and drew her attention home again. She added, "I kept a straight face then, but . . ." She explained that she had told Chowdhury that the armadillo's startle reflex would give his Armadons problems, and they had caught him checking the idea out with a small pistol. She described the scene and its outcome, and Nick laughed too.

At the same time, both of them shook their heads ruefully. The situation had clearly had all the slapstick humor of a pratfall. But like any pratfall, no matter how ludicrous, it had involved pain. Pain for both the Armadon and its creator.

If he wondered that his wife seemed to be dwelling on another man, he said nothing. She showed no sign of romantic or sexual interest, and besides, modern marriages varied broadly in their openness. Some couples orbited each other only loosely, returning home like explorers to a base camp. Some, like Nick and Emily, hewed only to each other. Yet, he knew, neither of them had ever tested their bond. If and when such a test arose, their marriage might have to change.

Later, once Andy was in bed and asleep, they had another drink. They read a bit in separate easy chairs. Then they shifted to the couch, side by side, his arm around her shoulders, one hand playing with her buttons, her hand against his chest toying with his, to watch a veedo show.

The show proved boring, but one button led to another. Soon they tuned the veedo's sound to a low murmur and paid attention only to each other:

"Do all poets have quill pens?" she began. "Feathers here . . ."

"Ballpoints."

"Fountain pens."

"Gengineers have test tubes."

"They need genes too."

"How do they get them?"

"With pipettes." A pause. "Did you know that once upon a time, long ago, lab workers used to suck on pipettes. With their mouths?" They shifted their positions, and there was a longer pause. "But now they're safety-conscious. They use electronic pumps."

"Poets use electronics too."

"Not tonight, they don't. We want those genes . . ."

"Put that pipette . . ."

"In the test tube . . ."

"Click that ballpoint . . ."

"Fountain pen!"

They had perfected the game long ago, when they were still in school, before they were ever married. Still they loved to play it.

Chapter Eight

WHAT HAD AWAKENED her? Morning light—*early* morning light—filtered past the curtains. The clock radio had not yet turned on. There was silence from Andy's room. Nick was still, his head on her shoulder, his breath warm on her chest, his hand spread on her belly. She twisted in the bed, let his head fall to the pillow, and smiled tenderly at his oblivious face. He had always been a heavy sleeper. When baby Andy had cried in the night, he had never noticed. She had been the one to rise and feed the baby and change the diaper and rock him back to sleep.

She wouldn't really have minded, except for the loss of sleep. For a few months, before Andy had begun to sleep the night through, she had been so exhausted that she had spent her days at the lab in a fog. But she had also done some very good work then, including the groundwork for her Bioblimp. Nick had suggested that the exhaustion had loosened the restraints on her creativity. Perhaps he was right, though she had not realized that that was a side benefit of a wakeful baby until much later. At the time, she had had to content herself with the realization that the nighttime house had been pleasantly quiet, and the dawn hours, alive with birdsong, had been relaxing, peaceful, mellow. She had come closest, then, to understanding the lives of her ancestors, their days and seasons timed by the rhythms of the sun.

What had awakened her? Some sound? She peered at the clock across the room: Its glowing numerals announced smugly that the time was a quarter to five in the morning. It would be another hour before the radio turned itself on to get them out of bed.

But there was light. Dawn was breaking outside, and there was no birdsong. Was that what had awakened her? That absence of normality? That silence?

No. A soft crunch sounded overhead, a scritch of avian claws as they stepped along the peak of the roof.

That goddam Chickadee!

"I believe you," she said. "You said you called the airport, and you said they came and got the Chickadee, and I believe you.

"So why is the damned thing still here?" Her voice was so tense it was almost a scream. "I want it *gone*!"

"Me too!" said Andy.

Emily suppressed a glare at her son. Like most children she had ever met, he did not know what to want for himself. He learned, he built himself, by modeling himself on those who meant the most to him. He was heartbreakingly loyal, and there were times when that loyalty made her heart turn over in her chest. But right now he was staring yearningly at the window, clearly wishing that the Chickadee would come down off the roof for him to watch. His loyalty was so obviously just that, no more, unreal, a lie for whatever in-built reasons, that, for a moment of irrationality, she wanted to strangle the little bastard.

Her toast and juice sat untouched before her. Her coffee quivered in its cup when she lifted it to her mouth. A swell of tears hovered on the brink of her lower eyelid. She dabbed at the moisture with a hanky from the hanky bush.

Nick stared at his plate. Yes, he had called. Yes, they had come. When he and Andy had returned from their shopping trip, Mrs. Palane across the street had said so, describing the truck, the crew, the bait that had lured the bird into the truck, and the sigh of relief that had seemed to emanate from the trees, where presumably the local—and diminished—population of swallows was hiding out. If he wasn't sure about the sigh of relief—Mrs. Palane did have a tendency to hyperbole—he did believe the airport crew had come for the Chickadee. But, yes, here it was again. He had clearly failed.

He said: "They can't be securing it very well."

"I'll say! This is the second time it's come back!" She jerked her head sharply to one side, making her dark hair fly as if to emphasize her anger.

He explained why he didn't think they were tethering it at all. "It has to be a hangar bird, and the hangar door can't be latching properly. Either that, or someone is letting it loose at night."

"Don't tell me about it. Tell them!"

"I will." He set down his cup, brushed a crumb from the front of his white shirt, carried his empty plate to the sink, and made the call on the spot. He didn't want her doubting him, or accusing him of more failure than he had earned. She was, he thought, too prone to anger, even with a good excuse, and he felt his real failures keenly enough without her comments.

The airport clerk, once more, was sympathetic and promised immediate action. Nick suggested that once they had the little jet back, they check the latch on its hangar. He did not suggest that anyone was letting the Chickadee out deliberately, for that seemed unlikely.

When he was done, his wife nodded as if he really had solved the problem. She took a bite of her cold toast, drank her juice, and pushed the dishes away. Then she said, "It's time to go."

"I'll go out with you."

She shrugged, as if to say, "Suit yourself," and left the room for her briefcase. Andy followed, stretched to reach the garage-door control, and held the door for his parents.

Together, they waited on the walk while the Tortoise ambled from its cave and positioned itself for boarding. But Emily did not board. Instead, she stared at the Chickadee on the roof, and her mouth set in a rigid line. The bird shifted its weight from one leg to the other. A shingle came loose, slid down the slope of the roof, and fell among the rhododendrons.

"And now the roof is going to leak," she said.

"I can fix it," said Nick. "I will."

"But look at that!" She pointed at the streak of birdlime. "Look at *what* it's going to leak!"

Nick laid a hand on her arm. "It'll wash off the roof. I'll take a hose to it today." With gentle pressure he turned her to face the oak that overhung the lawn. He pointed. "But look there."

"Where?" She searched the shadows among the great tree's branches.

"There!" cried Andy. "I see it!" Nick lined his arm up beside her head so that her gaze could follow its line.

"Is that it? It's pretty." The strange, bitternlike bird was there again, or still, its beak thrusting into the shadows above its head; its small eyes, like beads of sparkling ebony, blinking in the morning light.

Now that bird turned, focusing those dark eyes upon them. Its beak swung to the horizontal. Its wings lifted as if in a shrug. They flapped once, twice, and it dove off its branch. Its course carried the bird, a heavy flier, low over the lawn before it could rise and circle close above their heads.

"It's right over you, Mommy!"

Indeed it was. It was so close that they could feel small gusts of breeze from its straining wings, and the shadows of its passage across the sun were passing waves of coolness. But now its circle was rising and broadening, and its eyes seemed aimed at Emily alone. She moved to one side, and the bird's orbit shifted to remain centered on her. The Chickadee moved too, cocking its head to watch the little drama below it. It sidled along the rooftop as if to be closer to the action. Its beak gaped, and in the brief glance she spared it, Emily could see the tongue within its mouth.

The strange bird suddenly broke off its circling, uttered a raucous shriek, and dove straight for Emily, its beak an outthrust dagger. Andy screamed. Nick grabbed his wife and pulled her toward him. She felt the buffet of the bird's heavy wing against her arm as it missed.

It did not give up. As Andy, still screaming, grabbed his mother around the legs, hobbling her as effectively as quicksand, and as Nick, cursing, tried to pry him loose and get them all into the house, the garage, the Tortoise, anywhere safe, the bird bent its course around again. It flew up between the oak tree and the house, performed a graceful Immelmann looping turn, and arrowed back toward the target it seemed to have chosen so deliberately.

This time, it did not make it. It did not even come close. Its course took it over the roof of the house, and as soon as it was within reach, the Chickadee lunged and caught it by one wing.

The smaller bird swung on its suddenly forced pivot. There was a snap of breaking wingbone. It struck with its beak, stabbing, and the Chickadee's throat blossomed red.

The Chickadee cried out in apparent pain. As its beak parted, the bittern—if that was what it truly was—fell to the roof, its beak and one good wing flailing. One huge foot clamped it into place, while the Chickadee's shorter, blunter beak struck once, twice, three times. As blood spattered on the roof, Emily felt a droplet of something wet and cool strike her cheek. Another droplet struck Nick's white shirt, and she knew that hers too must be blood, blood that had lost its warmth in its voyage across the intervening space.

The Chickadee cried out once more and leaped, more clumsily than usual, into the air, leaving its victim behind. It flew off, heading this time in the direction of the airport, presumably going home to nurse its wound.

The dead bittern slid slowly down the slope of the roof to land in the shrubbery. It was accompanied by two more broken shingles.

Nick finally got Andy loose from his mother and scooped him up to hold him safe, his thighs enwrapped by one paternal arm. The boy began to cry. "Let's go back in the house," said Nick. With his free hand, he tried to steer Emily toward the door they had just left.

"No," she said. She patted his hand with her own, understanding his protective feelings. But she was a biologist, a genetic engineer, and she had just been attacked by something whose behavior was not natural.

She looked down, at the hand that still gripped the handle of her briefcase, and noted without surprise that her knuckles were stark white. Deliberately, she loosened her grip, scooched, opened the case, and extracted a tissue. She dabbed at her cheek, stared briefly at the spot of red upon the tissue, wondered which bird the blood had come from, and crossed the lawn to the bittern. Two rhododendron branches, broken from their parent bush, lay beneath the body. A pungent odor declared that that body had fouled itself as it died.

Emily used the bloody tissue to cover her fingers as she drew the bittern into clearer view on the lawn. Even in death, its orange-on-grey color scheme gave it a kind of beauty. But, close up, that beauty was the stark beauty of a weapon designed for a single job. Now, finally, when it had almost been too late, she recognized it.

The back of the head bore a small, implanted plug of the sort that on the Tortoise received a cable from the controller computer. The beak was as long as her hand from wrist to fingertips, sharp, and stained, as if it had been dipped in some sticky substance. The claws were talons whose specifications probably had been lifted from the genome of a hawk or eagle. Around one ankle was a metal band.

A shadow fell over her. She looked up at Nick and Andy. "An Assassin bird," she said. "But why was it after me?"

The police arrived half an hour later. Nick had called them immediately, while Emily made herself and her husband another pot of coffee. Now here they were, their Roachsters hogging the driveway and forcing the Tortoise back into its garage. Nick, Emily, and Andy had been herded onto the walk by the front steps, where they would not interfere. The police themselves were stomping all over the lawn, taking samples of the Chickadee's dung, retrieving feathers of the Assassin bird from beneath the oak tree and the bird feeder, sliding the body, looking much smaller than it had in life, into a plastic bag. The officer whose responsibility was this last task was being very careful not to touch the beak.

Nick was explaining: "It showed up first by the bird feeder—my son spotted it—but then the Chickadee chased it off . . ."

"A chickadee?" The tone of disbelief that escaped around

the officer's wad of gum was thick enough to bottle. It smelled of peppermint.

"An escapee from the airport. We just thought this, this Assassin bird, was just a pretty bird. We looked it up and figured it was some kind of bittern. Then it showed up in the tree there . . ." He pointed.

One of the cops, dark-skinned, grizzle-haired, with a weathered look to his lined face, kicked at Emily's briefcase, still on the ground, and said, "Bitterns don't roost in trees. They're a swamp bird."

Nick shrugged. So he had thought, Emily knew, but there the bird had been. "That's where it was today too. And when we came out, it flew around her, in circles . . ." He gestured overhead with one arm. "Then it attacked, and the Chickadee got it."

"So where's the Chickadee?"

"It flew off. I guess it's back at the airport."

A shadow swept overhead. They all looked up, and Emily said, "A Hawk!" The police insignia were plainly visible.

The Hawk, fanning its wings and tail, descended onto the lawn, braced its legs, and darted its head to left and right. The bubble-shaped pod on its back opened, and a figure familiar to both Nick and Emily emerged. He waved to the other officers and approached the Gilmans, leaving the Hawk alertly scanning the neighborhood.

"Detective Bernie Fischer," he said to Nick. "We met on the expressway. Damned birds." To Emily, he said, "I thought I'd asked you every question I could think of yesterday. Now . . ." Someone passed him the bagged Assassin bird. He gestured with it. "This gives me a bunch more. What happened?"

Nick watched Emily as she answered: "It was no accident, Bernie. It can't have been. Someone had to aim it at me. Me!"

She looked from the detective to her husband. If he had been a cat or dog, she thought, the fur above his neck and shoulders would have been bristling suspiciously. She could almost hear his thoughts—Bernie? Bernie? My wife is not *that* informal with strangers.

"Wait a minute," Nick said. "This detective was the cop who interviewed you at the lab?"

Emily and Bernie both nodded. Emily said, "Why not? He found out I was a gengineer at the expressway, and then he needed to talk to a gengineer."

He was clearly unable completely to restrain his skepticism that that was enough to explain his wife's familiarity with the other man. But in a moment, he relaxed, and Bernie asked Emily again, "But what happened?"

She went through the whole story again, just as she had for the other cops. When she came to the Chickadee, Nick interjected, "I don't see how it could keep escaping. Maybe someone's been letting it loose on purpose."

"We'll look into it," said Bernie. Then, when Emily had finished her report, he asked her, "Why did someone have to aim this bird at you?"

"It's an Assassin bird. Programmable." She pointed at the plug in the bird's head. "The military uses them."

"Ah," he said. He looked at Nick. He shifted his gaze to Andy, standing between his parents. "Then we should be able to track it down. I'll get right on it." One hand lifted as if he would like to squeeze Emily's shoulder, but he redirected the intention movement toward the boy. "Your son?" As they nodded, he patted Andy on the head. "We'll keep your mother safe," he said. "That's our job."

Bernie lifted off in his Hawk shortly thereafter. With him went the Assassin bird in its plastic bag. After him went the other cops, leaving behind footprints, a cigar butt, and a handful of gum wrappers.

"Andy," said Nick. He made a show of examining his watch. "The Chickadee's gone. Isn't there a veedo show you like about now?" When the boy, thus reminded of his favorite *Warbirds of Time*, rushed toward the house and veedo, Nick added, "Should I be jealous?"

Emily bent to pick up her briefcase. She stared at him. She said, "At a time like this you can ask such a question?"

"The way he looked at you . . ."

"And the way I called him Bernie?" Her wide mouth contracted into a disgusted moue. "Yes, we got fairly friendly yesterday. But not *that* friendly." She tucked her briefcase under one arm long enough to clap her hands once, sharply. The Tortoise emerged once more from the garage.

The door to the house opened suddenly, slamming against the side of the house. Andy yelled, "Daddy! Phone!"

"I'll see you tonight." Emily climbed into the Tortoise, and the vehicle began to move immediately. She did not look back. Nor did Nick, staring after her, yearning, resisting the pull of the phone, cry anything after her.

Only later did she learn that the phone call had been from the local airport. The Chickadee had returned just as the retrieval crew had been about to leave. Unfortunately, before they could get it back into its hangar, it had dropped dead. *What* had Nick done to it? *Who* was going to pay? And did he know, *he* could be arrested for destroying other people's expensive property?

As Nick told her that evening, it had taken him ten minutes to explain, though his explanation did little to soothe his caller.

Chapter
Nine

So HER HUSBAND was jealous.

When Bernie Fischer was in a hurry, he didn't waste time soaring. He used the jets to get as high as he could. Then he blasted straight across the sky until he could put the Hawk into a dive to his destination. The practice wasn't recommended, for even with its composite skeletal implants the Hawk was more fragile than an all-metal jet, but it was fast.

He snorted to himself. He was not in a hurry now. He had lifted off quickly enough, but as soon as he had gained some altitude, he had turned the jets off. He would take his time and glide, soaring, back toward headquarters while he thought about Nick Gilman's reaction to him.

"Jealous," he muttered to himself as the landscape pivoted about his vantage point. "Hah!"

He had never thought of himself as a ladies' man, but Connie *had* said Emily had a yen for him, and maybe she did. Maybe her husband was right to worry.

Mentally, he slapped his wrist. Bernie, he thought, your mama raised you better than to think like that. Like a typical male fat-headed skirtflipper.

The Hawk's passenger pod had a rearview mirror much like that in a road vehicle, though its purpose was more to give the pilot a glimpse of whatever might be in the small space behind him. Sometimes he carried prisoners. Now he bent the mirror so that he could see his own face. Was he handsome? He supposed so, or close enough. Sexy? Ask Connie, or Emily.

The radio's buzzer sounded. He picked up the phonelike handset and spoke: "Fischer here."

"You still anywhere near the Gilman place?"

He peered through the pod's transparent wall. He could already make out the roof of the Aerie. "Almost home, now."

"Litter! We have a complaint from the county airport. They have a dead Chickadee."

He had said he would check out the hangar, hadn't he? "Get a gofer up to Platform 3, then. I have an Assassin bird for the freezer. Evidence. Then I'll go see." Maybe it was the same Chickadee. If so . . .

"Thanks." The dispatcher's voice sounded relieved. "Everybody else is busy."

"Ten-four." Two-way radios might now be more like phones, but some things never changed.

The airport that had housed the Chickadee was an antique. Once, surrounded by fields, it had served crop dusters. Later, suburbs had grown up around it, the worn, brown grass of the runways had been paved, and it had been a base for commuter airlines and air freight services. Now grass struggled to reclaim the cracked and rutted pavement. The arch-roofed metal hangars were streaked with rust. A few small private planes, lifeless and mechanical, gathered rust on the parking apron near a dilapidated terminal building. Even fewer modern bird-planes were visible, though their lost feathers and other litter testified that more must wait in the sun-baked hangars or be off on flights.

The airport manager was short, round, and bald, except for a thin fringe just above his ears. The hair that tufted above his eyes and in his ears and nose seemed much more plentiful. His name was Frederick Conal, and in between wide-eyed glances at Bernie's Hawk, he was complaining: "Yah, sure, it kept getting away from here, and he kept calling, telling me to come get it. And we did. Twice. But now— Look! Look at it, Officer! He says an Assassin bird did it, but I think . . ."

"He's right," said Bernie. His Hawk stood next to a snow-white Dove. A twisted-wire cable bound the Dove's neck to a ring set in the concrete of the apron. Its interior—white leather and velvet, with black accents—looked very comfortable, but that was not what appealed to the Hawk. Bernie wondered if his predatory vehicle would try to take a bite. So did the Dove, apparently, for it sidled a few steps to one side, getting as far as its tether would allow from the Hawk's hooked beak.

Bernie did not choose to put the Hawk into dormancy. Conal was anxious for some reason, far more anxious than a dead Chickadee would seem to warrant. The detective wondered whether he might not play upon that anxiety. Scare him, he thought, and he might reveal something useful. And he wouldn't even have to try hard. Conal was a rabbit. And he, Bernie, was an official predator. He was, he thought, a Hawk himself. He liked the image.

"A beak this long," he added deliberately, using both hands to show how long he meant. "It was trying to kill a woman, but the Chickadee grabbed it."

"That's what he said." Conal shook his head as if amazed at the heroism of a mere Chickadee, or at the fact that someone could tell the truth.

Bernie pretended to ignore the man as Conal gave the Hawk one more terrified glance. The Chickadee's carcass, one wing splayed, eyes already glazed, lay on the pavement not far from where they stood. No one had bothered to rig a tarp to shade it from the sun, and already the flies were gathering. Happily, so far there was no stink. He squatted beside the dead bird's neck and used a ballpoint pen to probe the wound. It was not the full depth of the Assassin bird's beak, he found. Nor did it seem to sever any major blood vessels. He looked closely. The edges of the wound were discolored in a way that did not seem due to mere drying. He sniffed. The odor was off as well.

He stood again, dusting his palms over his uniform knees. "Where's its hangar?"

Conal's eyes flicked left while his right hand flapped at the air. "What do you want . . . ? What's that got to do with . . . ?" His voice squeaked. "Do you have a warrant?"

Bernie stared at the man. Conal's eyes had gone to the

nearest hangar, so close that the Chickadee must have been trying to reach it when it died. Why had his panic suddenly increased? "I don't need one," he said. "You called me in, remember? And I want to know how this Chickadee could keep getting loose."

"But . . . !" The day was hot, but the humidity was mercifully low. Bernie had not noticed any great accumulation of moisture on his own body. Now, he noted with interest, Conal's bald head bore noticeable beads of sweat.

"You have the right . . ." Conal shut up as Bernie read him his rights. Then the detective turned toward the hangar. The door was held by a simple padlock-and-chain arrangement. He shook it. The door was solidly fastened.

"Unlock it."

When Conal refused, he drew his .357 magnum, held the muzzle close to the padlock, and pulled the trigger. The padlock shattered, and the Dove and other small planes parked nearby, startled by the report, spread their wings reflexively. Only his Hawk failed to respond. He pulled the door open.

"Lights?" Bernie kept the gun in his hand as Conal pushed past him, one arm extended to the right. There was a click, and a bank of overhead fluorescents came on.

The hangar was not much larger than the Chickadee itself. The floor was dirt, though a drain received the overflow from a metal sink whose single tap ran constantly, if slowly. Bernie supposed any bird confined to such a sweatbox would need plenty of water.

There was room in the hangar for the plane, a wheelbarrow, a food trough crusted with the remains of the Chickadee's recent meals, and a table. The jet's engine and pod hung from the ceiling. Maintenance tools decorated the walls. A few chairs were scattered around the periphery. A dungheap marked the Chickadee's customary parking position, and Bernie wondered why. At the Aerie, at the city's main airport, litter was never allowed to accumulate. Then he recalled the mess outside, and its revelation that what picking up was done here—which clearly wasn't much—had to be done by human hands.

"Don't you have litterbugs?"

Conal twitched, satisfyingly rabbitlike. "They cost too much. We're just a small operation."

The hangar's corrugated metal walls concentrated the sun's heat pitilessly. Bernie thought that that alone, even with the water, might be enough to drive a plane to run away during the day. So might the stink the heat cooked out of the dung-heap. He scowled at signs of spilled jet fuel, and Conal said, "We do put 'em outside during the day, you know. On the line, out there. The hangars are for foul weather, and night, and winter."

With an abrupt wave of one hand, Bernie cut him off. Sweating now, and still scowling, he stalked through the hangar. He didn't know what he was looking for, but there was a faint touch of something strange to the stink in the hangar's air.

In the back, under the small wooden table and close by the dungheap, the dirt floor looked disturbed, as if someone had been digging. He scanned the hangar's walls. There was a shovel, its blade marked by ordinary soil, not the litter one might expect, or wish.

When he moved the table and reached for the shovel, Conal began to back toward the door. "Uh-uh," said Bernie. He raised the gun in his other hand as a reminder of the strength of his position. "Stay here." He whistled, and the Hawk's shadow moved to block the hangar's doorway.

He put the gun away and began to dig. Moments later, he had the answer spread out on the tabletop: two wooden boxes, each one twice the size of a shoebox. Each one was full of small vials. Each vial contained a gelatin capsule that might once have held vitamins. There were no labels, though the capsules were of various colors that might encode some meaning.

Bernie's voice was disgusted. "Hedonic parasites," he said aloud. He bent over the table to sniff the vials. He sensed nothing but the odor of freshly turned earth, and then he realized what the strange scent had been. It was not the smell of contraband, but—in a hangar that normally reeked of litter, jet fuel, and old bird food—that very scent of dirt.

Smugglers, he thought. Coming in at night to bury the

goods, or dig them up while money changed hands. Though the quantities of money could not be great. It was too easy to get the parasite eggs from another addict. Or might this be something new? He held a vial to the light. Through the translucent wall of the gelatin capsule he could see a small round dot that looked more like a seed. He knew about the nettles that had come on the market in just the last few months. Was that what these were? Whatever, the smugglers had been here, and they presumably had let the Chickadee out to give themselves more room in which to work.

The airport manager was huddled against one wall of the hangar, his body folded in upon itself as if he were cold. But he was sweating too, and even more than could be credited to the hangar's saunalike atmosphere. Bernie ignored him as he threw the shovel down and went to the Hawk. There he used the radio to call the dispatcher and request a warrant and a crew. They would search the terminal and the other hangars, collect the evidence, arrest Conal, and stake out the cache in hope of catching the smugglers that night, or the next. The hope was slim, he knew, for surely there was another of the gang watching the hangar now, noting his presence, and warning off the rest. But they would try.

The necessary reports had taken time, but it was still morning when Bernie set his Hawk down in the Neoform parking lot and toggled it to sleep. He grinned when he noticed the Gilman family Tortoise not far from the slot he had chosen. He had some information for her, perhaps he could learn something more about gengineering, and maybe . . .

The Grey Lady at the reception desk kept him waiting just long enough to let him know that everyone called her Miss Carol, that it was an awful shame what happened on the expressway just the other day and she hoped he, as a policeman, would see to it that it never happened again, and that Dr. Gilman was such a nice woman, didn't he think? When Emily showed up on the other side of the turnstile, he could just barely restrain an effusive "Thank you!" until they were out of sight.

"She has that effect on everyone," said Emily. "I've heard Security took a year to find her."

He stopped dead in the hallway and swung to face her. "You mean it's an act?"

"Oh, no!" Her wide mouth parted in a laugh, and he noticed the way the floral print of her dress swayed as if in a breeze and her pens bounced in the pocket on her bosom. She touched his arm to push him into motion again. "Oh, no! They wanted a genuine yenta. I'm told the idea is that she can keep any intruder talking—or listening—until the guards arrive."

"As long as she's on duty."

"Oh, well. There's someone else on the desk, but we lock the doors at night." He supposed the company's armed guards were on more visible patrol then, as well. "There's the lab." She pointed. As they began to slow down for the turn into her lab, a man emerged from a door on the other side of the hall, and a little farther from them. He was slight, short, and brown-skinned, and when he saw them, he scowled viciously. Bernie thought he recognized the man, but he had to grope for the name.

Only when they were in the lab could he say, "What's Chowdhury mad about today?"

"Probably the same thing as yesterday. He holds grudges." She gestured toward a young black man seated before a complicated array of control pads, glass tubing, and test tubes. "You met Alan. He's putting together an artificial virus for a gene transplant."

"How does that work?" he asked.

"Wild viruses can plug genes into DNA, but they put them anyplace. The ones we use can be designed to insert a 'cargo' gene wherever we wish in a genome. They can also be targeted to any type of cell in an animal's body. We have viruses for plants too."

When he said nothing, she added, "The key is simple. DNA is built as a sequence of simpler chemicals, or nucleotides. And it can bind to matching sequences. Since the virus is also DNA, all we have to do is tailor the appropriate piece of it to match the target area we want, and the virus will do the rest.''

Now Bernie looked confused. Alan grinned up at them. ''We use them the way mechanics use pliers,'' he said, ignoring her little lecture. ''You shouldn't have scared Chowdhury's Armadon for him.''

''You heard, huh?''

''We all did, though it didn't help that you were with her at the time.''

When Bernie looked puzzled, Emily explained, ''There's a certain amount of rivalry between us. He wants those Armadons of his to be the next big product for the company. I want . . .'' She told him about the Bioblimp.

''And the chowderhead hates everyone anyway,'' said Alan. ''His parents were South African.''

''Alan!''

He grinned sheepishly. ''You know I can't resist.''

Bernie admitted to himself that the epithet seemed inevitable. He knew just enough history to feel that Alan's description made sense, though he could not, at the moment, spell out that sense. He shrugged, smiled, waved a hand, and followed Emily to her office corner. ''What's that gadget?'' he asked, glancing over his shoulder.

''A DNA splicer,'' she said. ''Have you found out something about that bird already?''

He shook his head, let his gaze drop to her ankles, and scratched one temple. ''Not really. Though we know it's a government genimal, and the beak was poisoned.''

''That stain!''

He nodded, watching her face, the wide eyes, the parted lips that let the words escape so quietly, almost in a whisper. ''It stabbed the Chickadee.'' She nodded. ''This deep.'' He showed her with his fingers. ''And that was enough to kill it. I had the call even before I made it back to the office.'' He told her what else he had found in the hangar.

''Then Nick was right. It must have been in the way, and . . .''

''They were letting it out.''

She stood up and said, ''Coffee?'' The coffee maker was

on the windowsill. She had to step behind him to reach it, and as she did so, her belly brushed the back of his head. Was it deliberate? He let his head lean into her, and she said nothing. But when she had poured the two cups and handed him his, she retraced her path without touching him.

Shrugging mentally, he said, "The Assassin bird—you saw the band on its ankle? That carries the bird's serial number. Unfortunately, the number wasn't readable. Whoever sicced the bird on you defaced it."

She sipped her coffee. "Why didn't they just take the band off?"

He shook his head. "They tried. But the band is fiber-reinforced metal." He meant, she knew, the same material that was used to strengthen the skeletons of jets and other genimals against the consequences of the square-cube law. "All they could do was gouge a few of the digits badly enough to make them unreadable."

He then began to explain how an Assassin worked: Its handler showed it two photos, one of the intended victim, one of some landmark near which that person could be found, and released it not far from the landmark. The bird would then locate the landmark and lie in wait until the target appeared. Often, as in this case, the beak would be poisoned, although the beak alone was quite sufficient if the bird hit a vital spot.

She let him get about halfway into his explanation before she stopped him with a chopping gesture of one hand. "I know," she said. "I looked them up this morning, when I got here. Neoform designed them for some government agency—I don't know which—years ago, when I was still in school. We still breed them, though that's a different operation from this." She pointed her chin toward the rest of her lab. Her expression said that she didn't like the idea of clandestine assassinations, whether directed at her or not.

He hadn't known, he told himself, that Neoform was responsible for the Assassins. That bit of information hadn't been in the data base he had been able to tap that morning once he had established his "need to know" as a law-enforcement officer. He supposed that she had been able to consult company files more easily.

But all he said was: "I'm getting hungry. Lunch?"

When lunchtime came to the police department, its clerks, administrators, and officers streamed steadily from the building's main entrance, slowing only when too many people tried to get through the door at once. At Neoform, Bernie therefore thought the rush of employees through the halls toward the main entrance entirely normal, at least until the traffic flow slowed and halted not far from the turnstile.

Emily had just introduced him to one of her coworkers, Frank Janifer. When everyone stopped, he asked the man what was going on.

"Miss Carol," he said. "The dragon at the gate making sure that everyone signs out properly."

"Security," said Emily. "They tried electronic cards once, until the day a summer intern showed up with six of them. She said she was supposed to put them all through the scanner. Their owners were in a rush."

Yet the technology of signing out was not obsolete. Electronic cards may not have worked, but no one had felt that meant a return to pen and paper was necessary. As each person came to the turnstile, they bent and worked an electronic wand over a plastic-coated surface connected by a cable to the company's main computer. Their signature was instantly compared with a template in memory, and the machine kept the essential records of who came in and went out, and when. The process took no one long. Soon Bernie and Emily were outside and walking toward a nearby restaurant. "I don't know much about gengineering," he said.

Emily sidestepped as a girl, perhaps ten years old, sped past them on a bicycle. "It began almost a century ago," she said. "Biologists first learned how to snip genes apart in the 1970s. The key was chemicals—protein enzymes—that cut DNA only at certain points. Very quickly then, they learned how to add genes taken from one organism to the genome of another. They used everything from microscopic shotgun pellets coated with DNA copies of genes to viruses, which would carry a gene into a cell and plug it into the cell's DNA.''

The restaurant featured a broad flagstoned patio overshadowed by a trellis supporting a heavy growth of vines. Most of the patio's tables were occupied, but they found a small one for themselves. Menus were already on it. When it was obvious that the waiter would be a while in getting to them, Bernie said, ''And now you use those artificial viruses.''

''Like the one you saw Alan assembling.'' She took a moment then to scan the headlines on a newspaper spread across a chair at the next table. They concerned a demonstration against bioforms in another city; the demonstrators had built a bonfire and roasted a litterbug. Done with that, she glanced at the menu and raised a hand to attract the waiter's attention. He nodded distractedly, as if to say, ''Soon! Soon!''

''But they're a convenience, really,'' she went on. ''We could do without them, if we had to, though it would make the gengineering go much more slowly. By the late 1980s, the early gengineers had already made bacteria that would produce human hormones and other drugs. They had even transplanted growth genes from trout to carp to get larger, faster-growing fish.''

''Is that all?'' said Bernie. It was hard to believe the technology had ever been so primitive.

''They were timid,'' she said. ''Scared. There were groups that sued every time someone proposed doing anything more challenging. Very few dared to speculate about Roachsters or hanky bushes. Or . . .''

The waiter finally reached their table. ''Or potsters?'' asked Bernie. They were a hybrid of lobster and potato, with all the flavor of the former and the convenience of the latter. Emily nodded and ordered a glass of white wine and a potster salad. He asked for a beer and a hamburger and fries, made the old way, with potatoes.

When the waiter had left, Emily said, ''Potsters were a very early development. I was thinking more of this.'' As she reached overhead to finger a dangling vine leaf, she stretched the bodice of her dress across her chest. Bernie felt his attention focus, but so did she, and the arm drew back. ''I've been here at night," she said. "The leaves glow brightly enough to provide all the light this place needs. But things like this were only for the tabloids then."

"I'll bet they loved them."

"They would have loved the Sparrow too."

"That reminds me . . ." That morning, after he had finished at the airport, when he had gone to the office to write up his reports, he had found on his desk a note from the Air Board's Alan Praeger, saying that they had finished their analysis of the chip they had found in the Sparrow's controller. And yes, it was indeed responsible for the liner's behavior. A timer had activated it on the Sparrow's approach to the airport, and then a simple program had directed it to the expressway and stimulated its hunger center. "You were," he said, "quite right."

Their drinks came, they sipped, and she twisted the stem of her wine glass in her fingers as if uneasy with his compliment. "It was simple," she said. "It couldn't have worked in any very different way."

He laughed and touched her hand. "Enjoy your strokes, Dr. Gilman. We never get enough of them. And then tell me what it took to get gengineering from bigger carp to Tortoises, Sparrows, and Armadons."

As she then explained it, while they ate and while they walked back to her Neoform laboratory, the simplest part of gengineering was finding and transplanting the genes that gave an organism the ability to make a new substance such as a drug. But that ability was useless for designing new creatures such as Armadons. Patterns of growth, of size and shape, depended much less on individual genes than on large complexes of genes, including genes that controlled just when, in the course of development, various other genes became active. And synergy was crucial. Much of natural evolution, she told him, seemed to be due to changes in these controllers, which then changed the way all the other genes knitted together into a functional whole. The genes of a human and a chimpanzee were 99 percent or more identical; the vast differences between the two species resided in less than one percent of their genomes, in the controlling genes that shaped the interrelationships of all the rest.

"We try," she said, "to mimic this natural process. We don't just transplant single genes. We change the way they are controlled, their timing, their interactions. And it's difficult work. It takes time to build, or rebuild, a genome that really works. And there are always bugs, just as in a computer program."

"Those wheels," said Bernie. "On the Armadon."

They were in the Neoform parking lot now, standing beside his dormant Hawk. "But don't underestimate Chowdhury. He's a better gengineer than I am." She shook her head. "I wouldn't dare to tackle making those Armadons. But he can do it. He's good."

Bernie looked perplexed. "What's so tricky about a giant armadillo?"

She pointed at the Hawk. "Big is easy, and that's mostly all we do to make many of our genimals. But he's also re-shaped it to get those wheels, and the internal passenger compartment."

He shook his head. "It sounds like a Roachster."

"He likes to remind us that General Bodies had it easy, and he's right. They had a shell to work with, while an armadillo's armor is bone buried in its skin."

He opened the hatch in the Hawk's pod, stepped up and into his seat, and toggled the creature awake. It stretched, gaping its beak and extending its wings. "Gotta go," he said.

"Me too."

He kept an eye on her, appreciating the lines of her body, as she began walking toward the building entrance. He watched her stop and turn when the Hawk's hatch slammed shut. But then he had to look away, to pay attention to his controls. He snatched only a glimpse as the Hawk set its wings, fired its engines, and leaped into the air, and he was delighted to see that she was still there, one hand shading her eyes, the other holding her fluttering skirt against her thigh. He wished he could remember what ancient movie had first shown him that sight.

Chapter Ten

ON SATURDAY, BERNIE Fischer and Connie Skoglund went to the Roachster races.

For Bernie, it began when Connie stopped him in the hall on Friday afternoon to say, "You look depressed. What happened?"

He told her about finding the boxes of capsules, which had indeed turned out to contain nettle seeds. "We set up a stakeout at the airport, but it was a bust. Someone passed the word."

She made a sympathetic face. "Sounds like you need a break. I won big last weekend. C'mon and share the luck."

"I don't bet," he said. He really didn't bet, and she knew it, for always before he had refused her invitations to the track, but he often played the game of deliberate balkiness. At the same time, his mind was dwelling on another woman.

"So come anyway. You'll have fun. And you need it."

The Roachster races were not just for Roachsters. There were events for Buggies of all kinds, including Hoppers, Beetles, and even Tortoises. The paved, oval track had been built nearly a century before for the gasoline-burning stock cars and dragsters that now made the stands tremble with their bellowing roars only on nostalgic special occasions. Most weekends were now much quieter affairs, though the crowds made as much noise as ever. Some things never changed.

Bernie thought that racing Tortoises looked just plain silly, as did the Hoppers and Beetles. He favored the Roachsters, though he had never been able to decide which version he preferred. The wheeled Roachsters, with their stubby legs pushing on the wheel tops, made him think of wheelchairs built for paraplegic galley slaves. Legged Roachsters were derived from the spiny lobster of the Caribbean instead of the North Atlantic table lobster. They were so long-limbed that Bernie wondered how they could possibly run. In repose, their limbs jutted like the masts and yards of some prickly sailing ship. In action, they flailed the ground to every side like a berserk bundle of knitting needles.

He was not the only one to note the similarity, or to realize why "stilters" were rare on the highways. He didn't bet, but Connie did, and she was shouting, "What do you think of 'Tatter's Hope'? Or 'Orkney Nightmare'?"

"What about 'Kentucky Whizzer'? Or 'Derby Dervish'?" he countered, speaking as loudly as she to be heard above the crowd. They were wheelers, and though they would not compete in the same races as the stilters, he knew she would bet on them as well. He had heard enough talk of her coups and setbacks to know.

Connie disappeared to place her bets. "Waste of money," he said and stayed to hold their seats. When the vendor passed nearby, he bought beer for both of them. He handed her hers when she returned and said, "It's a hot day. They should do well." The gengineers had made their arthropod-based designs more or less warm-blooded, with metabolisms that would function even in a temperate winter, but they remained true enough to their ancestors to work best in hot weather. They were useless in more northern winters, and Bernie sometimes wondered why the gengineers had bothered, except to prove what they could do and demonstrate their power over the square-cube law.

She glanced sidelong at him, most of her attention on the track, where the first race's stilters were taking their positions. She leaned closer; he bent to put his ear near her mouth. "How about you? Made a move on that Emily yet?"

The starter's gun banged in the distance as he shook his head. She squeezed his knee with her free hand and leaned forward to watch the race.

The crowd roared as the stilters began to move. The start was slow, much slower than for wheelers or other Buggies, for the track was so narrow that the stilters had to set their flailing legs among their neighbors' limbs to move at all. They managed it, however, and somehow without tangling, and as first one and then another broke from the pack's leading edge, the pace picked up.

He was left to wonder whether he had imagined a sense of satisfaction, even of possessiveness, in that squeeze. Connie had egged him on with Emily, but she had also invited him into her own bed. And this trip to the races *had* been her idea.

Later events only kept him wondering. For dinner, they bought take-out ribs near one of the city's parks and found a grassy niche beside a pond. There, Connie kicked off her shoes, stuck the toes of one foot up his pants leg, and said, "Go ahead, Bernie. Make a pass. I'll bet you score."

He had called himself a predator, but not of that kind. He was not a skirtflipper. But why not go along with Connie, just to see what happened? "Maybe I will," he said. He pointed at her with a rib bone, a scrap of meat dangling from one end. Connie had very little surplus flesh, and he didn't dare to touch her with his sauce-coated fingers. "She's bigger there."

The toes withdrew. Connie stuck out her tongue and turned her back on him. She was much leaner than Emily; Bernie could count the knobs of her vertebrae, though now he pointed somewhat lower.

"And there."

She turned back. "I'll bet it's all flab. She doesn't work out."

"She's got a sit-down job. What do you expect?"

"She'd be a marshmallow in bed. All soft and . . ."

He grinned deliberately.

"And weak!"

His grin grew broader, but only for a moment. He stopped teasing her when she began to turn red. She was proud of her strength. He knew it, he enjoyed it, and she knew he enjoyed it. But there was an insecurity to her pride that left her vulnerable. He was beginning to doubt that she really meant it when she urged him to pursue Emily Gilman. He was beginning, in fact, to sense a cattiness, a jealousy of whatever time he spent with the attractive gengineer, even of what might in the future come of all her urging him in that direction.

He watched her flush fade away, watched her turn to face him once more, watched the toes creep back up his leg. How jealous was she? he wondered. How jealous could she get? Might she be the one who had sicced the Assassin bird on Emily? But where would she have gotten it?

He dismissed his suspicion. He recognized that she was by her behavior staking a definite claim upon him, and that if she were ever to get nasty in any competition over a man, she might get very nasty indeed. But he thought that she would be more direct, more explicitly confrontational. She was a traditionalist. She would look for a woman-to-woman, hair-pulling, knock-down scream-fest.

Suppressing his sudden urge either to laugh aloud or to speak, he took her hand and carefully, thoroughly licked every trace of the rib sauce from her fingers. She did the same for him, her eyes sparkling at him above her busy lips. When they were done, they walked the city's streets hand in hand, window-shopping, debating the attractions of bars and movies while knowing that only one end to the day would suit them equally.

He liked her. He did. He even told himself that if he ever chose to marry, another cop, one much like Connie, Connie herself, would be ideal, for she would understand the life, and the risks. She might, unlike his mother, even be able to survive his loss. He winced within as he realized that he had not considered the possibility that the loss might go the other way, especially if he married another cop. Could *he* survive such a loss? He did not know.

He said nothing. He told himself that he had long since sworn himself to a single life, one without hostages, and besides, there *was* Emily. She had more status in his mind than Connie; she was a gengineer, a shaper, not a mere guardian, of society. She also probably had more money than either of them. Maybe he *would* make that pass Connie kept urging on him.

* * *

Bernie had flown over the suburb of Greenacres before. Now
he was on foot, circling the neighborhood where that girl,
Jasmine, had been so brutally murdered. Lieutenant Alexander had braced him that morning, saying, ''You've been
spending too much time on the Sparrow case. Let the feds
have it. I want you to go over the ground again on that rape.
Search the neighborhood. Look for witnesses. Look for *anything* unusual! Check the garbage!''

Garbage searches had been routine for decades, ever since
the Supreme Court decided they were not an invasion of pri-
vacy. But the criminal they wanted had been smart, or lucky:
There had been a pickup in this neighborhood even before
the body had been found. There would be another early tomorrow morning, Tuesday. There would be nothing now. Nor
would he find witnesses this way, unless he was very lucky.

He had perched his Hawk on the lawn of the house where
the crime had happened. Now his path brought him around
the block to see it before him, the Hawk stropping its beak
on the tree trunk to which he had tethered it. The house was
a small, six-room pumpkin that had been grown on the lot
that spring. Once it had reached the proper size, it had been
cut from its stem, levered onto a concrete foundation, and
allowed to dry. Then workers had cut holes, sprayed the shell
with sealants and preservatives, and installed doors, windows, insulation, interior walls, plumbing, and appliances. It
had been empty when the rapist had broken in with his victim. The owners had planned to move in later in the month.
Now there was a ''For Sale'' sign on the lawn. Bernie was
not surprised.

There were three other pumpkin houses on the block, with
curtains in the windows and children's toys in the yard. Across
the street, a beanstalk twined around a concrete pillar that
supported a Swiss chalet. A gengineered baobab tree swelled
grotesquely to contain a two-story duplex. A flowering vine
dangled giant seed cases equipped as apartments above a
shallow pool in which flickered Japanese koi, colorful carp.

The lawns around the apartment vine and the baobab duplex were entirely a lush and normal green. That around the

beanstalk was divided into two zones, an outer one of normal green and an inner of green with a tinge of pink, like new oak leaves. A stray dog lay sprawled just within the line that separated the two zones.

This was cannibal grass. Once the householder had sprayed it with an "ID acceptor" pheromone, the whole family and its pets lay on the grass long enough for it to "learn" their odors. Reprogramming it required simultaneous exposure to both the pheromone and one or more of the original family members. Lacking that, whenever strange people or animals stepped onto the tinted grass nearest the house, its sharp blades would penetrate shoes, clothes, and skin, inject a paralytic agent, and sip away the victim's blood. Death would not come for at least a day; the resident family therefore could, if it wished, rescue wandering neighborhood children, birds, and dogs. They could also deliver would-be burglars, peeping toms, and other undesirables to the police with neither hazard nor objection. The drawback was that temporary guests had to stay outside the protected zone; it was thus not practical for apartment complexes and public buildings. Nor was its sale legal, for the Bioform Regulatory Administration feared—probably justly—the consequences if it ever escaped into the woods and fields. The seed, like that for the cocaine nettles, was contraband.

Greenacres held more conventional structures as well, but the "genurb" was a very good example of the new architecture. It was also not a cheap neighborhood. From the air, most of the dwellings vanished in the greenery of ample lawns and plantings, providing a landscape in which only the scattered orange dots of pumpkin houses and a few ordinary roofs stood out. The overall impression was of a carefully tended garden. Bernie thought that impression quite suitable for a place where so many of the houses were gengineered garden plants, though he supposed it wouldn't last. Future developments would be more crowded. In this one, the lots might someday be subdivided, and the greenery might grow unkempt, while the masonry pillars that flanked some of the driveways would become covered with graffiti. It had happened to older neighborhoods of hand-built houses. In time it would be the turn of the grown houses. In time, the neighborhood might decay as far as any neighborhood could, into the human wilderness of an urban or suburban slum.

As the detective in charge of the case, he had a key to the house. He used it, and once inside the door, he sniffed. The slaughterhouse odor of blood, feces, and urine was now almost undetectable, canceled by vigorous applications of soap and bleach, its remnants covered by perfumed sprays. He stepped into the living room and stood with the broad bay window at his back, letting the morning sunlight illuminate the scene. There were still traces of bloodstains on the hardwood floor and plaster walls. There were even a few spatters on the dome-curved ceiling. He could also make out remnants of the chalk lines that had marked out the body and its parts. He shook his head sadly. The "For Sale" sign would, he was sure, be fruitless until the owners applied new paint and installed a carpet. The new house's brief but unfortunate history was far too visible.

He settled against the windowsill and withdrew a packet of photos from a pocket of his uniform shirt. The Scene of the Crime—he could not help but add the capitals—as it had first been seen. Close-ups of the dismembered body, forlorn, pathetic. A single footprint on the floor, stamped in blood. It was small, as if made by a woman, but still too large for the victim, as if she could have walked. Or as if the killer had played puppet with her dying body. It had worn a man's shoe, though, and it was clearly his. But definitely small. Was he a boy, not a man? Or . . . ?

He tapped the photos against the palm of one hand to align their edges. Man enough, he thought. He guessed. It must have been a man. He wished there had been some semen, even on the floor. If they ever found a suspect, DNA analysis would then quickly prove whether the semen was his. Bernie was not the first cop to wish that society had chosen to put tissue or blood samples—DNA samples, either way—of every one of its members on file, frozen in liquid nitrogen. DNA was far more individual than fingerprints, and it would be quite convenient if they could simply ask the evidence to whom it had belonged. Semen, bloodstains, sputum, skin scrapings from beneath a victim's fingernails, even a hair or two, all would be able to tell the tale.

Unfortunately, victim's rights had advanced not at all in the last century. Suspects claimed the right not to incriminate themselves and court rulings robbed solid evidence of its potency. It was no wonder that so many people circled their homes with booby traps such as cannibal grass.

The photos went back into his pocket. He explored the house, seeking any clues that might have been overlooked before. But the place had obviously been cleaned thoroughly, if not quite thoroughly enough to remove all the bloodstains. There had been a few neglected scraps of lumber and wallpaper, sawdust, bent nails, and the like in the corners of the rooms. Now they were gone.

There was a wastebasket in the kitchen. Remembering the Count's instructions, he checked and found it half full of the missing rubbish. On top of the basket's contents, he saw a withered leaf. He picked it up, felt it, sniffed it, and identified it as a nettle leaf. When he realized that it had done nothing to him, he peered at it closely. The myriad fine hairs that covered nettle leaves were on this one all mashed flat, drained of whatever they had once contained.

So there had been a junky on the premises. Maybe even the murderer. He tucked the scrap of evidence in a plastic bag and stored it in a pocket.

Then he looked into the basket again. He thought he had seen . . . Yes, there they were. Two of the plastic wrappings from instant film packs, and though the police had taken many photos on these premises, they had used electronic cameras. Not the sort of thing most citizens would have.

He put the scraps of plastic in another bag.

Over the next three weeks, nothing happened. The Air Board made no progress on finding whoever had put the override chip in the Sparrow's control computer. Bernie found no more clues that might lead to whoever had treated Jasmine Willison so cruelly. And neither criminal made any mistakes that might have swung their fates against them. Life was, reflected Bernie, not a novel, in which one could count on some coincidence that would precipitate the mystery and lead directly to a satisfying resolution.

Later, he repeated that thought to Emily. They had lunch from time to time, whenever she was not in Washington, sculling her patent application slowly through the bureaucratic shoals, and their schedules meshed. Sometimes she went to lunch with her coworkers, or with representatives of van lines and other shipping concerns. Sometimes he was busy himself. But often enough he was able to find an excuse—some question about controllers, chips, neural overrides, reflexes, even how the firm for which she labored worked—to enjoy her company.

"Tee gee aye eff," said Emily. "Thank God, it's Friday!"

They were coming back from lunch, navigating Neoform's hallways on the way to Emily's lab. Ralph Chowdhury turned a corner ahead of them, approached, and passed. His slight, oriental frame was leaning forward, fists clenched, mouth twisting around a glowering scowl. "Is he still worked up about the armadillo?" asked Bernie.

Emily shook her head. "Uh-uh. I think he got that licked." "So?"

"He hasn't been saying much." She turned to look down the hall after the other man's departing form. "I suppose something hasn't been going right for him, but what it is . . ."

She was reaching for the door to her lab when it opened. An older man, grey-haired, his round cheeks just beginning to sag, reached for her hand. "Emily," he cried. "My dear! You'll never guess!" Bernie smiled to himself at the sound of the other's British accent. It seemed so pure, so ancient of nobility, while the permanently tanned skin and the prominent blade of the nose bespoke a recent immigration. He guessed that Gelarean's parents or grandparents had come from the eastern Mediterranean, or perhaps from somewhat farther into Asia. Certainly the last century had seen enough people departing the lands of Palestine, Lebanon, Syria, Iran, Iraq, Afghanistan, Pakistan, and the like.

"Sean. What's happened? Oh . . ." She introduced Bernie as the detective investigating the Sparrow incident.

"I didn't realize that was still unsolved."

"This is my boss, Bernie. Sean Gelarean." She stepped forward, forcing Sean to give way until all three were in the lab. Alan Bryant stood near the room's window, grinning broadly.

"Word from Washington," said Sean. "We'll have to celebrate."

"You mean . . . ?" Her voice rose in a breathless note of excitement. Alan grinned even more broadly and nodded furiously.

"The Bioblimp patent, yes!" Sean Gelarean showed a mouth as full of teeth as any horse's. "Sunday, at my place. We'll have everyone!" He seized her hand again, pumped it, said, "Everyone!" once more, even including Bernie in his inclusive glance around the room, and left.

"Where does he live?" asked Bernie. As he spoke, he wrinkled his nose. He did not much care for hearty Englishmen. No matter how pure or impure their Saxon blood, they always struck him as having some shameful secret to conceal. He supposed many of them really did—didn't everyone?—but why did they have to be so obvious about it?

"You've already had a call from Mayflower," said Alan. "They want to know how long."

"Greenacres," said Emily. "I'll get you the address." She turned to Alan. "I hope you told them it would take a few months to grow and equip the things."

"The eggs are in the tank already."

"Have you ordered the control boards? The crew cabins? The engines? The . . . ?"

At each item, Alan bobbed his head, his smile as wide as ever, until he struck Bernie as nodding like some small dark bird gobbling seeds from a feeder. Yet there was nothing of subservience in his manner. He was Emily's technician and assistant, but he was more than an underling.

When Bernie looked at Emily, her mouth was splitting her face with as broad a band of white as Alan could possibly have shown. The way the two were sharing their relief and pride and joy was palpable.

He must have looked as puzzled as he felt, for when the

excitement had calmed a little, they led him to a computer workstation, called up the necessary diagrams, and explained just what a Bioblimp was.

He shook his head in wonder. "It seems," he said, "as difficult as Chowdhury's Armadons."

"Oh, no!" said Emily. "This is just a scale-up, like I was telling you. Except for the pouches. And they weren't that difficult. Were they, Alan?"

"Fussy, maybe. But not hard."

"Ralph is definitely the best of us."

Bernie had talked to professionals before and found that they often felt they did not deserve their status or pay. What they did was easy, for them. What someone else did always seemed harder and more worthy. He wondered if Emily Gilman was deceiving herself in the same way.

Chapter
Eleven

"DADDY!"

Nick was reading a news magazine. The lunch dishes were done. The house was clean. And he had just finished shoveling out the Tortoise's stable for what seemed the ten-thousandth time. He deserved a break, he felt, but now here came that small, insistent voice. He had been told, years before, that there was for mothers and fathers a basic and incontrovertible law: Nature abhors a resting parent. It applied especially when the children were young, but when they were a little older, old enough to tiptoe from the room or house in search of unwatched mischief, their silence could be enough to bring a parent out of a coma.

"Coming." Andy's voice had seemed to echo from the kitchen. With a sigh, he set the magazine down, lurched from his easy chair, and headed for that room.

"Daddy! Hurry up!"

Yes, there he was, kneeling on the chair by the window, nose against the glass, staring toward the bird feeder. A coloring book and box of crayons sat neglected on the kitchen table. Nick grunted to signal his presence.

Andy turned his head enough to confirm that he was indeed there and paying attention. "Where's the Chickadee, Daddy?"

The boy must have asked the same question three times each week ever since the Chickadee had flown off. It, and Nick's patient, loving, sympathetic answer, had become a ritual that required periodic repetition. Was the boy, Nick wondered, rejecting, repressing, any hint that his mother's life could have been in danger? Or did he simply have to hear again and again the news that his mother was indeed safe? And that therefore *he* was safe?

Cautiously, watching for signs of upset, wondering whether—when?—they might have to take their son to a psychologist, Nick explained once more that the Chickadee was dead. The bird that had flown at Mommy, the one with the orange stripes, had stabbed it with its beak, and the beak had been poisoned. The Chickadee had flown back to its home, at the airport, and died there. It had been a hero, for it had saved Mommy, and she would be home soon from work.

Not long after the incident, they had taken Andy to the local airport to show him where the Chickadee had died. He had not been impressed by the place's unkempt runways, its dilapidated state of repair, its general air of decay. He might have been more impressed by the small airplanes and living jets that had once been based there, but with the arrest of the airport's manager, the airport had closed and its tenants had left.

The boy turned his back on the window. "When I grow up, you know what, Daddy?"

"What?"

"When I grow up, I'm gonna have a Chickadee. Just like that one. All my own." He looked thoughtful for a moment. "And I *won't* keep it anyplace like that airport. *That* was a dump." The wisdom of a five-year-old. "I'll keep it in my yard."

This too was part of the ritual, as was the silent sequel, when Nick wondered anew each time at the workings of the unconscious mind. He guessed that Andy's final resolution must reflect some conclusion that a Chickadee in the yard might preserve him too from harm. It would be a talisman, a luck piece, a charm against disaster.

And come to think of it, Nick's own more private ritual continued, that might not be so far from the unconscious reason why he and Emily had installed the bird feeder in their yard in the first place. Certainly, when for some reason the birds went elsewhere and the feeder stayed empty for a day or two, or more, they felt bereft, as if their luck had abandoned them. When avian activity flurried around and on and under it, they felt blessed. They felt doubly blessed when the birds at the lunch counter they provided included unusual species. And triply so when something unique appeared. The Chickadee, seed-hog, devourer of swallows and other birds, had at first seemed more like a curse, but as events had developed, it had indeed been a blessing.

The slap of Tortoise feet on the surface of the driveway announced Emily's return home. As Nick stepped outside to meet her, he thought he could still detect the faint odor of the cleaning solution he had had to use to get the stain of the Chickadee's litter off the brickwork of their house. He was glad the genimal would not be returning, for that, and repairing the roof, and washing the roof, had been work for which he had no enthusiasm.

The door to the Tortoise's quarters slid down with a screech that announced a need for oil. He sighed at the thought of more work, even though the task was not a large one. Then he grinned at the sight of his wife running toward him.

"The patent! We got the patent!" Her voice was joyfully excited, and her impact against his chest almost knocked him over.

"Mommy!" The door banged behind Nick, and Andy pushed between them, holding up his arms. Emily scooched to hug their child. In a moment she looked up at Nick and told him the rest of the story: They already had orders for the Bioblimp, and there would be a celebration at the Gelarean house, in the Greenacres genurb.

"It'll be interesting to see that place," said Nick. "I wonder what kind of house Sean has."

She shook her head. She didn't know.

"Can I go too?" Andy's voice was plaintive.

"It's a work thing," said his mother. The boy pouted, but he quieted immediately. If the occasion were not a "work thing," he might persist and even win. Otherwise, he knew, he might as well forget it. "We'll get the baby-sitter."

* * *

Sean Gelarean's house proved to lie among fruit trees, lignum vitae, and summer-green forsythia bushes set in a carefully trimmed lawn. A Victorian gazebo of wooden latticework overlooked a small fishpond not far from the road. The house itself was a crook-necked squash that, once it had been grown to size, hollowed out, and dried, had been hoisted onto a stand that let its neck jut high into the air, above the surrounding trees. Later, that neck had been fitted with narrow windows and a spiral staircase. It had become a tower, and the chamber at its apex had become Sean's den. Broad windows were visible in its rounded roof, and lush greenery that suggested a love for houseplants.

The rest of the squash, painted white with dark brown crisscrossing lines, bulged like some Tudor tumor beside the parking apron at the head of the driveway. In it were the living and dining rooms, the kitchen, three bedrooms, and more. A porch, its construction echoing the lattices of the gazebo, framed the main entrance. Roses bordered the porch and spread their fragrance like a fog over the nearby lawn. A caterer's van had rutted the turf near a side entrance.

Nick had met Sean before. He knew the man had come from England, and when he saw the house, he recognized immediately its restatement in the modern idiom of that English architectural theme, the towered manor house.

The driveway and the small parking area were filling rapidly with cars. Gelarean's guests, most of them Neoform employees, most of them in pairs with friends or spouses, were wandering the nearby fringes of the yard, eyeing the plantings, the house, and the gazebo before trickling toward the porch, where their host and his wife awaited them. From what Nick could see of facial expressions and overhear of conversations, the consensus was that the Gelarean manor was a remarkable monstrosity.

When Nick and Emily finally reached the porch, Sean was wearing a rueful expression on his face. Grasping their hands, he introduced them to his wife, Victoria. She was a short, round woman, dressed in a red silk monk's robe, its hood raised, whose mouth jerked into a smile nearly every time he spoke. Then Sean said, "It *is* a horror, isn't it? But we couldn't resist it when we saw it."

Cool air flowed from the open door of the house behind them and made the fabric of Victoria's robe sway. Nick welcomed the promise of relief from the heat of the outdoors, but he stayed on the porch long enough to laugh at his host's pleasantry and say, "You must have been homesick."

The other nodded, his cheeks shook, and his accent thickened briefly. "That I was, wasn't I, Vicky? But it's comfortable." He leaned over the porch railing to pluck a newly opened rose, pinched off the thorns, and held it out. "Emily, my dear. Put it in your hair." As she obeyed, he gestured toward the interior of the house. "Drinks on the left."

In an alcove off the entranceway, one of Wilma Atkinson's genetic sculptures moaned and writhed as people passed it by. Nick paused to examine it and found a pair of flexible rods that twined around each other to form a double helix, emblem of heredity, that twisted into a complex knot. He petted it, luxuriating in the short, silky fur that covered its surface. Its voice became a purr, and its motions grew less random, as if it were butting for attention. "This must be half cat," he said softly to his wife.

"I wouldn't be surprised," she answered. "Although she's never said."

They found the bar, dominated by an octopoid genimal whose arms were pigmented with green and white stripes, like sinuous barber poles. It was taking verbal orders, and the arms worked in pairs, serving four customers at a time, pouring, mixing, shaking, wiping up occasional spills.

"I've never seen one of those before," said Nick.

"I saw a description in *Genginews*." That was the industry's trade paper. "But I didn't know they were on the market yet."

"They aren't."

Emily turned toward the speaker and cried, "Frank! What do you know about it?"

Frank Janifer lifted his glass to them with a grin. "I hear our host let a friend do him a favor."

They laughed, and then they turned to note the buffet the caterers were assembling, vast seas of food surrounding is-

lands of flower arrangements, and survey the rooms within
their view. Polished tables, antique chairs, flower-filled vases,
deeply cushioned sofas, thick carpets as soft as moss beneath
their feet, all impressed Nick, and he murmured to his wife,
"Much more tasteful inside." They accepted small bits of
meat wrapped in pastry crusts from a tray proffered by a
perambulating waiter. And then people were leaving the circulating flow of guests to congratulate Emily on the patent,
to speculate among the clinks of glasses on the applications
of her Bioblimps, to wonder how they would contribute to
the company's fortunes.

"I hear the stock went up a bit already."

"Have you thought of designing a walking suitcase?"

"Or an incubator for preemies."

"Wait till the word about the Mayflower order gets out!"

"You could start with an ordinary kangaroo . . ."

"Should be something four-legged."

"Use your options now!"

"Like a wallaby."

"Delicious appetizers! You should try . . ."

"Whatever. Leave it just enough brains to follow you on
a leash. And a couple of big pockets on its sides."

"Make a great baby carriage!"

"Make it an imprinter, so if anyone else tries to open the
pockets . . ."

"Chomp!"

Laughter. A small bell invited everyone to the buffet, where
Nick found the centerpiece to be a whole roast litterbug, easily identifiable by its distinctive jaw. The roast, steam rising
from its crusted back, was presided over by a Japanese chef
wielding a carving knife the size of a samurai's short sword
and saying, over and over again, "Don't worry. Grain-fed,
perfectly healthy, very tasty!"

No one seemed to have trouble believing him, for the carcass was rapidly diminishing beneath the strokes of the carv-
er's blade. Nick obtained portions for himself and Emily,
passed her a plate, and then, realizing that she was quite
absorbed in her conversation, found a quiet corner beside a
bookshelf on which he could rest his plate. Not far away, he

recognized Bernie Fischer, the cop, likewise by himself, a plate in his hand, surveying the crowd.

He wondered how the detective had managed to be invited, but then he forgot the matter. A small man—grey-suited, his skin a shade darker than any tan could reasonably achieve, flat, reflecting panes of glass revealing only intermittently his dark brown eyes—was approaching. He was apparently looking for a niche like Nick's own in which to eat his meal.

"You're . . ." He groped for the name. "Ralph Ch . . ."

"Chowdhury. Ralph Chowdhury. I have a lab just down the hall from your dear wife's." He pushed a polished crystal knickknack aside and set his plate on the shelf below the one Nick was using.

Nick blinked in surprise before he realized that, of course, the man was shorter than he. "The armadillo man," he said.

Chowdhury beamed as if delighted to be so known. "Your wife has told you of my poor efforts! I hope she hasn't made too much of our silly rivalry. I am delighted that she has her patent!" He raised his glass in a gestured toast. Then he tasted his roast litterburg. "Delicious!"

"I didn't see one outside," said Nick.

Chowdhury's laugh seemed strained, as if he were trying hard to be congenial. "I walked! I live not far away, right in the neighborhood. Besides, my Armadons are not yet ready for the road. Nor are they quite ready to take to Washington. But they will be. Soon! And then Neoform will dominate the transportation market in the sky and on the ground. Both!"

"It surely won't be long before Sean is throwing a party like this for you."

Chowdhury shrugged as if it didn't matter, or as if . . . "Not for me. He likes your Emily much better." A grin. "She's prettier."

Nick grinned back. "She is, but . . ." What could he say? He brought the subject back to the Armadons, and then, while Chowdhury described his genimal, concentrated on his food. The roast was indeed delicious, and he finished his serving quickly, but when he looked toward the buffet table, wondering whether there might not be a little more, he saw nothing but an empty space. The remnants had already been re-moved.

Chowdhury followed his gaze. "We had our share," he said. "Though I too would like some more."

A thought occurred to Nick as he nodded. "Neoform doesn't make the litterbugs, does it?" When the other indicated that he was right, he added, "Then serving one is quite symbolic, isn't it?"

"Devouring the competition, you mean?" Chowdhury stared at him for a moment. Then his gaze flicked to the nearby policeman. "You have a poetic mind."

Nick shrugged. "Perhaps I give Sean too much credit."

"Or perhaps not." Chowdhury's tone became quieter, almost musing. "And you make me wonder. Are the police making any progress?"

"On . . . ?"

"On those attempts on your Emily's life."

Bernie Fischer, just a few feet away, suddenly assumed a more erect posture, as if something he had just heard or seen had made him more alert. The movement drew Nick's eye, and he wondered what the reason might have been. But he did not pursue the question. Chowdhury's query still awaited an answer.

As far as Nick knew, the police had made no discernible progress at all. At least, no one had told him that they had any clues to who had programmed the Assassin bird to attack Emily. Yet, for some reason he did not himself understand, he said, "I'm not in their confidence." He gestured toward Bernie Fischer. "There's the one in charge, and he does his talking to my wife. But from what she tells me, they're getting very close."

"How nice!" Chowdhury showed his teeth in a broad, beaming grin, but Nick could see the corded lines in his neck that said his jaw muscles were tense. His body odor seemed to carry a touch of spice that Nick thought made it seem to fit the other man. The spice was . . . what? Then he had it. Curry.

"I expect they'll have him very soon."

The other drained his glass abruptly. "It would be a shame if anything happened to Emily. You have a child . . . ?"

They chatted for a few moments more while they emptied their plates. Then Chowdhury left, saying he wanted to find a sweet. Nick remained by the wall, watching the crowd, glancing from time to time toward Bernie Fischer, who in turn seemed to be following Chowdhury with his own gaze.

According to Emily, Chowdhury was abrupt, abrasive, abusive, temperamental, secretive, impatient, and intolerant. But he had been quite cordial just now. He had been willing to speak at least a little about his Armadons. He seemed interested in the search for whoever had programmed the Assassin bird to attack Emily. He seemed sympathetic and concerned.

Nick preferred to believe his wife. She was not the sort of person who could convince herself that a thoroughly nice person was so awful, and then describe that person so to others.

Chowdhury therefore had to be dissembling. But why? Was he hoping to get on the good side of Neoform's current fair-haired girl? Did he wish that some of her good fortune would rub off on him and make his Armadons as great an initial success as her Bioblimp? Or . . . ?

Nick left his plate on the shelf and wandered through the house. Where was Emily? There, talking animatedly to her technician, Alan. She saw him and waved her glass. Beside her was another Atkinson sculpture, a dozen narrow stalks thrusting from the dirt in a plain, brick-red flowerpot set atop a baby grand piano. The stalks merged to form two linked rings that were covered in fine scales picking out a colorful mosaic. He could not see the details clearly enough to tell what, if anything, the pattern signified, but he could hear the thing's metallic, chiming voice.

There were more conventional artworks as well—paintings, prints, antique scientific instruments, small carvings in wood and stone, each displayed to good advantage but safely set behind glass barriers, all originals, all expensive. Either Neoform was very successful or, as he had heard from Emily,

Victoria Gelarean had indeed brought money to the marriage. There were very few houseplants other than the sculptures.

Nick would have liked to climb the tower both for its view and for the sense of power, of overlordship, that he thought might accompany having such an extension of one's house. He would also have liked a look at the greenery there, and thus some sense of what Sean Gelarean might really be like behind the bluff exterior he showed the world. But locked doors barred all exits from the party's assigned rooms, except to the outdoors.

One of those locked doors turned a narrow hall into a cul-de-sac. He was testing the knob, thinking the door might open to the tower, when he felt a hand on his arm. He let go of the doorknob abruptly, embarrassed even before he realized that the hand belonged to Victoria Gelarean. The hood of her red monk's robe was back, revealing wrinkled skin, a vividly birthmarked cheek, and twinkling eyes. Her lips were pursed as if she were recalling something for which she did not care. She shook her head gently and said, "He doesn't let me go up there. Not even me."

Her hand exerted gentle pressure, steering him back toward the living room, where the bulk of the party still was concentrated. As they turned, he saw that Bernie Fischer was watching them. He had a drink in his hand, but he looked as if he too had been wandering curiously, trying doors much as Nick had been doing. Was Sean Gelarean then a suspect in some heinous crime? Or were police detectives simply just as nosy as he himself?

Victoria released him when they came to the bar, saying, "Why don't you have a little wine, dear?" Nodding, Nick filled a glass before turning toward the room to find her already gone from his side, circulating among the other guests. Gelarean was nowhere in sight, but there was Chowdhury, in a corner near a bathroom, so close against a stranger that their bellies were almost touching. Nick smiled at the sight. The stranger's pink tuxedo covered a mass of solid flesh that matched the slight gengineer three times over. He listened impassively, and when he spoke, when he reached out to pat Chowdhury's shoulder, his smile seemed a decal pasted into place to simulate approval. When the two men turned away from each other, that smile disappeared as if it had never been, and Nick glimpsed a coldness of soul that would have been out of place in an insect.

Nick had been to other Neoform parties, but he had never seen the man before. Was he a neighbor? If so, Nick thought, then Greenacres was a much less congenial place to live than its obvious wealth and stylishness might suggest. If he was a business contact—Nick hardly dared to wonder what sort of business, or how he must treat his employees. If he was a friend, then what sort of person could Sean Gelarean really be?

A hand clasped his arm from behind. He jumped.

"Did I startle you?"

It was Emily. "I was spooked. By a real creep. Over there, in the pink tux." He pointed, but the stranger was gone. He had to settle for describing the man. He said nothing about his attempt to open locked doors, or the way Gelarean's wife had stopped him.

Emily shuddered. "There's no one like that around the company, I know. You ready to go home?"

He was.

Chapter
Twelve

WHAT A WEAK-SPINED, pussy-whipped excuse for a man was that Nick Gilman! A jobless househusband! A pussycat, neutered and turned into a hearth rug for his wife to walk upon! Chowdhury pitied their son. A boy should grow up with proper role models, women who stayed home, content with children, kitchen, church, men who showed their strength, who dominated their women and the land as one.

Chowdhury could not help but think so. His parents had set the model for him, even though they had also violated it. Neither of them had been in any position to dominate anyone's land. And his Papa had worked in the kitchen as often as his Mama, for she had often been off with their fellow exiles, listening to their dreams of return and treating their illnesses, even confined as she was to a wheelchair. But he had been a man who knew how to use his belt and his fist. He had also told the boy stories of the homeland, where men were men and women knew their place, and he clearly wished that things had never fallen apart. He wished, indeed, for only such change as would let him join the dominant whites on equal terms. His Mama as clearly wished the same, though she could also say, with full and laughing awareness of her irony, that a proper man was a Boer-boar-boor, and his slogan a borborygmic grunt.

Chowdhury had had his reasons to make so nice to Nick Gilman. But it had been an effort, a severe effort. He was, he knew it, a snarler, a croc, as his Mama might have put it, in the river of life. His temper was worse because he had finished his latest illicit creations and turned them over to his

masters. Now he was waiting for their reactions, and patience
was not among the few virtues he numbered, in all honesty,
among his own. In fact, he counted patience as the antithesis
of what was necessary in the world's natural elite, its natural
rulers, *men* of genius like himself. Though he did realize that
just a little patience might help him bear the long wait for
recognition a little better.

Chowdhury shivered at the thought of what he had learned
by making so nice for so long to such an abysmal hearth rug
of a man. His master, the one who gave him most of his
orders now, was not far away. He could tell him things,
frightening things, things that would demand action, or flight.
But not here, not now. Later, later, the time would come. And
then, perhaps . . .

Chowdhury obtained a cup of coffee, fortified with a dol-
lop of Irish Cream, and a small square of cheesecake. He ate
and drank, wishing that his Indian half were less strong, or
that his inner mind could accept the fact of his professional
position and attendant prosperity. In India, in the old, pre-
Black South Africa, for all he knew in the modern post-Boer
South Africa, men displayed their wealth in their bellies, in
the fat that announced to all the world that *they* had enough,
and more than enough, to eat. But somehow, he could never
bring himself to eat enough to swell out with that commanding presence of the real man, Boer-boar-boor or not.

He watched the crowd around him. *There* was that cop,
always around, poking, prying, destroying. *There* was Victoria Gelarean, a woman unfortunate of face and figure but a
woman for all that, serving her husband's needs as a woman
should, quiet and self-effacing. She had one hand on the small
of the hearth rug's back, and she was pushing him gently
toward the bar. They had come from another room, and
Chowdhury wondered if Nick Gilman had been exploring
where he shouldn't. If so, perhaps he was less anemic than
he seemed. He had wanted to see the tower room himself
when he had first visited this house. Eventually, he had, but
he knew that it was normally kept behind locked doors.

A mass of pink gestured Chowdhury imperiously to join it
in the corner by the bathroom door. He obeyed, and as he

drew close enough to see the doughy face atop the pink, he recognized the gesturer as that man who had first set him the task of making the cocaine nettle. The pink was his tux. The mass was his torso, well fed and enviably unattainable. The smooth, round face was smiling thinly, coldly, though that did not disturb Chowdhury. He did not know the man's name—the thugs and dealers and waitresses at the casino had called him just "The Boss"—but his rank was clear. Chowdhury knew that he, like his predecessors in the Family, the Mafia, the Cosa Nostra, whatever the papers called it at any one time, was a manipulator of games, dollars, drugs, and lives. He was also, as Chowdhury's Papa—and Mama—would have recognized immediately, a real man.

When Chowdhury was within reach, a pink-wrapped arm extended like the proboscis of some parasitic beast. A heavy hand clasped his shoulder and drew him in to face, too close, the other's diamond tietack. The fingers kneaded Chowdhury's flesh painfully. The voice, all threat softened by careful layers of oil, murmured, "You've done a good job, Ralph. Good work." The thin smile broadened. "Fetch me a drink? I don't want to be obvious out there." He glanced toward the cop, Bernie Fischer, and his smile became more genuine. "I do believe he recognizes me."

"Of course." Chowdhury shrugged free of the hand, marveling that the casino owner could enjoy so obviously the stares of a policeman. Vanity! he thought, even as he felt the niggling truth that he might well react in the same way. If only he had the recognition he deserved.

"Just club soda."

As Chowdhury crossed the room to the bar, he noted the flushed faces and loud voices of the other people at this party. Many of them had been guests at the party thrown by that company lawyer. They were not avoiding alcohol or, perhaps, less licit substances, but he saw no sign of any nettles in their pots.

This man, his master, The Boss, the "baas" in the language of home, was carefully staying sober. He wondered how drunk he could get in private, or at his own parties. Or did he always keep his senses solidly about him, the better to control, to manipulate, his games and drugs and lives?

When he returned, the other accepted the glass of bubbly liquid, raised it to eye level, and repeated, "Yes, good work." He sipped, and the toast was done. "I came to tell you so myself, though ordinarily we let him"—a flick of the eyes— "handle you."

Then, Chowdhury thought, they must have found his creations interesting.

"The nettle was fine. Though perhaps you could shorten its life?" The words came slowly, laboriously, as if, like Chowdhury, he too had to strain to speak soft words.

"But never mind. It's quite marketable as it is. A considerable success. But then . . ." He paused to sip once more from his glass. His dark eyes bored into Chowdhury's skin. "We weren't sure anything more was possible. You surprised us. Snakes and jellyfish!" Another pause. "We love them."

Chowdhury grinned nervously as someone passed behind them to get into the bathroom. He wondered if this love, proclaimed in such a coldly passionless voice, meant that he would be freed of his debts. He suspected not. He was more valuable than ever to these people. They would surely refuse to run any risk that he would escape. Freedom was not in the cards.

When the bathroom door closed, the other said, "We want two thousand of those jellyfish. Immediately. And two thousand of each of the snakes."

"I've already started the jellyfish." They had been easy to start. He had simply left the lights over their tanks on a little longer to convince them it was time to breed and then released a burst of pheromones into their water. They had promptly generated millions of gametes, eggs and sperm. Overnight, almost, he could have more larval cnidarians than he could possibly raise to maturity, or supply with tanks. He sighed at the thought that if they proved popular, there would have to be a factory of considerable size just for the necessary aquaria. Breeding nettles, jellyfish, and snakes would need another sort of factory, rather more like a farm. He hoped he would not wind up in charge of it.

Chowdhury recalled the scene when he had introduced his creations. His immediate master had come to his lab, pushing, insisting, demanding tangible progress. Reluctantly, he had produced the disks on which he kept his plans, spec sheets, and notes. He had described what he had done. He had pointed to the aquarium and its contents. Then he had brought out the snakes in their terraria, the asps, the coral snakes, the mambas. Tiny things, sleek and colorful, loaded with hedonic venoms.

Within himself, carefully hidden from this underworld lordling all in pink, he smiled at the memory of his master's initial revulsion, of how intrigue began to show, of how the man had wished to try the venoms out. He had had to caution him, saying, "Be careful. With the jellyfish, you just leave your hand in longer for a larger dose. With the snakes, I linked the drug and pigment genes in reciprocal tandem. The paler the color, the less pigment, the more drug there is in the venom. You can start the customers off easy, and then sell them stronger and stronger pets. Don't take a light one."

"I understand tolerance." His master had reached for one of the darker, more brilliant reptiles and let it bite his arm, nearly as dark-skinned as Chowdhury's own. His eyes had closed, his mouth half opened, his breath moaned outward in an ecstatic groan. "I like that," he had said at last. "And so will they. I'll pass them on."

And indeed they had. "The snakes," Chowdhury said, "will take a little longer."

"What a pity." The man in pink shook his head. "Those will be much more profitable." He sighed heavily. "In fact, one of our board members was saying he wished we could retail them through legitimate channels. He even suggested an advertising slogan: 'Make an asp of yourself!' "

Chowdhury chuckled dutifully at this display of the other's wit.

But the lighter tone did not last. The other stuck the fingers of his free hand into the top of a pants pocket. Then, abruptly, as if the pocket concealed some secret switch, he asked, "How long?"

Chowdhury shrugged. They would grow quickly, but . . .

"I'll need a month or so to build up the breeding stock, even using hormones to speed their growth. Then, say, six months before you'll have many for the market."

The other shrugged as well, though he did not look surprised. Perhaps, Chowdhury thought, he had some small sense of biology. "*Que será . . .*" He patted and squeezed Chowdhury's shoulder once more. He said, "Then you'll have plenty of time to come up with something else," and turned away. The interview was over.

Something else? No, they would not let him go. Never, or never until he lost his touch or the competition proved more imaginative or the police caught them all. He told himself not to worry about that last possibility. He could always claim that he had been forced to do his work, though he did find it satisfying, if not as satisfying as his Armadons. And besides, as the lordling in the pink tuxedo had begun to say, "*Que será, será.*" What will be, will be.

Behind the door he stood beside, the toilet flushed and a deep, gurgling voice, like that of a drowning troll, rumbled, "Don't forget to wash your hands!" A more normal voice swore, and there was a rush of water in the sink. Chowdhury chuckled and moved away.

But what else was there? Nettle, jellyfish, snakes. Bees, wasps, and spiders were also venom injectors and could be tailored to deliver drugs that were effective in small quantities, such as hallucinogens. Even mosquitoes and other biting insects might work, for they injected a droplet of saliva when they bit. In fact, a snake's venom was a modified saliva in the first place.

But they were bugs. Nonusers, ignorant of their value, would swat them, smearing all their value on walls and arms and rolled newspapers. And people who would use them would surely be too few; bugs were not popular. What was worse, it might be difficult to keep them from escaping and multiplying endlessly. Then the world would have a drug problem!

He supposed it would be possible to come up with worse ideas. A porcupine? Its every quill filled with some mind-altering substance, standing ready to be plucked and injected? A hedgehog, its quills shorter and less prone to accidental removal and injection, would be a better choice. Color-code the quills, each color corresponding to a different drug?

Or a virus? Short-term and noncontagious to protect the market, just as his masters wished. One that would force the body to make its own supply of the drug, and then, after a few hours or a day, die out? Or a bacterium that could reproduce only outside the body? Either would have advantages over the more conspicuous genimals. They would be easier to smuggle, to conceal, to take surreptitiously. He would have to see what he could do along those lines.

Lost in thought, Chowdhury made his way toward the Gelarean's door. As he neared it, a billow of red converged upon him. He reached for the doorknob anyway, but before he could touch it, a soft hand seized his wrist. "Ralphie! You can't leave yet!"

He raised his eyebrows. The woman's crimson hood was up, her birthmark a mere shadow on her cheek. "But I must, Victoria."

"I know he wants to talk to you, and . . ."

"We can see each other at the lab tomorrow."

Her voice added to its quiet insistence just a hint of desperate wail: "But he told me to be sure . . ."

He shook his head. "Lovely party, Vicky, but I've had enough for now. And I'm sure he would rather relax with you once everyone else goes home."

Her voice went quiet. "I wish you were . . ."

Was she about to say "right"? He did not want to hear of the Gelareans' marital difficulties. He pushed the door open and slipped outside before she could say any more.

Dusk had fallen, but the heat still struck him like a wall after the comfort of the house's air-conditioning. He had been in Maine once, at about this time of year, and he had been impressed by how livable a place could be if only the day's heat gave way to coolness. One could recover.

He had a small air conditioner in his small apartment. It was a necessity of life much farther south than Maine. So was a wife, in Maine as everywhere else. Sean was fortunate. Hearth rug Nick Gilman was even luckier, for he also had a child.

It was too hot to rush. He walked slowly, ambling, looking at the bioform houses that he passed, studying the few other pedestrians on the walks. Not far away, he knew, there was an empty pumpkin house with a "For Sale" sign on its lawn. He had walked past it more than once in recent days, wishing that he could afford to buy it, or perhaps something more elegant, like the Gelarean place.

He had been married once. But she had left. She had called him cruel, abusive, mean-spirited, and worse. She had wanted him to see a therapist. They had drugs, she had told him. They can teach you not to hate.

He had refused. Of course. So had his Papa, when Mama had said the same thing, or close enough. So he too would sleep alone tonight. There would be no one to whom he might boast of his achievements.

Feet clicked on the walk behind him. He turned his head, and there—faltering as she noticed a stranger's perhaps hazardous attention, intention firming as she decided to take a chance, now again catching up so quickly—was a woman. Young, buxom, white teeth gleaming in her dark face as she smiled a greeting. The sheen of sweat. An aroma of musk. A schwartzer. What the Boers, and his Papa, called a kaffir. An Arabic word for infidel, once used to refer to the most intelligent of the Bantu groups, the Boer equivalent of "nigger."

As she drew abreast of him, he increased his pace enough to stay with her. He hated blacks, yes, as he hated whites. He always had and he always would, after what they—both of them!—had done to his parents. But he was lonely tonight, and his masters had approved of his work. He was feeling almost friendly, and in an unfeigned way quite unlike the act he had deliberately performed for Nick Gilman.

He waved a hand at their surroundings to catch her eye. "My apartment is lots cooler than this."

She looked at him. Their eyes met. She laughed. "So is mine. And it's not far away."

He felt something open up within him, brightening and relaxing. Was it possible? Could such a simple overture possibly have evoked any interest at all? A delicious thrill ran through the core of his being, and he told himself that she was not truly what he hated. Schwartzer, yes, but not kaffir, not the savage blacks who had taken over virtually all the continent of Africa and slaughtered whites, yellows, other blacks, everyone who was not of their tribe. Her ancestors had surely never been within a thousand miles of South Africa. In fact, they had been among the persecuted, just as had his parents. He could see it in her eyes, dark pools stained by generations of slavery, oppression, and discrimination. And besides, she was surely not a black, not a true black, not in this country with its centuries of miscegenation, recognized and unrecognized. She was a coloured, like him.

She touched his wrist as if by accident. He smiled. "I can hardly wait. A cold drink. A cold shower."

"Me too," she said, and her touch repeated. It was not an accident.

"But it would be so much nicer with company."

She nodded, smiling broadly. "I can hardly wait." A pause, just long enough for his hopes to soar like a police department Hawk. And then she lengthened her stride, drew ahead, and looked back to say, "My boyfriend's there already."

His spirits fell once more. She had been toying with him, and he would find no more satisfaction, of any kind, tonight.

Chapter
Thirteen

"FISCHER!"

Lieutenant Napoleon Alexander's office had one small window. On its sill was a dirty ashtray that dated from the days when the lieutenant had been a pipe smoker. On humid days, its carefully preserved encrustation of tar and ash added a strong note of stale tobacco to the office air. Until the year before, a rack of dusty pipes had held down papers atop the filing cabinet in the corner and made the stench even worse. Still more tobacco scent lifted from the walls, which would not be due for two years or more for an addition to their myriad layers of paint, visible in rounded corners and chip craters whose edges were bands of multicolored strata.

The rack of pipes had disappeared when the Count had decided they made it too hard to resist temptation. But the ashtray remained, together with the rumor that when the Count was alone and unobserved, he would lift it to his face to savor the aroma. This Monday morning, he would not need to touch it. The air was warm, and it was raining. The room stank of old tobacco.

The stacks of papers were still there, as clear a sign as Bernie's typewriter of underfunding. All the rest of the world was thoroughly computerized and had been for decades. The best the police could do was equip booking desks and evidence technicians with slow, cranky, limited-memory OS/2 machines from the last century. The officers had to write their reports on even older electronic typewriters, as their predecessors had once had to use manual typewriters. Obsolescence was a police tradition.

"Fischer!" the Count repeated.

Bernie was staring through the window at the rain that drew a grey curtain across the front of the Aerie. The bicycle rack was invisible. "Yes, sir!" As usual, Bernie's salute was sloppy and his stance was a far, far cry from the rigidity of the "Attention!" his superior had all but shouted.

The Count licked his bright red lips and said, very softly, "I had an alarming, a very alarming, phone call this morning." He stood and leaned forward over his desk, bracing himself with his arms. "An anonymous phone call. About you. And I don't generally put much credence in anonymous phone calls about my people. But do you know what that anonymous caller said?"

Both Bernie and Lieutenant Napoleon Alexander knew that such phone calls were part of any detective's life. Inevitably he stepped on toes. He came closer than they liked to people with guilty consciences. And they did everything they could to deflect attention. It rarely worked, for a detective's superiors always knew what such calls most truly signified.

What, then, could have the Count so worked up? Bernie could not guess, but he was sure he would learn very shortly. He said, "No, sir."

The Count glared at Bernie. "He said that you are neglecting your work. You are spending too much time at the Neoform labs. You are sniffing after Dr. Emily Gilman like a dog after a bitch in heat!" Spittle sprayed from his mouth to sprinkle the desktop. A few droplets landed on Bernie's shirtfront.

Bernie stepped backward at the force of his boss's explosion. First Connie, he thought. Now him. Emily was a sexy lady, yes, but why did everyone think he should be trying to get into her undies? "But . . ." He tried to speak, but he was given no opportunity.

The Count's next words were softer: "I've seen her picture. She's pretty. Good boobs. Nice ass. But you're supposed to chase that ass on your own time!"

Finally, he could say something. "It's work, sir, really. I'm . . ."

"Not anymore, it isn't. The feds are handling the Sparrow

case, and you don't need to do any more research on gengineering, do you?'' He didn't give Bernie a chance to reply.
''And I told you to concentrate on that mutilation-rape!''

''But they're linked!''

The Count, still leaning over his desk, blinked. For a moment, he looked almost owlish. ''Explain that.''

Bernie tried his best. ''The rape was in Greenacres, right?
And two of Neoform's major people live in that genurb.'' He
sketched Ralph Chowdhury, his hatreds, and his rivalry with
Emily Gilman over their creations. He told how he had happened to be invited to the party celebrating Emily's patent,
and he described Sean Gelarean, company founder, and his
richly furnished, limited-access house.

''Chowdhury,'' he said, ''may think he has good reason
to want Emily dead, and he would know how to fiddle the
Sparrow. And the Assassin bird, which is a Neoform product!
She may be the next woman we find in pieces.''

The Count settled back in his seat and shook his head
wearily. ''I doubt it.''

''And Gelarean's house. I'm suspicious. I'd like a warrant.''

Lieutenant Alexander shook his head again. ''No
grounds.''

''Greg Florin was there. In a pink tux.'' Bernie had indeed
recognized the casino owner. Because the state did not li-
cense gambling, Florin's operation was illegal. But the police
ignored his transgression, tolerating him as long as he kept
away from more socially disruptive activities. Because there
were rumors that he was not in fact avoiding those activities,
his presence at the party was ominous.

The Count sighed. Both men were aware that the drug
business was reviving with the aid of the same gengineering
technology that had almost destroyed it at first. They knew
of the cocaine nettles and the seeds that had appeared in the
hangar of the Chickadee that had saved Emily Gilman. They
recognized the potential of a gengineering firm such as Neoform.

''I was checking out that house the other day,'' Bernie
said. ''As you suggested. And I found a nettle leaf.''

The mood in the Count's small office had changed. Bernie was no longer on the carpet, no longer under suspicion of uncontrollable randiness. He was, instead, an official hound tracking prey through a maze of misdirection. He was a hawk indeed.

"Connections," said the Count. "You're right." He sighed heavily. "Stay with it, then. Carry on."

Before Bernie could close the door behind him, he added, "But no search warrants. Not yet."

The rain had ended by noon. The clouds had dissipated, and the city had steamed all afternoon in the summer sun. Now, Connie Skoglund's air conditioner hummed in the background.

"I still think she wants you." Connie's motions as she sliced onions and green peppers with a long-bladed knife were fast and efficient. In a moment, she would add them to the pepperoni-and-cheese pizza Bernie was taking from her freezer. They already had glasses of a cheap red wine that could pass for Chianti.

"That's the last one," said the freezer. "Should I put more on the list?"

Connie pitched her voice an octave higher: "Check!"

"Bull." Bernie set the pizza down on the counter and sipped heartily from his glass. "It's a strictly work relationship, and you know it." He had spent the day on a knifing, a burglary, a drug bust, paperwork, a court appearance, routine matters of the sort that had occupied police officers' lives as long as there had been police officers. He had barely had a chance to think about the Sparrow case or, for that matter, about finding whatever monster had murdered Jasmine Willison. Nor had he yet said a word to Connie about his confrontation that morning with the Count. She had brought up Emily's supposed infatuation with him entirely on her own.

She shook her head. Her brown hair, still glossy from a recent brushing, bounced. He smelled a flowery shampoo and wished he too had gotten away from work with time to shower and change. All he had been able to do was unfasten the harness that throughout the day had held his .357 magnum in its shoulder holster. His shirt was marked by still-drying sweat beneath the arms, the stain a simple, civilian moon under his right arm, but a moon extended by a shape that resembled the subcontinent of India beneath his left. He could smell himself. His scent was not much like flowers.

"Uh-uh," she said. "Bull, yourself. No way. You wouldn't be hanging around her so much if that was all it was. And she wouldn't be letting you."

"It's research!"

"You don't have to see her every day for research."

"I don't!"   •

"Near enough."

A thought suddenly struck him. He set his glass down. He laid one hand on her shoulder and turned her to face him. "Say. You didn't have anything to do with that phone call, did you?"

She stared back at him, her mouth a thin, horizontal line of annoyance. "What phone call?"

He did not let go of her while he told her what the Count had told him that morning. When he was done, she raised a hand to brush his arm away and turned back to the pizza. "Jackass."

"What do you mean?"

This time she turned around on her own. She held her slicing knife up between their faces and shook it. "I said, you're a jackass. A fool. You don't get it, do you?"

He shook his head.

She sighed. "It doesn't matter whether you've got the hots for her or not. You're hanging around Neoform too when you hang around your Emily, and you're making someone over there nervous."

She made sense. Of course. Someone wanted him out of there and they must have called the department. He didn't think it could be Nick Gilman, for though he might be jealous, he was also scared for his wife's life. Chowdhury? Gelarean? Someone else? He could not say, though he could guess. He had no real evidence, but there was, as he had told the Count, a personality, a history, and rivalry that could, together, lead to violence. Every cop had seen it happen more than once.

Bernie had come to talk to Emily about the phone call Lieutenant Alexander had received, but when she had ushered him into her lab, she would not let him speak.

"Look," she said. "Alan finally got the bugs out of those pouch genes." Her fingers moved over the keyboard of her workstation. A Bioblimp appeared on the screen. Ghostly fingers, barely visible on the screen, plucked at its flanks to open the folds in which it would tuck its cargo. There were only two, and their openings faced toward what, Bernie supposed, must be the front of the genimal. Ghost fingers poked into the pouches, their depth of penetration communicating internal size.

"I thought you already had the patent?"

Her dark hair jerked as she nodded. He caught a whiff of shampoo odor, clean and flowery, but not quite the same as Connie's. "Sure. But it describes the pouches in very general terms. This is design work, not invention. Details."

The next sequence showed the Bioblimp with its cabin in place, slung beneath the gasbag, tentacles dangling around it, except to the rear, where a missing tentacle left room for the propeller that jutted from the back of the cabin to push the Bioblimp through the sky. Bernie did not know whether the tentacle was missing because the creature simply did not grow one there or because it had been—would be, he thought, reminding himself that this was a simulation—cut away. It hovered over a house, anchored itself to a tree with one tentacle, used others to lift the roof from the house, and then plucked furniture from the exposed rooms. The furniture went into its pouches. As they filled, they bulged obscenely.

"It makes moving look easy," said Bernie appreciatively.

"Removable roofs are just the simplest of the changes that will make sense once this thing is on the market. Look here . . ." She keyed another animated sequence, and a Bioblimp, this time with the Mayflower logo visible on the side of its gasbag, floated through the air toward a high-rise apartment building bedecked with balconies, each one painted with a number. She pointed. "Addresses."

One tentacle wrapped around a balcony railing to moor the van. A human figure, so small on the screen that its gender could not be told, stepped out of the apartment, opened a panel in the wall of the building, and pushed a switch. The entire apartment slid out of the building like a drawer from a bureau, and the moving van began to pull furniture from its cargo holds and place it on the apartment floor. When the van was done, the human figure pushed the switch again, and the apartment slid back into the building.

Bernie laughed. "You could water the houseplants that way too. In the rain."

"Our patent lawyers are going nuts." She grinned at him. "We're remaking the world, aren't we?"

"As long as you don't redesign people so they don't need to eat. Lunch?"

"Where?"

"You choose."

"The Bed and Buggy Motel has a nice luncheon. It's just a couple of blocks away."

There was a moment's silence while they stared at each other, both of them fully aware that, whatever their purposes in going to a motel, most people went to such places for only one thing. Finally, he said simply, "Why not?" To himself, he saw that now, perhaps, he could tell her about the phone call. They would have a good laugh over lunch, and then they would come back here, to the lab.

To reach the motel, and its restaurant, they had to walk through a small neighborhood shopping center. There was a grocery, a hardware store, a liquor store, a cleaner, two small boutiques, a barbershop, a drugstore, and more. As Bernie and Emily approached the entrance to a shadowed bar, its door opened partway. A voice, warmly feminine despite its obviously synthesized nature, murmured, "It's awful warm out there. Why don't you come inside and be comfortable? The beer is cold." A free sample of the bar's conditioned air gushed refreshingly across their ankles.

They passed on, noticing that most of the stores were busy. The neighborhood was by no means crowded, but there were plenty of people on the sidewalks, and the doors to the stores were bouncing open and shut as electronic voices announced the day's bargains or wished good days as customers entered and left. A steady stream of Buggies passed down the street, wheels, legs, and occasional engines making their various distinctive noises, while litterbugs waited by the roadside, darting out to retrieve their prey as necessity demanded and opportunity offered. From time to time, the traffic slowed to eddy around a heavy-bodied, squash-nosed, bowlegged Mack truck that had stopped to load or unload cargo. Some, like airliners, wore both their driver's cab and a cargo pod strapped to their backs. Others wore just a cab, towing their cargo in long trailers.

As they walked, Bernie found himself talking about his meeting with the Count, the phone call that had prompted it, and what it meant. Seeing a couple on the walk ahead, their hands entwined, he wished he dared to take Emily's hand or to put an arm around her. To keep himself from doing so automatically, thoughtlessly, he sawed the air with his hands as he talked.

She moved closer to him as some other pedestrian passed them by. Their thighs brushed. She said, "You hadn't told me about that rape."

He described it as briefly as he could. She made a face. "Do you really think someone at Neoform could have done such a thing?"

"You can never tell. Chowdhury . . ."

"Hates everyone, black or white, I know. But . . ."

He shrugged. The motel they wanted, with its restaurant, was in sight a hundred feet away. He pointed, and his stomach rumbled. Emily laughed and touched his arm.

A blare of horns broke out behind them. They heard crunching noises and screams. Movement on the street and sidewalk abruptly froze. Those people who had been walking toward them stared, eyes wide, toward something behind. Those who had been going in their direction turned, and then they too stared. There were pointing hands, gaping mouths,

more screams, and then, only seconds after the opening fan-
fare of vehicular brass, people and Buggies alike were fleeing
in a panic-stricken rout.

Unlike all the rest, Bernie and Emily did not flee as soon
as they had turned to look. Half a block away, a midsize
Mack, the equivalent of the previous century's ten-ton trucks,
was accelerating down the street. Ignoring the Buggies already on the pavement, it brought its massive paws down
wherever it wished, accounting for the crunching noises and
a few, only a few, of the screams they heard. Blood and other
fluids ran in the gutters of the street. A litterbug, its stomach
burst, made a particularly messy smear on the pavement. The
Mack's bulldog jowls shook and quivered, and great gobs of
foamy spittle flew to strike the storefronts beside the road.

A brightly painted cargo pod was strapped to the Mack's
broad back, its forward end a bubble of clear plastic behind
which the genimal's driver, her face contorted, pounded on a
control board. Clearly, the beast was not responding as it
should. Emily gasped, "The Sparrow!"

Even as Bernie and Emily saw it, its broad jaws, full of
teeth, gaped. It growled, and then it uttered a deep-throated,
rumbling howl, as if a freight train were trying to bay. It
changed direction, swerving toward them across the road,
pausing only when the cargo pod caught on a lamppost.

Neither Bernie nor Emily could move, even though adrenaline was surging through their veins. The threat was too
great, too immediate, and all their energies were focused on
their senses as they sought some route for their escape. Small
details loomed large. Bernie noticed the cracks in the yard-
wide collar to which the forward edge of the pod was clipped,
and then, beneath the monster's throat, a dangling ornament,
a foot long, a box on wheels, and shiny with polished
chrome. In a moment, he recognized it as a model of an old,
engine-powered eighteen-wheeler.

The Mack braced its legs and tried its best to force its pod
through the lamppost. It tried again, and it succeeded. But
the necessary pause, while the driver's compartment collapsed and shards of plastic eviscerated her, gave Bernie the

chance he needed to unfreeze, draw his magnum from beneath his jacket, and begin to fire.

The Mack struggled and tore the lamppost through the remainder of the cargo pod. More plastic flew. Cardboard boxes spilled into the roadway. The Mack's jaws gaped wide again, and Bernie fired between them, trying with all the nerve and skill he could muster to put his slugs through the roof of the monster's mouth and into its brain, or through the back of the throat and through, severing, the spinal cord, whatever would end the onslaught of the berserk juggernaut this genimal had become.

With a final roar, it collapsed atop a Roachster whose driver had driven onto the sidewalk in his efforts to flee and now cowered in his seat. The pushed-in snout—each nostril larger than Bernie's head, the whole looming over him and Emily like a whiskery wave—was only feet away. A puddle of drool was already growing on the sidewalk. The smell was precisely what one would expect of something whose not-so-distant ancestors had been dogs.

The ululating screams of Hawks announced the arrival of Bernie's colleagues, almost in time. The first two landed on the Mack, their talons furrowing the genimal's fur, and promptly put their heads under their wings. The hatches of their bubbles popped open, and Connie and Larry Randecker emerged.

Connie scanned the now-growing crowd, stopping with a look of surprise when she spotted Bernie and Emily. "Look at the Great White Hunter," she said.

"Ferchrissake!" said Larry, staring. "Will you put that iron away?"

Bernie obeyed, but not until he had replaced the gun's magazine. He was not at all sure he would not need the weapon again before the day was done. "What are you doing here?"

"Pure coincidence," said Connie. "We were there when the dispatcher pushed the scramble button."

"What happened?" Larry gestured impatiently, and he and Connie switched on their recorders simultaneously.

As Bernie explained, more Hawks swept out of the sky to

land. The crowd gave way, and the new arrivals began to assemble crowd-control barriers, examine the Mack, photograph the scene, and look for the fragments of its control apparatus in the rubble that covered the street. As they found the pieces, they swept up the remaining debris.

"Where were you going?" asked Larry.

"Lunch."

"But where?"

When Emily pointed at the motel just ahead, Connie gave Bernie an appraising look and an exaggerated wink.

He sighed. "Just lunch."

However, when they finally got away from the scene of carnage, neither Bernie nor Emily had any appetite. They went into the motel's restaurant, and they ordered drinks, but then she said, "I'd rather just lie down."

Bernie looked at her. Her hair was disordered. Her blouse was sweat-stained. Her face was lined with recent stress, and her eyes showed far more white than usual. There was no trace of seductiveness about her.

He was not surprised. He felt none himself. "Sounds like a good idea," he said. He drained his scotch in a gulp. She did the same with her Gibson. He dropped a twenty on the table to cover the drinks, and then he led her to the motel's front desk.

When they were in their room, Emily proved as good as her word. She kicked off her shoes, flopped on one of the room's two beds, and closed her eyes. Bernie went to the window, held back the drape, and found that it overlooked the street where they had stood not long before. The Hawks were still there, Connie, Larry, the other cops, and a tow-Mack pulling a wheeled flatbed trailer. He studied the scene, passing quickly over the pile of mangled Buggies, lingering when he noticed the row of body bags on the curb. He counted them. Seventeen.

Abruptly he turned away, went into the bathroom, and knelt before the toilet. He vomited.

The cool hand that stroked his neck and shoulder was comforting. "It gets to you, doesn't it?" she murmured.

"I can stand it." He rose, unwrapped a motel glass, and rinsed his mouth.

"Your stomach can't." When he shrugged, she added, "Maybe you should lie down for a while too."

Later, she said, "I can't tell my husband."

Bernie held one breast in his hand and thumbed the nipple. It swelled in response, but not nearly to the extent that it had just a little while before. "Does he get violent?" Nick Gilman hadn't struck him as the type, but one could never know. That was a day-one lesson for every rookie, every police academy cadet. He had even recited it for her when she had asked if he really thought that someone at Neoform could have killed Jasmine Willison.

"No." She patted his belly, making his small roll of flab jiggle. "But he'd be hurt." She paused. "Or maybe not. He was telling me just a few weeks ago, when I thought I was in too much of a rush to look out the window and see the Assassin bird, that I seemed to have forgotten how to stop and smell the flowers by the side of my path."

"Some flower." He kissed her temple gently.

She sighed. "Maybe I'm remembering how, again? I used to be able to. Or maybe it's just shock."

"It could be both."

"I still won't tell him. And we shouldn't do this again."

Chapter
Fourteen

THE COUNT WAS waiting in the hallway when Bernie Fischer reached the station Tuesday morning. Beside him was a slender fellow whose grey mustache did not match his jet-black hair. He was wearing a white lab coat and carrying in one hand a small case covered in green-dyed leather. In the other hand, he held a cane.

Bernie had never had much to do with the man, but he recognized Daniel Addering, the vet who took care of the department's genimals. He needed the cane because a Hawk had once bitten his thigh; the leg had been weak ever since. "Hi, Dan," he said with a nod. He then looked at Lieutenant Alexander.

"I've asked Dan to look at that Mack truck that nearly got you yesterday," he said.

Bernie snorted. "You might as well call in the meatpackers," he said.

"You don't think I'll find anything?" asked the vet. His voice was heavy with the practiced softness of one who was used to gentling animals in distress.

"Not in the carcass." Bernie paused while he stared the Count in the eye. Finally, he said, "I'll bet you my next raise the problem's in the thing's controls. And it's an extra chip, just like the one in that Sparrow."

"I heard about that," said Addering. "I'd like . . . ."

The Count, ignoring the vet, stared back at Bernie. His red lips were set in a line that said as well as words that he was afraid his underling would win the bet. "It won't take long to see if you're right, will it? Though we'll need a computer jock to find it.''

Bernie shook his head. ''I know where to look. And I have a photo of the other chip.''

''Then get it.''

Bernie did, and the three men left the building, passed through the yard in front of the Aerie, and turned down the street. Addering's limp did not slow them enough to matter. A block away, they stopped before the loading dock of an old, brick-walled warehouse. A smear of something dark led under the dock's truck-sized main door. Set in that door, to one side, was a smaller personnel door, which Lieutenant Alexander opened with a key from his pocket.

A few small and filthy windows were set high in the warehouse's walls. Those that faced the sun admitted narrow beams of light across which drifted swarms of dust motes. The light that escaped absorption by the motes, and that more diffuse light that entered through those windows that did not face the sun, were just enough to reveal the warehouse's interior as a gloomy, shabby cavern. The room was still cool from the night, but the heat was already growing noticeably. The odor was of dust and mildew and dead meat.

Above were girders draped with wires and ancient spiderwebs. To one side stood three careless tiers of cardboard boxes, wooden crates, and plastic barrels. To the other slumped what had to be the Mack's carcass. Its back was toward them, one ear cocked absurdly ceilingward. They could not see its lifeless eyes.

The Count found the light switch, and banks of fluorescent lights slung beneath the distant roof came on. Half the fluorescent tubes were dead, and half the rest flickered dimly. The few remaining improved the cavern's lighting only enough to let them see that the smear by the door continued, ending in a pool of blood that had congealed around the Mack's head and neck, where Bernie's bullets had torn its vessels open.

Addering stepped closer to the beast. He stood near its shoulder, head bowed, one hand resting on the cold, stiff flesh. In a moment, he reached up with his cane and pushed at the base of the erect ear. It fell away from him, forward

and over the genimal's face, into a more normal configura-
tion. "It's hard to believe," he said at last, "that a handgun
did this."

"I like one with plenty of punch," said Bernie. He leaned
slightly forward as he spoke, belligerent• "And it had already
killed enough bystanders." He was proud of what he had
done, of saving Emily, himself, more bystanders. He did not
think that any animal-lover, even the official police vet, had
any right to criticize.

"A .357 magnum." His superior laid one hand on his
shoulder. The fingers bit into the flesh, drawing him back to
civility.

"Ah," said the vet. He still had not looked at Bernie, had
not noticed the effect of his words, but the moment passed.
He nodded sadly. "Poor thing."

Bernie turned away, toward a windrow of more mechanical
debris along the wall. Had Addering really meant to criticize?
He had certainly taken the man's first words that way, but
perhaps the vet merely felt sympathetic toward the dead genimal. He shrugged mentally. Here were the remnants of the
Mack's cargo compartment. Next to them was a stack of the
boxes that had been its cargo. "Where's the dashboard stuff?"

"There?" The Count pointed toward the other end of the
windrow. The Mack driver's bloodstained seat rose from the
rubble, surrounded by the crumpled metal of the cabinets that
had housed the Mack's control circuitry.

The cushions of the seat had been shredded by the same
flying shards of plastic that had killed the driver. On them,
Bernie found the bloody model truck that had hung from the
Mack's collar. The blood was dry, so that when he picked it
up, his hands remained clean.

"You should take it home," said Lieutenant Alexander.
"Great souvenir."

"I think I will." He set the truck down again, turned his
attention to the cabinets, and rummaged until he found what
he thought might be the right one. He pried at what had been
access ports with his hands, but he accomplished nothing but
a creak or two of protest from the distorted metal.

"Help me." The other two leant their strength to his, and

the metal gave. He reached in, felt, and pulled out a circuit board. He examined it, set it aside, and drew out a second.

"There." His grunt of satisfaction told Lieutenant Alexander and Dr. Addering that he had found what he sought. He pulled the photo of the Sparrow's chip from his pocket and held it beside the chip he had found on the board. He held both to catch the best light he could, and then he grunted again. "Same part number," he said. "It's a PROM, all right. And the serial numbers are even sequential."

Later, after a technician had dusted the Mack's circuitry for fingerprints, Bernie held the chip in the palm of his hand and stared at it. There had been no fingerprints, of course, just as there had apparently been none in the Sparrow. He didn't need them to know, as surely as if he had been present at the scenes, watching the installation of the chips, that one person was responsible for them both. And if they had been installed by different hands, then certainly the same mind had been behind them both.

The warehouse had become an oven in the time that Bernie had been in it. Sweat dripped from his hairline, and he breathed cautiously through his open mouth. The Mack lay in pieces now, its skin removed, the gases of heat-hastened putrescence escaping to the air.

One person, one man, behind both the Sparrow and the Mack. But he could see already that there were differences. The Sparrow had gone to a specific place at a specific time and there engaged in specific behavior. And that behavior had been perfectly normal, peaceful feeding, at least from the Sparrow's point of view. If the person behind the Sparrow had had a particular target, the method had been haphazard. It could have worked only by luck.

The Mack, on the other hand, had seemed to have a specific target in its mind. He had been convinced at the time that it had been coming straight at him, or Emily, or both of them. It had, like an Assassin bird, been programmed to respond to a specific image with a direct, unhesitating, straight-line attack. If he had been unarmed, he and Emily would now both be dead. Instead, there was the Mack, surrounded by the department's butchers, while porters hauled the first bins of meat to the dumpster backed up to the warehouse door. Both butchers and porters wore gas masks; Bernie wished he had one too.

The Count had left shortly after Bernie had found the chip, though not before telling him to find whoever was responsible. There was no hint that he should restrict his investigation in any way. Neoform would be fair game, and he could spend as much time with Emily as he wished. Not that the Count knew anything about the aftermath to the Mack's attack, but even if he did that might not matter. The Mack had attacked when Bernie had been with her, and that might well mean that Bernie was doing something very right in seeing her. He grinned at the thought that he might find his next clue in bed.

The vet had lingered to examine the Mack, patting its side as if it were not lying dead in a vast tomb, but merely ill and the warehouse a kennel of suitable size. Bernie had read of ancient chieftains, whose followers set them at their deaths in their vessels of trade and war, surrounded by weapons, goods, even servants and pets, and then covered all in a barrow of earth and stone. Watching Addering, he had turned his gaze upon the warehouse. There was stone and earth enough in its structure. And there, in the tiers of cartons, were goods enough for any ship-grave. The Mack was the trading vessel. All they needed was the chieftain who had directed it.

The vet had not left when the technician arrived to search for fingerprints. That had not disturbed him. But then the meatcutters had come to dismember the Mack. He had vanished as soon as he saw the first of their blades and bonesaws. He had, thought Bernie, known what was coming.

In cooler weather, those workers would be wrapping the meat they removed from the enormous carcass, packaging it as future meals for the police department's Hawks and other genimals. They would do the same for a dead Sparrow, a Roachster, a Tortoise, whatever came their way. Few owners wanted the meat for themselves, and insurance companies were all too willing to write off the value. It saved the cost of towing and disposal. But part of the deal was that in hot weather, when the meat spoiled overnight, or when the carcass must be examined and delays allowed the meat to rot, the department would handle the disposal.

Bernie tossed the chip in his palm. There was no reason why he should stand the stench a moment longer. Besides, he needed a phone. He wanted to ask Alan Praeger how he had managed to read the Sparrow's PROM chip.

The glass and concrete computer science building had been built many decades before. Most of the buildings on campus were a century older still, their gothic lines and ornamental gargoyles speaking of an age that had vanished more centuries before that. Tradition lay thick beneath the massive trees, though the people who strolled the paths, often with electronic or paper books in their hands, were mostly young.

Bernie Fischer parked the Roachster in a no-parking zone shaded by an American chestnut, a heritage of those early days when gengineers had defeated the blight that had nearly destroyed the species. There had been little money in the cure, he once had read, but students had needed a research project. Students had also been responsible for potsters and the first simple pumpkin houses.

He emerged from the Roachster and patted the vehicle's side. The chestnut tree seemed a slender sapling beside the ancient oaks that adorned the campus, but its shade was dense and cool and would protect his vehicle from the sun while he was gone.

He walked around the beast, comparing it with the Hawks he vastly preferred. The genimal's thoracic shell, mottled brown and greenish blue and orange-red, swelled to create a bubble equipped with seats, controls, windows, and doors. The doors were plastic blazoned with the department's emblem. The Roachster's head and mouth parts were protected by a steel bumper bolted to the shell. The creature's legs ran backward atop the wheels to propel them. Its antennae, at rest, curled back over the thorax. The massive claws, missing in the civilian models, projected forward, long arms of the law. They were the features that had first sold police departments on these genimals. General Bodies had given the first

ones away, and as soon as a cop had used those claws to tear
the wall out of an apartment building and seize a screaming,
flailing kidnapper, the market had begun to boom.

In its way, Bernie thought, it was as marvelous a product
of the gengineer's art as a Hawk. But he loved Hawks.
Roachsters he could barely stand, though he could drive them
when he had to, as he had today for the short trip to the city's
south side and the university.

He entered the computer science building to find air-
conditioned coolness and a wall-mounted, glassed-in board
that listed names and office numbers. Minutes later, he was
in the second-floor office of the man he had come to see, and
Henry Narabekian had plugged the Mack's chip into a circuit
board wired into his workstation.

Narabekian wore a thick mustache as if to compensate for
the near hairlessness of his scalp, but every hair was black
and glossy. He was one of those who go bald when young.
He was also very obviously a busy man, for his desk, book-
shelves, even the antique Apple computer that adorned the
top of his filing cabinet, were smothered in piles of papers
and disks that threatened constantly to tip and wash both
Narabekian and his visitor out the door. But he was also
willing to help.

"There," he said as lines of program code began to scroll
up his screen. "It took me an hour to get into the other one.
But this is just the same. Except in the program itself.
There . . ." He froze the screen and pointed. "Activates the
territoriality circuitry in the hypothalamus. It saw you as a
severe threat."

Bernie grunted. "But why us?"

Narabekian scanned the program further. "There. That
tight block of binary code is a stored image." He tapped
commands into his keyboard, and an inset on the screen blossomed into a face, Emily's. "Pretty lady. Not both of you
then. Just her. Introduce me? She doesn't *look* dangerous."

"She's married." He did not mention his own interest in
her. Nor the fact that his heart sank at this confirmation of
his fear. He had never really suspected that the Sparrow had
been aimed at her. But there had been no question about the

Assassin bird. And now this. The pattern was indisputable. Someone clearly wanted Emily Gilman dead.

But why?

Narabekian shrugged. "If it sees a match, bang. Push the turf button. And go for the throat."

"I thought it would be something like that."

"Have they caught whoever buggered the Sparrow?"

Bernie shook his head.

"Same guy then."

"But . . ." Bernie shrugged. "We have to find him."

Neither one of them was looking at the other. She was staring at the walls. He was scanning the restaurant's other patrons. Both were too aware of what they had done two days before. He at least—he couldn't speak for her—wondered if . . .

"Isn't that Chowdhury?"

Emily craned her neck to look where he was pointing, two tables to his right and a bit behind her. "It's lunchtime, Bernie. And our people eat all over this neighborhood." In other words, there was nothing alarming about seeing him here, in the dining room where they had been unable to eat after the Mack attack and before . . .

Then why was he watching them so intently from behind those flat, reflective panes? He stared, even while the waiter took his order. He leaned forward. He did not blink, even when Bernie met his gaze, and Bernie thought of a cat watching a bird it intended to have for lunch. All that was lacking were the erect, cocked-forward ears and the twitching tail.

Bernie was the one to look away, returning his eyes to the menu in his hand. When Emily said, "We didn't pay much attention to the decor before," he looked up again. The decor lived up to the Bed & Buggy's name: The ceiling lights were mounted on imitations of old-fashioned, wooden wheels, too narrow-rimmed to be wagon wheels. From each wall projected a relief molding of a four-poster bed. On one wall, the bed contained a Roachster; on another, a Beetle; on the third, a small, rounded antique automobile. On the last wall, the bed's covers bulged, and a horse's head, eyes shut, lay upon the pillow; behind the bed was the shadowed outline of wooden wheels and a high, fringed buggy-top. The dessert cart, waiting near the kitchen's swinging door, was another four-poster, high-canopied and on wheels.

He grunted. Then, as they ordered, he resolved to ignore Chowdhury. Emily had tried to refuse his invitation to lunch, but he had told her he had some information about the Mack and its chip. Finally, he looked at her. Her pupils were wider than the restaurant's dimness could account for. Was she worried? She should be. Or was she simply nervous about their return to the scene of their own crime?

"Someone," he said. "Someone is out to get you."

"I know that," she said quietly. "The Assassin bird had to be aimed. But yesterday . . . That was just random, wasn't it? Like the Sparrow?"

He shook his head. "The Mack was aimed too." He fished the Mack's chip from a shirt pocket and laid it on the table in front of her. She picked it up and studied it while he told her of the image Narabekian had found, and of what the Mack had been programmed to do if and when it found a match for the image. "The chip was identical to the one in the Sparrow," he added.

For her, he didn't need to spell it out any further. "Then they're trying harder," she said. She passed the chip back to him.

"I wish there were more clues."

Their food came, and they picked at it. "Are there any?" she asked.

"A few," he said. "Enough to let me suspect a particular person."

Her face brightened. "Who?"

He shook his head. "But not enough to let me say his name out loud. Or to arrest him. I need more evidence."

They finished their lunch in silence. Eventually, while they sipped at coffee, Bernie took a paper bag from the seat beside his own. Something in it clanked against a plate when he set it on the table.

"What's that?"

"The Mack had it around its neck." He pulled from the

bag the model truck. He had washed away the blood to reveal the gleaming chrome. "I thought your boy might like it."

"Would he ever!" Her grin was as wide and enthusiastic as he might have wished. But at the same time she was staring blankly at the truck. Finally, she stroked it once with her fingertips, slid it back into the bag, and drew the bag to her side of the table.

Bernie stared at her until she finally met his eyes. Then he asked her, "Would you like to lie down for a while?" He realized that he was wearing a grin that an onlooker might take for a fatuous smirk, but he didn't try to change it.

She looked away from him for a long time before she finally let her head jerk in a single abrupt nod.

Neither noticed that Chowdhury had left, his meal just half eaten.

Chapter
Fifteen

ANDY WAS DELIGHTED.

Weeks before, his father had set a wading pool up in the backyard. But he had never sat down in it with Andy, never sailed a boat, sunk a submarine, spouted a whale, never splashed.

Now his mother had come home from work, changed into her bathing suit, and climbed into the warm water. She didn't leave much room for him, but he didn't seem to mind. He pushed a boat toward her. She pushed it back. He wound up a whale and let it loose to thrash its tail. She bent, took a mouthful of water, and sprayed it into the air so that it showered down on both of them. He splashed her. She splashed him back.

They both hooted with laughter. And when she moved to a towel spread upon the lawn, to sun herself dry in the declining rays of the afternoon sun, he sat down beside her, blissfully ignoring the stickiness where skin met skin.

"What did that Mack truck look like, Mommy? When it was trying to get you?" She hadn't told him about the incident. When she had come home Monday, he had met her with the news that she had been on the veedo. She hadn't noticed the reporters and their cameras, although it did not surprise her to learn they had been there.

"All teeth, honey. All teeth." She made a face at him. He squealed. "It wore a collar," she added. "Just like a real dog. And on that collar . . ."

"What?" He bounced on the edge of the towel.

"It's on the front seat of the Tortoise. Go see."

He jumped up and ran. In a moment, he was back, in his fist a brown paper bag that sagged under the weight of something heavy. "Is this it?"

She nodded. Slowly, as if he were trying to draw out the special occasion, he spread the top of the bag, peeked in, and exclaimed, "Wow! The collar ornament!"

The door to the kitchen opened, and Nick stood there, staring toward them. She waved, and he said, "The wine's ready." He was not smiling.

"You play with that for a while, Andy," she said. Then, scooping up her towel and the empty bag, she went inside.

"What's wrong, Nick?" She was in tan slacks and plaid blouse now, her wine glass in her hand, watching her husband chop vegetables for a stir-fry. His motions were abrupt, reined-in, tense. His wine was untouched.

When he finally spoke, she could sense the effort it cost him to keep his voice calm and quiet. He lay down the knife, raised his glass, and took a hearty swig. "You don't give a damn, do you?"

She said nothing. Another swig. "You come home. You say hi. You go off with the kid. You don't even ask about my day, or say anything about your own. I'm just a fucking cook! And where the hell did you get that truck? It's off that Mack, right?"

She nodded. "Bernie got it for me. We had lunch . . ." She felt herself beginning to turn pink as she thought of what she had done. She wished desperately that her blouse would camouflage her guilty blush and he would fail to notice.

"Bernie!" he exploded. "You're seeing too damned much of him!"

"The investigation . . ."

"I don't give a shit about the investigation!" He stopped, looked at his glass, and realized that it was empty. Shoulders slumped, he went to the fridge, stared at the wine carton, and reached instead for a handful of ice. He found the scotch in the cupboard under the sink and poured as if it were amber wine. She said nothing.

"Yes, I do," he said more quietly. "I don't want a Mack

to get you." His control was back. "But this Bernie . . . He's drawing you away from me. Isn't he?"

She shook her head, but still she said nothing. What could she say? Nick was jealous, but not without reason. They had their problems in his joblessness, in the fear of losing his wife to a murderer. And he was right about Bernie. The detective had drawn her from the start, and the Mack had weakened her, allowed her to step over the line. Or was it that their narrow escape had triggered some basic urge to affirm or celebrate or simply reproduce once more her life? She had never believed that such a thing could happen, but . . . And she had succumbed a second time as well.

She set down her glass and reached for her husband. She wanted to hug him. She wanted to say, in actions if not in words, that she was still his. But he shrugged her off.

Then Andy came inside, looking for his small share of their evening drink. In unspoken agreement, as they had done before, as nearly every couple through all of time had surely done, they suspended their discussion, pretending for the child's sake that all was well. They knew there were exceptions, people who paraded every shred of anger and dissension before their children, but they had no mind to be among them.

The tension was still there Thursday morning. Breakfast was a silent affair, not helped by Andy's frequent glances toward the bird feeder and his wish, voiced just once, that another Chickadee would show up.

When they were done, when Emily had put her dishes in the sink, when she had picked up her briefcase, Nick said, "Are you going to see Bernie today?"

She shrugged. "We don't have an appointment, if that's what you mean." Or a date, she thought.

"Well." A hand twitched. His stiffness mounted, as if whatever he was about to say was difficult. "If you do . . . If you do, tell him thanks for the truck."

"Yeah!" said Andy. The doorbell rang, and he left his cereal bowl on the run. "There's a Hawk on the lawn!" he yelled.

She looked down at her still-seated husband, feeling his pain as her own. He had tried, hadn't he, to apologize for his suspicions? And as soon as he had done so, a Hawk had arrived to slap him in the face. Perhaps worse was the lift she had felt in her breast at Andy's words.

But the Hawker at the door was not Bernie. The figure that followed Andy into the kitchen was female, and Emily recognized her. "Detective Skoglund. Connie."

"I wanted to catch you before you left," she said. "I need your account of the Mack attack."

"Of course," said Emily. She set her briefcase down again. "Coffee?" When the other woman nodded, she turned on the kettle, saying, "The coffee maker takes too long," got out cup and spoon and a jar of instant and pointed to the containers of milk and sugar on the table. "I expected to see you Tuesday. At Neoform, like the last time."

Connie shrugged. "You know how it is. Busy." She studied first one of them carefully and then the other, and Emily wondered if she could sense the pain that had suffused the room such a short time before. The kettle whistled. Emily poured, and when both women had their coffee, she shooed Andy off to play and pointed at his chair. Connie sat down, turned on her recorder, and began to ask questions. Emily answered them all as best she could, until Connie asked, "And what did you do afterward?"

"We went on to the restaurant."

"I'm surprised you had any appetite left."

Emily hesitated. "I didn't." She glanced sidelong at her husband. He was watching Connie intently. "We just had a drink."

"And then?"

"I went back to the lab. There was work to do." When Connie stared at her, she felt herself blush. How much did Connie know? How much had Bernie told her? Were they close? Had she interviewed him yet? *Did* detectives interview each other?

She looked again at Nick. He was watching her now, not Connie, and on his face she thought she saw just a hint of a forlorn puppy that knows it is about to be given to a new owner. He hadn't missed a thing.

Connie was looking at him too. "I have some questions for you as well, Mr. Gilman."

"Why? I wasn't there." His tone was glum.

"But you're close to your wife, and . . ."

"You mean I'm a suspect?"

She nodded. "That's the other reason why I'm here. Now, is there any reason why you should wish your wife harm?"

He looked shocked. "Of course not!" He clearly meant what he said, and Emily's heart warmed.

There were more questions, probing for his knowledge of PROMs and genimal controls, for any history of emotional instability or violence, for possessiveness and jealousy. At the end, she grew explicit: "How would you feel if you learned your wife was sleeping with another man?"

As Nick's mouth fell open, Emily felt her face turn pale with shock. She watched as Nick stared at Connie, who in turn was watching Emily, a slight, knowing smile upon her lips. She waited for the explosion that had to come, now that someone had all but spilled the beans. But why? Why should she do that? Did she want Bernie for herself?

Finally, he said, "That is none of your business."

"He's right, you know," said Emily. "I think you'd better go."

Connie had the grace to look down as she said, "That *was* out of line. Sorry." She clicked off the recorder, said "Thanks for the coffee," and left.

Emily and Nick stared at each other across the table. They could hear Andy talking to himself in the other room, the thudding boom as the Hawk's wings grabbed air for its take-off, almost each other's thoughts.

As the Hawk noise faded, Nick said, "You *are* spending too much time with that cop."

She shook her head. "Not as long as someone's out to kill me. He's protection."

"But what if they're trying to get *him*!"

"They're not." She felt awful about deceiving him, but she did not dare to tell him the truth. She could not face the

possibility that he would leave her. Misdirection, the truth
but not the whole truth, was her only option.

She reached across the table to cover his hand with her
own. "I'm the target." She told him of the image Bernie had
found in the Mack's chip.

He sighed. "I still get jealous," he said. "So does that
other cop."

"You saw it too?" She smiled at him. "Yes, I like Bernie.
But I'm not about to walk. And if I did . . ."

"She might plant a chip or two herself?" He grinned boy-
ishly, and she felt a tide of relief wash through her, removing
tension, at least for a while.

The Tortoise accelerated smoothly down the entrance ramp,
its legs pumping vigorously in the periphery of Emily's vision, and merged into the flow of traffic on the expressway.
Emily's hand was tense on the tiller as she steered, but not
because she was now late for work. That was no problem.
Neoform was not that rigid an outfit, at least at her level in
its hierarchy, and there was nothing urgent awaiting her.

No. The problem was what she had told Nick. Did she
have no intention of walking out on him? Was she so sure?
Was Bernie just a momentary passion, born of a congruence
of novelty and shock and fear and opportunity? Would he
disappear as soon as the villain responsible for the chips in
the Sparrow and the Mack, and for the Assassin bird, had
been caught? Or was there something more between them?
More than between her and Nick? And Andy. How could she
fail to think of him?

The traffic was especially heavy in the three lanes bound
eastward toward the city center. That would change later on,
when the commuters flowed the other way and choked the
three lanes Emily now followed. Not for the first time, she
felt fortunate that Neoform lay even farther west of the city
than their neighborhood, so that her commuting kept her free
of the worst of the inevitable traffic jams.

Still, "free" was a relative term. The traffic on her side of
the narrow strip of grass that separated the eastbound and
westbound sides of the highway was quite bad enough. Every

lane was a steady stream of Buggies, gas-burners, and Macks, the fastest vehicles in the leftmost lane. She had maneuvered the Tortoise into the center lane, where the speed was comfortable and she could, if necessary, pass to either side. Now she glanced at the median strip. It was concave, a drainage ditch deep enough to stop wheeled vehicles from crossing freely, by accident or design. As she passed one of the flat, paved turnarounds for official vehicles that periodically interrupted the grass, she reflected that legged animals would not need them. They could trot as easily across the ditch as across a sidewalk. She smiled at the thought that her Bioblimps would be able to ignore even the roadway.

The smile didn't last. The Tortoise's head began to sway minutely back and forth. Normally, it held steady until she bent the tiller left or right. Then the neck and head followed her command, and the reflexes built into its nervous system by eons of natural evolution, no thanks at all to the gengineers, brought the limbs and body in train. She loved to watch the process: first the movement of the head, say to the left, then the left-side limbs bent a little more, taking shorter steps, while those on the right took longer, and the beast would pivot into a shallow curve or a sharp turn, just as she, its master, its driver, wished.

But now—something was wrong. She had, when young, driven a few old gas-powered automobiles. This was not the wobble in the steering, not transmitted to the wheels, that came from a loose coupling in the steering column. This was more like the constant overcorrections of a novice driver, for the Tortoise indeed seemed to be hunting for some proper path.

How bad could it get? Would she, she wondered, be unreasonably paranoid if she uncovered that switch Nick had used to protect them from the Sparrow? She eyed the median strip and the traffic beyond it, the trucks, fuel-driven and gengineered. If the steering went . . .

She glanced in the rearview mirror. A gap was coming up on her left. As it reached her, the Tortoise's head stopped swaying, and the beast swung smoothly into the other lane. She had not turned the tiller.

Now the median was right beside her, and the opposing traffic and its massive trucks, heavy steel and toothy Macks, were mere yards away. Adrenaline surged through her. Her heart raced, and her mouth went dry.

She tried to steer back into the middle lane, back to the comfort of being surrounded by a horde of people going in the same direction and insulating against opposition.

The Tortoise did not respond.

She yanked at the tiller, but it made no difference. She stabbed her fingers at the ''pull-in'' switch's panel, expecting resistance such as Nick had met, but there was none. With a sigh of relief, she punched the switch. If it worked, she knew, she would suddenly become an obstacle in a steady stream of high-speed traffic. She would be hit, buffeted, rolled, bruised, perhaps more seriously injured. But she had her belt on, and she knew it would be much worse if the Tortoise crossed the median.

Nothing happened.

The panic rose still more. She punched the switch again, and again, as fruitlessly as the first time. She crested a rise and faced a mile of road gently descending and then rising into a leftward curve. She stared at the oncoming traffic, and she saw that a gap in that traffic was on its way. On the far side of that gap, a juggernaut belching smoke and noise, was a truck, all steel and engine, not flesh, not teeth, but just as deadly.

The Tortoise's nose swung just enough to align with that truck. Thereafter, it moved just enough to track it in its progress toward her.

The situation was eerily familiar. She had only seconds left, but they seemed to stretch interminably. She had all the time she needed to search the panels below the dashboard, find the one whose ventilation slits suggested the presence of electronics, open it, identify the motherboard, and yank it out.

The Tortoise promptly stumbled to a halt. She gasped with relief. She had hoped only to snatch any foreign chip that might be on the board and thereby return her vehicle to normal. But now a memory rose to tickle at the back of her mind: Somewhere, the source would come to her, she had read that Tortoises and some other Buggies were designed to function only as long as they received signals from their controlling computers. The computer didn't control all the genimal's functions—it ate and defecated and scratched without command—but without some signal, the beast could do nothing at all. Deprived of its computer, it was paralyzed.

Horns blared behind, and a swerving Roachster slammed the Tortoise's shell, bumping Emily's now-inert vehicle onto the shoulder of the road. Another buffet slammed her into the median, tilting helplessly. There were more horns, and in the vehicles that now swept past her she could see purple faces, mouths open, fists waving.

If they only knew how little she cared for their anger! She fell back in her seat behind the useless tiller. She grinned, feeling the stretching of her face as if it were some strange and independent thing, knowing that with her wide mouth she must look as foolish as . . . as foolish as she felt. She was safe. Already her charge of adrenaline was draining from her system and her body was returning to normal.

In a few moments, she was able to lift her hand, and the Tortoise's motherboard, to her lap. She turned it over, and over again. She studied it, savoring the luxury of time. And there, a little less dusty, a little newer in appearance, was a chip that reminded her of the one Bernie had shown her. The one from the Mack.

Could she trust her memory? What if she pulled the chip and put the board back and replaced the panel and started up, and the Tortoise remained intent on killing her?

But she was a gengineer. She knew how genimals were controlled. She had been the one to teach Bernie all he now knew. And her memory was reliable. It had better be.

She yanked the chip from its socket. Then, hesitating only briefly, she put the motherboard back where it belonged.

The call had to be routed to his vehicle, somewhere in the city, but within moments of entering her office, Emily was telling Bernie what had happened. "I'm afraid I got my fingerprints all over it," she said. "But it worked. I plugged the board back in, and the Tortoise was fine."

She had ignored Alan Bryant when she had come in, too intent on reaching Bernie. Now he leaned against the wall, listening as he waited for her attention, his eyes wide, his mouth pursed in an "O."

"What about you?" His voice was tinny in the phone's earpiece.

"Pretty shaky. I got all the way over in the right lane as soon as I could. I stayed there too."

"You did the right thing." He hesitated. "I should be done here before lunch. A burglary and rape. Then I'll come by and get the chip."

She wished he was there, or Nick. Either one would be a comfort, and she should call her husband soon, to tell him too, to hear his concern. For that matter, she should have called him first, but . . . To her surprise, she found herself thinking that Nick's comfort would be worth more to her than Bernie's. It would be more comforting.

She had two men in her life, as she never had had before. Someone else was trying to kill her. There were just too damned many complications. But now she had a clue to how she should resolve at least one of those complications.

She looked up as her assistant pulled himself away from the wall. What did he want? More complications?

"Gelarean's called a meeting," he said. "At ten. And we have no problems with the Bioblimps. The new babies are growing fine." When she sighed in relief, he added, "Glad you're okay."

Then, pointedly, he looked at his watch. "It's very nearly ten now."

Chapter
Sixteen

BERNIE TURNED THE chip over and over in his hand, staring at it, studying it. Finally, he said, "We're getting quite a collection of these things, aren't we? The Sparrow, the Mack, now your Tortoise."

He had had to wait in Emily's lab for half an hour. Alan Bryant had explained that she was in a meeting, and yes, it was running late. Then he had turned back to his work, and all Bernie could do was watch the pretty pictures on the workstation screen. When she had eventually arrived, she had led him to what passed for Neoform's company cafeteria, a row of vending machines in an alcove near the second-floor stockroom. One wall bore a collage of dusty photos displaying to all who cared the company's past triumphs. Beneath the display was a counter equipped with racks of paper napkins, wire bins of salt, pepper, and sugar in paper envelopes, and bowls of tiny packets containing catsup and mustard. A line of stools waited beneath the counter.

They had the room to themselves. Everyone in the building apparently preferred to eat out, at one of the local restaurants. They came here only for occasional snacks, or when they were working through the night and needed sustenance. And sustenance, Bernie thought, was surely all they would get. The machines' displays did not promise much culinary excitement.

There had been an uneasy silence when they first sat down, choosing the metal folding chairs at one of the two small tables instead of the stools. Eventually, she had said, "That meeting. Sean wanted progress reports on our work, but that wasn't all.'' As she spoke, she watched the hallway outside the alcove, not him. She seemed to be looking for some particular person. ''He said you didn't seem to be getting anywhere and were just wasting people's time. He meant mine. He wanted to bar you from the premises.''

''Does he have a guilty conscience?''

As she shook her head, releasing a flood of odors—perfume, shampoo, the smell of the back of her neck, which he had tasted twice now—he snorted. A warrant would get around such a ploy too easily. Or if he wanted to see Emily, a phone call, and she would come to him outside. They had both enjoyed their encounters on the sheets, and he hoped there would be more. She was wearing a light blouse that let him see the straps of her bra and a skirt of some thin, summer-weight fabric.

''I told them about the Tortoise, though. And he gave up,'' she said.

''You made it clear that the problem wasn't over.''

She nodded vigorously, her wide mouth smiling at her victory over her boss, and produced the chip. She held it out to him. He took it, and he saw immediately that it was as identical as she had thought to the others. When he gestured for her to go on, she told him the rest of the details.

Now she said, ''And I didn't have to shoot it.''

He grimaced. ''I wouldn't have thought of that. Pull the board and yank the chip. Instant repair.'' He looked up from the chip, ignoring the plastic-wrapped sandwich and cardboard cup of coffee in front of him. ''Very quick. Very cool. Congratulations.'' He meant it all. She had done the perfect thing under the circumstances.

''What would . . .''

''Shot it.'' She seemed cooler toward him, as if she did not look forward, like him, to going to bed together again. Was she having second thoughts? ''Pulled out my gun and blown its head away. That would have stopped it.''

She made a face and looked at her food. She had chosen salami, cheese, onions, and green peppers on a sesame-seed bun. ''But I still have the Tortoise, alive.''

''That's true.'' He eyed his sandwich at last. He had pushed the button for tuna fish on rye, but it looked more like canned cat food on dirty foam rubber. "Do all genimals stop like that when you pull the plug?"

She held one hand palm upward, fingers spread. "I knew the Tortoise would. I read the owner's manual after Nick and I got married, and I thought I remembered that. But others? Some Buggies, I think. But I really don't know for sure."

"I suppose it would make sense for private vehicles. But what about jets?" He was, quite naturally, wondering about the Hawks he loved to fly. Would the same ploy, if it ever became necessary, work for him?

She shook her head. "Probably not. They would need some control in the air, wouldn't they? In case of accident." She paused while she unwrapped her sandwich and took a bite. He followed suit, first setting the chip on the table between them. Then she said, "Of course! The Chickadee! They can't possibly turn off the same way."

He made a disappointed face. She laughed around a mouthful of sandwich, but then she choked the sound off abruptly. He looked at her curiously, and in a moment she said, "Your colleague came by the house this morning. She wanted the dope on the Mack attack."

"Connie?" he asked.

She nodded. "She also laid some heavy hints on my husband."

He winced.

She reached out one hand to touch his wrist. "I don't believe you'd brag about your women, Bernie. But . . ."

He sighed. "Yeah. We've been pretty close."

"So she wants you for herself. She's jealous."

"So's Nick," he said.

She reached out one finger to touch the chip. "Would she . . . ?"

"No." He hesitated. "She'd probably try for me." He set down his sandwich, sipped his coffee, and picked up the chip. "And not this way. I'm willing to bet that when I take this down to the university, Narabekian will say it's set to activate on the expressway, and then watch the traffic until just the right situation comes up. Those 'hunting' motions you no-

SPARROWHAWK 167

ticed. It was looking for gaps in the traffic, and maybe an oncoming truck. When it found them, it moved left, and . . ."

She shuddered.

"Whoever we're looking for, he doesn't care about by-standers. Your response was perfect, and just in time," he said. "But you were still lucky."

"Very lucky," she agreed.

"He couldn't have known . . ." He stopped suddenly.

"Not Nick," she said softly.

"Of course not," he murmured gently.

She stared at the sandwich in her hand. She nibbled at a bit of meat that stuck out between the halves of bun. "He's suspicious," she finally said. "But only partly because of Connie. He thinks I'm seeing you too much. More than the investigation calls for."

"Let him." Had he been behind the call to headquarters? The one that accused him of chasing skirt when he should be chasing murderers and rapists? "Grown-ups have a right to have friends of their own. Even outside marriage. Even bed-type friends."

She set her foot down and clenched her hands together, staring at them. "But not in secret," she said. A tear glistened on the lashes of her right eye. She looked up, her gaze meeting his squarely. "That's not fair. It's dirty."

"You feel guilty."

She nodded, her eyes still meeting his. "And we really shouldn't keep it up." She shook her head, so hard that her hair swung wildly. "We're not, we're not, really compatible. Are we?" The tear was back in her eye, and her broad lips were pinched with pain.

She was right, of course. Connie was much more his type. But . . . "What do you mean?"

"I thought you were sensitive. You are. But you also have a cruel streak. I saw it with Ralph's Armadon first. Then the Mack. Now you say you would just have shot my Tortoise. Nick's Tortoise."

He could have left the Armadon to Chowdhury's own tender graces. And she had shown him what else was possible with the Tortoise. "What else could I have done with the Mack?"

Her hair flew again. "That's not the point. You're like that Hawk you fly. Bloody-minded. A predator."

He sighed and looked away from her, fingering the chip. "You're right. I even think of myself that way."

"And I prefer a gentler man."

"Like Nick." Now he knew who she was wishing would walk down the hall.

"Like Nick."

When Bernie had arrived at Neoform, he had been pleased to find a parking space for his Hawk beside Emily's Tortoise. The genimals cared nothing for each other, unless his Hawk might look upon a shelled reptile as food. He didn't think it would. It was crows, wasn't it? Or ravens? Whatever. He once had heard of a bird that carried turtles aloft and dropped them on rocks, as seagulls did with clams.

He had, however, enough of a romantic streak to wish that their genimals might, like their riders, at least enjoy each other's company. At the same time, he was practical enough not to forget that the other vehicles in the lot might seem more tasty fare.

Laughing at himself, enjoying the sparkle of sunlight on the water flowing in the trough between the rows of genimals, the small puffs of cloud overhead, even the scent of dung, he had given his Hawk and Emily's Tortoise a moment in which to recognize each other. A moment more, while he soaked in the lushness of the nearby plantings, surely fertilized with the sweepings from the lot, those the litterbugs missed, and he had admitted that in truth they barely seemed to notice. Then he had laughed and toggled the Hawk into dormancy. As he had walked toward Neoform's entrance and his appointment with Emily—his date, he had felt, with his mind on what might come, once more, after lunch—he had told himself that surely he fooled himself just as much by insisting whenever possible on the same Hawk. It never recognized him, or if it did it did not care.

Now, telling himself that perhaps the Hawk had known better than he all along, he climbed aboard again, awakened it, and strapped himself into his seat. Carefully, he inspected the panels of the control board, the papers on the other seat beside his own, the litter on the floor. There was no sign of tampering or intrusion, and he laughed at himself. Emily's Tortoise had been sabotaged. Now he was wondering about his Hawk. He reached forward and gave the panel that hid the control computer a tug. When it popped loose, he tunked it back. It was enough, for now, to know that the panel was not locked or jammed in place. He could, if that action became suddenly necessary, yank it free, find the motherboard, and remove the foreign chip. There should be no problem, for gengineered aircraft could continue to function without the carrier signal from their computers. If, for some reason, Emily's conclusion on the matter proved faulty and the Hawk froze up as had the Tortoise, well, he would still be high in the air. He would have plenty of time to repair the problem while the Hawk fell.

Still, he was not sure. He checked the Hawk's pod again, and again he saw no signs of trouble. He felt the edges of his seat, and, yes, there was the button that would eject him from the pod if necessary. There was a parachute beneath the seat that would lower him, seat and all, safely to the ground. But there was no piece of paper that offered him a guarantee of long life and happiness. There never was.

He manipulated the controls. The Hawk spread its wings for takeoff. The engine roared, pressing him back into his seat, and the bird leaped into the air. The wings tipped, warping its flight into a climbing spiral, and the Neoform buildings diminished below, shrinking to the incongruity of a child's playroom, a modern office building set beside a farmer's red and white barns, the bulging blue and yellow stripes of a fabric dome, all among white fences and green paddocks surrounded by city streets, stores, and tracts of homes.

Bernie looked toward the city center, now ahead, now to leftward, now to rightward. His office and the Aerie were there. His apartment. Connie. She might be jealous, but she *was* a cop. A predator herself. Like him, a hawk—his mind flashed that ancient line, "She stoops to conquer," into his consciousness just long enough to evoke a dusty memory of

high-school English class and forgotten plays. He wondered
if she would be free for the evening.

With one hand on the steering yoke, he bent the Hawk's
course toward the Aerie. It rolled, throwing him against the
straps of his seat belt. Had he oversteered? A gust of wind?
It rolled again, pitching abruptly to the right and back again.
He felt the pod in which he sat slip against the Hawk's
back, and adrenaline surged through his system. His pulse
raced. His palms grew damp and his mouth dry.

The sensation was familiar. He felt it anew every time he
faced a criminal. He had felt it when the Mack had been
bearing down on him and Emily. He was sure she had felt it
when her Tortoise had headed for the median.

He eased up on the throttle and jerked at the yoke. For a
moment, he thought he had solved the problem, whatever it
was. But then the Hawk pitched forward, back again, from
side to side. He could feel the movements of his pod and the
strain on the straps. Those straps were heavy. They were
strong enough for all foreseeable strains. They had to be. But
they could not possibly be infinitely strong. They could be
broken.

Or torn. He was reaching for the computer cabinet, the
truth having penetrated that his Hawk had indeed been sabotaged. Emily had rejected him, but still he could learn from
her. But before he could open the panel, much less remove
the motherboard or cleanse it of its parasitic infection, the
Hawk pitched into a forward roll, like a diver from a board.
It bent, and it tore at its breast with its great hooked beak.

Bernie seized the yoke. It was, he knew, too late to remedy
matters in Emily's way. If he let go, the Hawk's gyrations
would slam him back and forth against the straps that held
him in his seat. He would not have the stability, the steadi-
ness, he would need to pop the panel, find the board, and
remove the chip that was surely there. But, he thought, it
didn't matter. The Hawk would shortly sever the straps that
held the pod to its back, just as it and its fellows had severed
the Sparrow's straps. And the saboteur's influence would have
to end.

He hung on, while the Hawk's gyrations spun the blood to

his head and his vision darkened. He barely noticed when his bladder let go. His face distorted into a rictic grin, but that grim expression was due only partly to the g forces he was experiencing. He too, he told himself, was a hawk. He would survive. He would triumph.

The straps gave way. The pod leaped from the Hawk, its tangent course quickly curving into a parabolic plummeting toward the ground. Bernie grunted relief at the sensation of free-fall, but his rictus remained.

He pressed the ejection button. Explosive charges shattered the clear shell of the pod and propelled his seat and him into space. Wind struck his face. He tumbled, and nausea flooded his stomach. When he faced the ground he saw that he was above a residential neighborhood, one whose street pavements had been replaced with turf. Where other neighborhoods were blocks of green embedded in a lattice of grey tar or tan concrete, here the lattice was light green, the blocks darker, and there, to one side, was a square of tar, beside a building of red brick, a schoolhouse, a playground, and the wreckage of his pod was tumbling slantwise, pushed by wind, toward it. He thanked God that it was summer, school was out, there would be no kids at recess. Then, realizing, remembering his own childhood, he prayed that none of the neighborhood children would be on the playground anyway.

He extended his arms and legs to slow the tumble and let air pressure stabilize his position. He looked for the Hawk, afraid that now it would see him as prey on the wing and . . .

And ''Eee kai vai!'' There it was, screaming its siren call, already stooping toward him, and the favorite curse of the few Franco-Americans among his childhood playmates sprang to his lips. *''He! Calvaire!''* or ''Oh! Calvary!'' He had not thought of it in decades. He wished he too believed. He crossed himself anyway, just as those playmates always had in moments of stress.

His magnum was, as always, under his arm. He fumbled, cursing the seat straps that got in his way, and drew it. He aimed and fired, and the recoil renewed his spin, but not before he saw the Hawk shy off.

The Hawk swooped past him while he spun. It screamed.

It climbed. By the time he had himself stabilized once more, the Hawk was attacking again. He fired, missed, and spun. Frantically, he squeezed off another shot as soon as he swung into position anew, and again, and again.

The Hawk's scream stopped. Bernie felt a buffet of air at his back, and then the Hawk, his Hawk, his soaring, swooping, stooping steed of air, was falling past him, already tumbling. Less dense than the pod, offering more surface area to the wind, it would strike the ground well past the playground.

Once more he stabilized his fall, and then he felt for the D-ring that would activate his parachute. He pulled it, knowing that the wind would carry him much farther than it did the pod or Hawk. He might never see either again, or until he visited them in the warehouse, surely the same one that had held the Mack, to retrieve the chip, the evidence of sabotage.

In a moment, the chute yanked at his seat. His seat straps yanked at him, squeezing his chest and stomach. He began to sway, and it was all too much. He vomited.

Chapter
Seventeen

THE COUNT, LIEUTENANT Napoleon Alexander, was a martinet with delusions of grandeur, but he did care about his people. Bernie had to give him that: Just as soon as the word reached headquarters, the Count himself would come to pick up the pieces.

Bernie wished it would do him some good.

He had had paratroop training long ago, in another war, and he knew how to land. But only when his legs were free, not when he was strapped to a massive, stinking pilot's throne, unable to cushion the blow on bent knees, or to roll. All he could do was grit his teeth, ignoring their taste, and clutch the arms of his seat, his gorge convulsing at the touch of what his stomach had expelled. The wind of his fall buffeted his face and chilled his soaking legs.

He waited, staring alternately at the rapidly nearing ground and the canopy of nylon that billowed above his head, thinking that the Hawk had cheated. It had kept on attacking even after the loss of the pod had broken all connection with the saboteur's subverting chip. Was it because the new programming had somehow taken root in the genimal's brain? Had the chip simply activated reflexes that had to run their course? Had it seen him, tumbling in the air, as irresistible prey? Or did it hate its masters and seize its opportunity for vengeance?

When the impact came, he felt it in his butt, jarring up his spine. His teeth bounced apart, despite his clenched jaw muscles, and whammed together again. His vision blanked.

When his eyes agreed to work again, they showed him a

broad expanse of green, a lawn splashed with color, trees onto which the chute canopy was settling. There was a house to one side. He tried to blink the daze out of his eyes as he looked closer, and he realized: He was neatly embedded in a cluster of thorny rosebushes. Their pale pink blooms nodded away from him on stems bent by his presence. He assumed they had the fragrance typical of roses, but at the moment his nose was as stunned as his butt.

He remembered a movie that had featured hapless cinematic aviators plunging into thickets of barbarian swords. He untangled himself from his seat straps and the cords that had suspended him beneath the parachute. He struggled free of the rose thorns, swearing that his magnum would at least have given him a fighting chance against the barbarians. He tugged the chute out of the trees beside the lawn, used it to wipe his hands, face, and shirt clean, and wadded it up. Then he yanked the seat out of the roses and weighted the chute down.

Finally, he turned toward the house. It was a green cylinder rounded on the ends, with small windows studding its low length. "A goddam zucchini," he said aloud. Except for the color, it reminded him of the antique Airstream trailers that still, from time to time, queued up to tour the countryside and the pages of travel magazines.

A young woman clad in a skimpy bathing suit leaned on the railing of the house's central porch. A screen door stood ajar behind her. A gaily striped towel, one corner rucked up where a parachute cord had brushed it, marked where she had been sunbathing. A glass lay on its side beside the towel, as if she had knocked it over. Perhaps, he thought, she had heard the Hawk scream, looked up, seen the fight and its end, and then run for the house to get out of the way of falling objects.

"I saw it all," she said. "Wow! Do they do that often?"

Bernie shook his head. He was still dazed. "It keeps the job interesting," he managed. "Got a phone?"

"I called already." She waved a hand toward the street and the other houses of the neighborhood. "So did they, I guess." He turned to look. A dozen people, men, women, and small children, were standing there, carefully staying off the lawn, not approaching, perhaps wondering whether there would be more gunfire. Two dogs stood spraddle-legged, howling their defiance of his invasion of their turf. A few other people were trotting purposefully down the greenway, away from him. He was still too disoriented to know which way was toward the city center, or where his Hawk had come down. He presumed they knew just where to look.

Sirens echoed across the sky and down the nearby streets. Four Hawks swept into view and stooped, two toward him, two beyond the trees. A Pigeon ambulance howled into view, and half a dozen Roachsters rattled to a stop by the curb.

The Count was in the first of the Hawks to land. He tumbled from the pod, tripping on the edge of its hatch, catching himself, running toward Bernie, his dignity forgotten for the moment. "Bernie! You're okay! What happened?"

Briefly, he told the tale, while the woman on the porch listened and his fellow officers—Larry Randecker was one of them—shooed the bystanders away. "Find the computer," he concluded. "There'll be another of those goddam chips in it."

The Count gripped Bernie's biceps with one hand and gestured with the other. "That's what they're looking for," he said. "Don't need a cargo hauler for a Hawk. They've got nets."

"Did you bring a body bag for me?"

Lieutenant Napoleon Alexander looked uncomfortable. After a moment's hesitation, he said, "We didn't know what to expect, so . . ."

Bernie laughed. "So you did!" Then: "Where's Connie?"

"We couldn't be sure, but she was afraid it was you. She wouldn't come."

"Excuse me?" Larry Randecker clapped Bernie on the back, but he was speaking to the Count. "We've got a veedo reporter."

"Tell him we'll have the story later. At headquarters." He sniffed at Bernie, then at the crumpled chute. He wrinkled his nose as if to say they both stank. They did, though most of the obvious mess was now embedded in the chute's fabric. "Maybe we should put the chute in the bag. But come on."

He led Bernie toward the waiting Hawk, one free of sabotage, well behaved, normal, safe.

"I didn't dare." Bernie had showered and changed his uniform for a set of overalls belonging to one of the Hawk handlers. When he emerged from the Aerie's locker room, Connie was there, seizing him in arms like steel bands, laying her head on his chest, saying, "I just didn't dare go out there. If I had to help shovel you into a bag . . ." She choked on tears, and he struggled not to pat her on the back. Instead, he squeezed her as hard as she was squeezing him.

"Come on," said the Count. "They've got it all, and . . ." Both of them followed, their arms around each other's waists, as he led the way out of the Aerie, across the yard, and down the street toward the warehouse. No one worried that they were not upholding the proper image of a police force.

The warehouse was as gloomy as ever, its lights as dim, its walls as darkly shadowed. Bernie's Hawk lay where the Mack once had been, and the department's butchers labored over it. The meat was fresh this time, and there was no need of delay for inspection. They were reducing the carcass to slabs of meat for the Aerie's genimals. Probably, Bernie thought, some of it would find its way into the cafeteria. That sometimes happened; it always did when the dead vehicle was a Roachster, the meat of which was indistinguishable from lobster.

The wreckage of the pod lay in a pile to one side, set off by a line of official sawhorses from the residue of the Mack's debris. There were shards of the plastic that had been the pod's bubble. There was the seat Bernie had ridden down, and the parachute. There were the straps the Hawk had torn. There were the crushed and mangled remnants of the control board and cabinets and computer.

"Looks like you needed a shovel," said Bernie. He let go of Connie when she tugged at his arm. He watched as she approached the butchers' area and retrieved a tail feather.

"Damn near," answered a young technician. She stirred a mass of small, black fragments. It looked like a pile of dead beetles. "The composition board material shattered. These are all the chips we could find."

Bernie knelt and sifted through the pile with his fingers. Each chip—or rather, its epoxy, contact-legged housing—was intact, and its code numbers were legible. But he could not recall that numbers that had identified the PROM chips the saboteur had used. He had no hope of finding the evidence he craved, not unless he trekked back to the office. He did not feel like exerting himself when he was so certain of the result.

Another technician opened a case. "Intact boards from a Hawk controller," he said. "A full set."

Connie returned, carrying the feather over her shoulder as if she were a carpenter lugging a board. She murmured, "A souvenir," and took Bernie's hand. Then, while she, Bernie, and the Count watched, the two technicians carefully matched each of the loose chips to those mounted on the boards. In ten minutes, there were just two chips on the boards for which they had not found matches, and they had one loose chip that did not correspond to either one of them. Wordlessly, one held it up to Bernie. He accepted it, studied it, and thought the numbers looked familiar. Finally, he nodded. "I'll check it against the others. But, yes. This has to be it."

"What now?" asked Connie.

"Back to Neoform," he said. "It had to be put in while I was there this morning. So whoever it is . . ."

"But how will you find him?"

Bernie looked at Connie until she blushed lightly. "Or her," he said at last. "They keep good sign-out records."

"Want a Roachster this time?" offered the Count.

Bernie shook his head. "I'll be brave. I'll stick with Hawks. Just make sure it's got a good chute."

He had arrived there before lunch and stayed through the lunch hour, Bernie told himself. Surely no one would have dared to tamper with the Hawk while Neoform's people had been passing through the parking lot on their way to their favorite restaurants. But there had been a little time before lunch, and then a little more when the lot had certainly been quiet, waiting for the return flow of people and their genimal vehicles.

He had checked the chip. It had indeed been identical to the others, and as he had with the one that had made Emily's Tortoise go astray, he knew, without looking, exactly how it had been programmed. Had it been just that morning, that noon, that he had been telling her what someone had done to her? Now he could tell her that that same someone had tried a similar trick on him. Later, before the case came to trial, if it ever did, he would have to see Narabekian for confirmation. On both chips, his and Emily's. But he had no doubts. The modus operandi was far too clear.

The new Hawk had lifted from the Aerie roof as if someone had lit a fire under its tail. Had that been nothing more than the thrust of the beast's jet engine? Or had Bernie's determination leant it impetus? It did not matter. It was enough that the jet spread its wings and pushed him through the sky at speed. Soon the Hawk was banking obediently to circle above the Neoform estate. There was no hint of sabotage, no least suggestion that someone had plugged some subversive hidden program into the beast's circuit boards, waiting for its first chance to get him. Bernie grinned mirthlessly. He hoped the sonuvabitch would try. The afternoon was winding down—it was after four already—and he could see that the Neoform parking lot was already emptying. He would land in a vacant area—that one, there, to the right, not too far from the building's entrance—and leave the Hawk awake, not toggled down.

The bird's head was up, cocked now this way to look at clouds above its head, now that way to watch the traffic on the road that bordered the parking lot on two sides, now peering at genimals beyond its reach, now at people leaving the building, now at Bernie as he approached the entrance. Bernie felt confident that, this time, he was safe. If anyone approached the Hawk without him, there would be no need for a trial. He had come too near needing a body bag himself. This Hawk would leave so little that a baggie would be enough.

Neoform employees were trickling past the reception desk.

As each one paused to scrawl his or her name on the sign-out pad, a light glowed and the company's central computer checked the signature against the template it had on file. If the signature checked, a tone sounded, and Miss Carol released the turnstile.

A woman as grey-haired as Miss Carol stood behind the receptionist. Bernie, presuming she held down the evening shift, ignored her as he moved over the counter that separated her from visitors. "Miss Carol . . ."

"I just called her. She's coming down."

He shook his head. "That's not what I'm here for. I need to see the sign-in and sign-out records for earlier today."

Her eyebrows rose. "You can't do that!"

He sighed. "I can get a warrant if I have to. Someone here sabotaged my Hawk this noon, and I want to see who had the chance."

"But that will take hours!"

"I doubt it," he said.

"And besides . . ." She glanced at a clockface set in her console, and then at her replacement, who simply shrugged and said, "I'll go get a cuppa."

Emily arrived as the other woman left. She looked puzzled, but Bernie quickly explained what had happened. When she said, "Oh, no!" and put a hand to her mouth, he flapped a hand. "I'm all right," he said. "There was a moment there when I was saying good-bye to my descendants, but . . ." He shrugged and said what he was after.

When Miss Carol objected once more, Emily said, "There shouldn't be any problem. It's on the computer." She moved behind the receptionist and pointed to a slot in the side of her computer terminal. The printer was built in. "And it shouldn't take very long to get a printout."

It didn't. Though she grumbled as she worked her keyboard, Miss Carol was able within minutes to elicit a list, two single-spaced pages long, of all those who had signed in or out between 11:00 A.M. and 1:00 P.M. Beside each name was the time that person had left the building and the time he or she had returned.

"Thank you," said Bernie.

"You can look it over in the lab," said Emily.

They were alone in the lab. Alan Bryant was gone. The broad screens of the workstations were dark, and the papers, books, computer disks, and pieces of apparatus atop the lab's desks and benches had been carefully straightened. Clearly, Emily and Alan wanted to be able to get straight to work when they arrived in the morning. The desk and bench tops were not empty, though Bernie supposed sensitive material must be kept in a vault at night. At least, that was how it had worked in other labs past cases had taken him to.

"I *was* about to leave," said Emily. She led him across the lab to a bench with more clear space than most. When she reached it, she pulled out a chair for him. Then she kept moving, circling the bench until, safely untouchable, she could face him from its other side.

Within himself, Bernie winced. So short a time ago . . . "Sorry," he said, and he was, for everything. "It shouldn't take very long. But it can't wait."

"Why on earth not?" As if despite herself, Emily leaned forward over the bench. Her blouse gaped, and he deliberately kept his gaze on the sheets of paper in his hand.

"Because it's the first solid clue we've got." He pushed aside the few pieces of workaday clutter that occupied even a relatively clean bench. Then he spread out the pages of the computer's printout. "Whoever planted that chip had to do it when the Hawk was here. They couldn't have done it at headquarters."

She pulled back, found a seat at another bench, pulled it into position, and sat down. "Couldn't they have done it on an earlier visit?"

He shook his head. "Too unreliable. I don't always have the same Hawk. I try, but . . ."

He leaned over the papers, scanning. He cursed when he realized that the names were in alphabetical order. "I wish it had listed folks in the order in which they signed out."

It was her turn to apologize. "I should have realized."

He found his own name. "Here," he said, handing her a

page. "Cross out everyone who left before 11:23 A.M. or after 12:47 P.M." He did the same on the page he had retained. Those were his times, and they bracketed the vulnerable period. No one here could possibly have sabotaged the Hawk before he arrived. And the deed had been done before he left.

Together, they studied the names that remained. One had "returned" before she left. "On vacation," said Emily. "She comes in for her mail." Most of the rest clustered near twelve noon. Only one left after 12:15, and that one signed out at 12:20 and back in at 12:29. A delay, perhaps, to allow the parking lot to clear, and then just enough time out of the building to do the job.

Bernie sighed in satisfaction. "The only one." He pointed at the name on the sheet of paper, the damning numbers beside it. "The only one who had a chance. I was afraid there would be more. Or that he would be cleverer."

Emily stared at the page. "But why him?"

Bernie shook his head. "I don't know. But at that party, he asked about attempts on your life." When she looked puzzled at the significance of that clue, he explained: "Attempts. Plural. More than one. And at that time, there had been only one that we knew of, the Assassin bird. No one suspected the Sparrow had been aimed at you. That's when he became a suspect."

"But . . ." Her eyes widened, as if even now it were inconceivable that anyone would really want to kill her. "But why?"

He picked up the printout, folded it, stuck it in his shirt pocket, and shrugged. "Rivalry, perhaps. Or part of his general mad-on for everyone in sight. You told me about that. Or maybe . . ." He hesitated.

"What?"

It had occurred to him that if Chowdhury were truly capable of trying to kill Emily, and of doing so with no regard for hapless bystanders, he might well be capable of other evils. And he lived, he had told Bernie at the party, not too far from the Gelarean place. That put him in or near Greenacres. He might have been the one who had treated Jasmine Willison so poorly.

Bernie said nothing to Emily about his additional suspicion. It might be sheer coincidence. There was nothing except his personality that made him think the man was even capable of such an act. But if she met the man before Bernie could gather the final shreds of evidence and make the arrest, her reaction to him, involuntary though it would be, might give away too much.

In fact, he regretted what he had said already. But that was done, past changing, and he would have to make the best of whatever came next.

"He must be scared," she said. "He left no tracks before, but now . . ."

"I've been around too much," said Bernie. "He must have thought our affair . . ." She winced when he said the word, and he hesitated. "Our affair was just a blind, while I snuck up on him. Of course he's scared. They always are, and when they panic, that's when they slip. And we get them." It was, he thought, a cliché right out of centuries of detective stories. And though writers often thoroughly fouled things up, some things they could not get wrong. They were just too real, too inescapable as basic aspects of reality. They were clichés, yes, but no less true for that.

"What next?" She licked those broad lips, and Bernie looked away.

"I'll need to get a pair of search warrants. Then, tomorrow, I'll go over his lab and his apartment. Wherever I find him, I'll arrest him. And you'll be safe." And back with Nick, he told himself.

"Can I go with you?" She stood and began to edge, crabwise, toward the end of the bench. The distance between them increased, but Bernie realized that, really, she was drawing closer to him, diminishing the length of the perimeter between them. He held his breath for a moment, though he knew he was being an idiot. She was Nick's. He was, he knew it now, Connie's.

Would she be safe with him? Taking her would not at all resemble standard operating procedure for a cop nailing a suspect. But she was certainly concerned, and he did still feel something—more than *something*—for her. "Why not?"

Chapter
Eighteen

A LITTLE AFTER Emily had left the house that morning, Nick had busied himself with doing laundry in the basement. Andy he had left in the living room with the veedo running and his plastic Warbirds within reach.

Emily denied it, but he was sure she had a yen for that cop. Maybe more. He wouldn't be surprised if she actually had something going with him. He had, after all, seen her face when Connie Skoglund had asked her last question. And if she didn't, or hadn't, she wouldn't have said she wasn't about to walk. But she *wasn't* about to. She said so.

He sorted the clothes as his mother had taught him once, long ago, thinking. The cop was lucky. Two women. That Connie wanted him too. Which one did *he* want? Lucky bastard.

Or was he? Was he, Nick, luckier than he thought? Bernie could have Connie, she had made that clear. But not Emily, after all. She had said she wasn't leaving.

Nick grinned at the sense of relief that rushed over him. She loved him. She must. And he loved her. He always had, he always would. He should tell her so, now.

He set dials, pushed buttons, and waited a moment while the machine began its noisy labors. Then he went upstairs and checked on Andy, who had folded a throw rug into a mountain range and poised his Warbirds on the edge of the couch. He was launching the 'Birds one by one to strafe and bomb the range while invisible ground forces strove to shoot them down. At the end of each run, the Warbird would scream, roll, and crash noisily before returning to the couch.

The phone was in the kitchen. He punched the Neoform number, got the receptionist, and asked for Emily. The answer startled him: "Oh, Mr. Gilman! She's in a meeting right now, but she's all right. Really, she is!"

For a moment, he could not speak. Why shouldn't she be all right? He was happy that she was, of course, but . . . But . . . He almost shouted the words: "What happened, Miss Carol?"

"I don't know the details," she said. A "yet" seemed to linger behind the words. "I'm sure she'll tell you all about it later on. But she *is* all right!"

He hesitated once more, as uncertain as he had ever been of what to do. Finally, he said simply, "Tell her I love her."

"Of course you do!"

"What's the matter, Daddy?" Andy was at his knee, looking up, eyes wide, drawn inevitably by the tone of panic in his voice. "Did something happen to Mommy?"

Of course he would think that. Nick shook his head. "She's all right," he said, straining to sound normal, hoping that was the whole truth. "Want to go for a ride?"

"Yeah!" The boy grinned. "But Mommy's got the Tortoise."

"So we'll take the bus."

"The airport?"

"Why not."

Nick had heard that the gengineers had, in the name of historical aptness, experimented with turning greyhounds into mass-transit vehicles. Unfortunately, their long, lean bodies had buckled too easily under the weight of loaded passenger pods, and it had been impossible to correct the problem without losing the greyhound look entirely. Most buses were therefore based, like trucks, on bulldogs. A few were based on Saint Bernards.

The local bus line used Bernies, and the nearest stop was just two blocks away from the Gilman home. After one transfer, Nick and Andy were on the route to the airport, and Nick was saying, "The bus may not stop, you know. The airport's closed."

But the bus did grunt to a halt at the airport. Nick was surprised to see construction crews at work, tearing down hangars and sheds and tending fast-growing squash vines. The young fruit, already visible, were long and thin, like zucchinis, and their upper, sun-facing surfaces were a translucent yellow.

Father and son left the bus and walked past the small, obviously abandoned terminal building. Nick pointed out the bioform bulldozers, enlarged box turtles whose shells had been modified to serve as earth-moving blades; the Cranes that positioned the young squash next to their foundation cradles on the runways; the antique Mercedes parked, a gleaming, maroon intrusion from another age, behind the terminal. Beside it stood a trio of lean, black-suited, hard-eyed men. They were clearly supervising the efforts of the construction crews, though they did not seem necessary.

They saw Nick and Andy as soon as they rounded the building. The youngest of the three turned, smiled stiffly, and said, "What are you doing here?"

"Just looking." Nick was suddenly cautious. He put a hand on his son's shoulder and held him close. "There used to be an airport here."

"Yeah. The boss bought it when it went bust."

"The boss?"

The other's eyes narrowed, as if Nick were being too inquisitive. "Florin. *Greg* Florin."

The name meant nothing to Nick. He shrugged. "What's it going to be now?"

The man sighed. "A farm." He gestured at the growing squashes. "Greenhouses. And aquaculture tanks. Barns. They figure it'll be close to the market, you know?"

Andy's mouth hung open. "Can we come back later? I wanta see everything!"

The other laughed, a short bark that cut off as if it were against the rules to be amused by anything at all. At the sound, the oldest of the supervisors swung around. He wore a pencil-line mustache, and his hair was greying neatly along the sides. He said, "This is private property, kid. Get lost. And tell your father it ain't smart to ask too many questions."

* * *

Andy's mouth had still hung open, but no longer with delight.
Nick had stifled words that surely would have been unwise to
speak aloud, considering the way the strangers had carried
themselves. He had turned the boy away, back toward the
airport bus stop, and they had left immediately.

Once safely on the bus and heading home, Andy had
wanted to know, "Why, Daddy? Why were they so mean?"
Nick could only shake his head and repeat the question to
himself. Were they just litterheads? Or were they involved in
something that could not stand public scrutiny? Or both?

Andy was still upset about the rebuff he had suffered when
it was time for Emily to arrive home. Nick was in the kitchen.
The boy was in the living room, pretending that his Warbirds
were the real thing. As best Nick could make out from the
other room, they had come to town to visit Andy himself.
When they found the local airport's runways blocked by
growing farm buildings, they used their laser cannons, fle-
chette bombs, and poison sprays to clear away the obstacles.

Nick could not help but be amused. Children's fantasies
were free, direct, and often violent, and they effectively
vented feelings and relieved frustrations. If only adults could
use fantasies in the same way! Some could, he knew. But
most, most thought that fantasy was for kids. For grown-ups,
its only justification was as planning for the real thing.

"Where's Mommy?" The cry seemed plaintive. When
Nick checked the clock on the wall, he realized that she had
not pulled the Tortoise into the garage on schedule. She was
late. He left the makings of dinner scattered on the counter
and joined Andy in the living room.

By the time Emily did get home, father and son had been
standing by the window overlooking the drive for twenty minutes. Nick, remembering how Miss Carol had alarmed him
with her reassurances, had said nothing aloud. He had simply
joined the vigil and let the boy lean against his leg.

When Emily finally walked into the house, she was obviously tired. She slumped, and her hair needed the touch of a
comb. There was a hint of future bags in the drooping of her

lower eyelids, but her eyes remained bright. Her voice was even lively as she said, "You wouldn't believe . . . !"

She threw her briefcase toward the couch and opened her arms. Nick held her tight. "Try me," he said. When Andy tried to push between them, he let her go long enough to reach down and lift the boy into his arms. Emily kissed their son.

In a moment, she looked at Nick curiously. He told her about calling, and what he had wanted to say. She kissed him and said, "It was the Tortoise."

"What happened?"

She explained, accepted his congratulations and hug, and let him lead the way to the kitchen. "Dinner's on hold," he said. "And the wine . . ."

Nick set Andy down on the counter beside the sink. They fetched the wine, poured, and positioned themselves on either side of the boy. She said, "But that wasn't all. Bernie's Hawk had a chip too, and it went berserk in the air. He had to shoot it."

"I'll bet he had a parachute!" said Andy. She nodded and squeezed his shoulder. Thus encouraged, and reminded of the death of the Chickadee, he said, "We went to the airport today. And it's gonna be a farm! But they chased us away."

She let him interrupt. When the story ran down, she squeezed his shoulder again and returned her attention to her husband. "And then Bernie had to check the computer at work. That's why I'm late. He didn't even get there till almost five." They clicked their glasses in a silent toast to survival. She went on: "The saboteur made a mistake. He left tracks." She explained how Neoform's people signed in and out, and how that procedure had let them identify the guilty man.

Andy tugged at his mother's blouse. "Who was it?"

"I don't think you've met him, dear. I hope you haven't." She looked at Nick. "Chowdhury."

"The chowderhead." He said that natural corruption of the name as if it were a curse.

"We'll get him tomorrow. Bernie's getting the warrants tonight." She hesitated before adding: "I'll be going with him. He said it would be okay."

"Can I go too?"

They each put a hand on Andy's knee. "Uh-uh." Nick's smile, so confident that he loved her and that she loved him, that she was his and not this other man's, slipped. It became a frown, and then a scowl. He said. "I'm not surprised you want to be there. But . . ."

She straightened and drew back from him, just a little, as if chiding him for his suspicions. "He almost killed me, Nick!"

"And *he's* your protector."

"That's what I called him this morning. It's true. And I'm certainly concerned with this case. I want to be in at the end." She tossed back her wine, lifted her butt away from the counter, and stepped to the fridge to refill her glass.

He watched her move, thinking of the past. There had been a time when his thoughts had centered on that butt, her body, for hours and days at a time. He had prized as well her intelligence, her independence, her determination, her drive. He was getting old. The body still drew him. But the rest of her, the mind and spirit, seemed more important. There were plenty of bodies in the world. The rest . . . ? He did not want to lose her.

She held up the wine carton and cast a quizzical eye in his direction. He nodded, emptied his glass, and held it out. She poured, a wing of dark hair falling past her cheek.

He sighed. What did Bernie value in her? Mind? Spirit? Body? Or even less? Was she perhaps, only a momentary focus of attention, attractive because she was part of a case, there, ready to his hand?

She spoke: "That's all he is, you know. There might have b . . ." She stopped herself with a visible effort. "He's not really my type."

His voice was gentle. "What do you mean?"

"He's a man," she said. "He even smells like one." Her eyes half closed and she smiled softly, while Nick wondered whether he should feel insulted. "But he has a mean streak." She told him what she meant. "He's not gentle. Like you."

Andy was watching them carefully, head turning, first right, then left, to face them as they spoke. "Daddy's nice," he said. "Isn't he?"

Emily wrapped one arm around the boy's shoulders. "We want you to grow up to be just as nice," she said.

He wiggled under her arm and said, "I'm hungry."

Nick laughed. "Then I'll get supper back on track."

When Emily fell asleep on the couch after supper, Andy said, "That's funny, Daddy. Mommy never takes naps."

"She had a hard day," his father told him. "The Tortoise . . ."

"Why did it try to kill her?"

"Someone told it to."

"I know. He reprogrammed the computer."

He nodded. "Sort of. But she fixed it in time."

"Then it's okay now?"

"For sure. No problems. And right now, it's time for you to head for bed." He reached as if to swat a young behind, and the boy laughed, dodged, and ran for his room to change into his pajamas.

Nick let his wife sleep. She *had* had a hard day. It wasn't the first, what with the Sparrow, the Assassin, and the Mack attacks, but this one must have been the worst of them all. Their own possession, the Tortoise, always and unquestionably trustworthy, had turned on her. She had won the battle, but surely the stress had been far worse than the less traitorous attacks of strange genimals could ever engender. And then the discovery of who had done it, the resolution, the relief of suspense, the letdown. He told himself that he too would collapse under the circumstances.

She did not wake until, near their normal bedtime, he decided to move her to their bed. As he slipped his arms under her and lifted, her eyes opened and one arm went around his neck. "Honeymoon time?" she murmured.

"Bedtime," he said, smiling down at her.

"Hokay," she drawled. Her arm tightened to draw his lips to hers. "But can I wash up first?"

"You smell fine."

"So do you." She kissed him again. "But I still want to wash up."

Chapter
Nineteen

MORNING SUNLIGHT POURED through the broad windows of Sean Gelarean's spacious office to puddle on a golden carpet. The walls, paneled with Honduran mahogany, were splashed with original landscapes. A sideboard held three of Wilma Atkinson's biosculptures. The cooled and filtered air smelled faintly of polishes for wood and leather, of lime aftershave, and of potting soil.

Gelarean himself sat at the broad desk in a high-backed seat of padded leather. His face was dark in silhouette against the window behind him. A single unmarked pad of paper was centered before him, a pen beside it. A computer screen and keyboard rose out of the desktop at comfortable angles. A phone was pushed to one side to make room for a glistening rectangle with rounded corners. The strange object's surface was a mottled green. In the center of its top was a ring of eight eyes. Near each edge was a mouthlike slit. No legs were visible.

The desk was a slab of wood that, at first glance, seemed to float in air. Then the watcher realized that Gelarean was visible only from the desktop up, the rest cut off as if by a knife, or blocked as if by a solid desk. The desktop's apparent defiance of gravity was an illusion: The desk had supporting sides like any normal desk, though they were holographic veedo screens that faithfully repeated the view of rug, wall, and window behind them. It was as close as technology had ever come to invisibility.

Bernie stood before the desk, thinking that Gelarean was just the company's head of research. He knew that the com-

pany depended utterly on research for its products, but still
he wondered what sort of quarters Neoform's president enjoyed. Could the difference be as simple as thicker carpeting
and more expensive paneling? Or would the president have a
private sauna behind a door, say, right there?

"A warrant," Gelarean was saying. He held the paper before his face, reading. "For today, Friday. But why?"

The briefcase from which Bernie had taken the warrant still
hung from one hand. He lifted it six inches and let it fall.
Carefully, as if Gelarean were totally ignorant, he explained:
Someone had been sabotaging genimals, apparently trying to
kill Dr. Gilman. There had been the Sparrow, the Mack, the
Tortoise. And, of course, the Assassin bird, which underlined
the seriousness of the criminal's intent, and the fact that Emily was indeed the target. The target image in the Mack's chip
was mere confirmation.

"But what makes you think . . . ?" Gelarean's tone was
that of a businessman who had nothing at stake but face—
giving nothing away, expressionless except for a faint air of
confidence. The police were in his office, but he had done
nothing wrong and could not be touched. At worst, the company might falter for loss of a key employee, while he might
blush in embarrassment.

"Yesterday that someone put another chip in my Hawk
while it was in the lot outside." His voice had grown biting,
angry. "And only one person left the building at the right
time." After a moment's pause, Bernie added, "Your security system produces very good records." He did not say that
there were other reasons for suspicion too.

"Ah. Well, in that case . . ." Gelarean's seat creaked. The
hand nearer the telephone twitched, as if Gelarean suddenly
wished to place a call. Bernie did not miss the intention
movement, but he did not credit it with any great significance. The reason, he later thought, was that the executive
smoothly changed the motion's course to open a drawer and
produce a small vial with a perforated lid. Gelarean held the
vial near the green oblong on his desk and removed the lid.
A fly buzzed free and circled briefly. Then one of the oblong's

mouths opened, and a long, cordlike tongue flicked out to snatch the fly.

Gelarian explained: "A flytrap. We developed it from a frog to sit on a table, or hang on a wall and . . ." He flicked a finger. "It should do well in warm areas."

"On picnics too."

The other gestured, open-palmed, toward the door to the suite. "I won't keep you. Go to it. Though I hope you're wrong. We'd hate to lose the man."

He met Emily at the door to her lab. "Just down the hall," she said. "I saw him come in earlier."

They faced each other, motionless, for a long moment. No, he thought, she was not for him. And she clearly still thought the same, for her mouth was clamped, looking uncharacteristically narrow, and she was leaning back, slightly increasing the distance between them. They could enjoy their bedroom sports. They had done it. But they had nothing in common outside the bedroom. Their society was supposedly classless, but the difference between them was, in truth, one of class, even of caste. The caste marks were education, physicality of occupation, even favorite entertainments. He could *not* imagine her at the Roachster races.

He hooked a thumb over his shoulder. "He was playing with a flytrap when I left."

She made a face. "That was developed by one of our technicians. The patent's in *his* name."

"Let's go," he said. She turned and started walking down the hall. He fell in beside her. At first, then, he thought they were both leaning away from each other, just enough not to touch. But the rhythm of their walking fought their separating; within a few steps, their arms were brushing companionably, almost as if they were still bedroom friends.

Ahead of them, a door slammed open. A slight figure darted into the hall. A white lab coat hung, half on, half off, from his shoulders. A small case was in one hand.

"That's Ralph!" cried Emily as he dashed toward them.

"Stop!" When Chowdhury paid no attention, Bernie spun and grabbed. He caught a glimpse of wide, staring pupils surrounded by rings of white, a half-open mouth, drops of sweat on a dark upper lip. Then Chowdhury was twisting toward the wall. His lab coat came off in Bernie's hand, and he was past them, racing toward the stairs. The case was still in his hand.

Bernie sighed. If they hadn't paused to chat about flytraps! Emily was already beginning the turn back to her office and the phone. "Don't bother," he said, one hand on her biceps. "He's probably past Miss Carol by now. And we'll get him later, anyway."

The door to Chowdhury's lab was still open. When they stepped in, it was to meet the stares of his three technicians, seated at two computer workstations and a DNA splicer. "He's not here," said one. "He had a phone call."

"He said he forgot an important meeting," put in another.

"He was in an awful hurry," said the third, the one woman. All three had black hair and brown skin. Hers was the brownest.

Bernie tossed the vacant lab coat on a workbench. He remembered that twitch of Gelarean's hand toward the phone. He should have realized that Chowdhury might be warned. Now it was too late. Then again, they would catch up with him soon enough. He breathed deeply. They would not be here long.

He stared around the room, struck by the differences between it and Emily's lab. The furnishings were far more idiosyncratic, more reflective of its master's personality. He was dismayed by the high lectern at the front of the room, the stool on which Chowdhury must have sat just a little earlier, the lesser stools on which the technicians sat at their higher-than-normal desks and benches. How could anyone in this modern age use such ancient, uncomfortable perches? He barely noticed the freezers and incubators, the potted plants that occupied the benches nearest the windows, or the aquaria and terraria near the walls. They fitted perhaps too well his image of a biologist's laboratory.

Emily introduced the technicians. Sam Dong, his skin, now that Bernie knew his name, actually seeming more yellow than brown, was the one at the keyboard nearest the door.

Micaela Potonegra was working the splicer. Adam Chand's
screen showed something that might have been a fish, or a
submarine. From the ceiling above him hung what looked
like a dried fish that had been inflated like a balloon. It was
studded with stubby spikes.

They rose from their seats and gathered near Chowdhury's
lectern. When Bernie showed them the warrant, Micaela
sighed. "It had to come," she said. She led them to a bench
in a shadowed corner of the room. It bore a row of terraria
whose contents were only dimly visible. She pressed a switch.
An overhead light came on to reveal a churning mass of . . .
Of what? They looked like worms in size and shape, but they
were banded in bright colors.

"Coral snakes," said Micaela. "There's heroin in the
venom. He had me implant the genes. I didn't know what
they were until . . ."

Sam Dong said, "I knew. He had me make some changes
in them, and I looked them up. I didn't tell her."

Bernie moved to peer into another terrarium, deliberately
ignoring the other man's attempt to defend his colleague.
"Rattlesnakes," Micaela said. "Amphetamines." She
pointed. "Mambas. Asps. Mescaline and angel dust." All
three technicians looked awkward, pained, embarrassed.

"The classics," Bernie said. His voice was quiet, depressed. There was no crime in giving a genimal the ability
to manufacture drugs, though the law would certainly cover
selling those genimals to drug users. And surely the Bioform
Regulatory Administration would object to the potential environmental impact. No wonder, he thought, that Chowdhury
had sabotaged the Hawk. He must have seen Bernie's interest
in Emily as a blind, his interest in the Armadon as a pretext,
his continuing presence as a threat. He must have panicked.
And today he hadn't dared to stay and try to bluff it out.

He opened an incubator, an upright cabinet like a stainless
steel kitchen refrigerator. It was filled with bottles of pinkish
fluid and trays of small eggs. "Snake eggs," said Micaela.

He moved to another bench and touched an aquarium.
"What's this?"

Adam Chand answered. "Jellyfish." He explained how they administered their drug.

Bernie bent to peer more closely. The water smelled of the sea and was full of dime-sized bells, mouths down, colored in faint pastels, trailing translucent fringes. "What's the drug?"

"We don't know. He did that one himself."

"They're so small," said Emily. "They can't give much of a dose."

"Just babies. He's kept us busy cloning the snakes. He said we could stop as soon as there were enough to handle the reproduction on their own. Like the jellyfish. They lay eggs. By the thousands."

"We think . . ." Sam Dong pointed at the aquarium, hesitation over the words. "We think it's a production run. As soon as they're big enough . . ." He looked away from Bernie.

Bernie stared at the three of them in turn. "Why didn't you report this?"

As one, they shrugged. "He's the boss," said Micaela. "And he's got a temper."

Emily touched his arm. "She's right," she said. "They were surely scared."

"I tried to mention it once," said Chand. "To Dr. Gelarean. He just told me to do what I was told." He hesitated. "And I like my job."

Bernie made an exasperated noise and moved toward the window. "And this? Nettles, by God! Did you make these too?"

"They were his," said Dong. "Just his. The first."

Bernie shook his head. He had not expected to find all this. A design shop for hedonic genimals and shrubbery. A goddam drug factory! The root of the new drug trade, and signs that that trade was ready to take off in new directions.

The technicians were dupes, browbeaten, intimidated into keeping quiet about their work. Surely, he told himself, they knew nothing more than they had already told him so freely, probably because all Chowdhury's threats had clearly lost their power as soon as Bernie had entered the lab with his warrant.

They would be interrogated later, just in case. For now, though, could there be any clues in this lab to the destinations of all these snakes and jellyfish and nettles? Florin had to be involved, but had Chowdhury left anything to prove it?

Bernie began his search with the drawers of Chowdhury's own desk. He found small models of Armadons and other genimals, diagrams, notebooks, spec sheets, including one for the coral snake. One of the notebooks held two sketches, one of a jellyfish, the other of something he recognized as a molecular diagram. When he held it out to Emily, she studied it for a moment, her forehead wrinkled intently, before she said, "Now I remember. Heroin."

He shuddered. The snakes were bad enough. "I hope no one ever dumps one in the ocean. Can you imagine a day at the beach then?"

Micaela Potonegra scooched before a workbench at the other end of the room and pulled from beneath it a cage. It held four baby Armadons the size of kittens. As the light struck them, they began to dash frantically and noisily about. "Armadilloes," she said. "They always have identical quadruplets."

He had heard of that peculiarity. Now he crossed the room to watch the small genimals, their bodies still unmarked by doors and windows, whizzing on their wheels around the confines of their cage. They had little room and kept banging into each other.

"Aren't they supposed to have tails?" asked Emily.

"Our first ones did, but we decided they just got in the way. We took the gene out."

Bernie felt sorry for the genimals, but they had nothing to do with the case. Leaving the technicians and Emily to watch the Armadons, he returned to the lectern and opened his briefcase. Within it was a rack of disks. He selected one and plugged it into Chowdhury's terminal. It carried a sophisticated ferret program that could check every file Chowdhury had ever recorded on the machine's hard disk, as long as he had not later overwritten it, for whatever he wished. Passwords did not matter, for computers were required by law to allow police overrides. They also had to keep internal records of uploads to networks and mainframes so that official ferrets could pursue files into all available hiding places.

Chowdhury's stool was much too high for Bernie's comfort. He stood at the keyboard while he gave the program every key word he could think of—drugs, heroin, nettle, cocaine, angel dust, mescaline, asp, coral snake, rattlesnake, mamba, jellyfish, hedonic, illegal, illicit, Emily, Gilman, sabotage, Sparrow, Mack, Hawk, PROM, chip, Assassin . . . He paused, and then he added Jasmine, Greenacres, rape, mutilation, pumpkin, murder. Finally, he turned the ferret loose.

Emily reached past his shoulder to point at the screen. "Why those?"

"I told you about that case," he said. "Her name was Jasmine. We found her body in an empty pumpkin house in Greenacres." He paused to watch the messages the ferret was throwing onto the screen as it searched, listing clean files, saying, "Nothing . . . Nothing . . . Nothing . . ." Occasionally, it would pause to display a file name accompanied by a suspect line of text. Each time it was an internal memo that mentioned Emily as a fellow Neoform employee. Innocuous stuff, so confirmed by Emily. If he thought the file important, he could easily tell the ferret to copy it onto its own disk for later study. But he simply pressed the keyboard's spacebar, and the ferret resumed its search.

"And Chowdhury lives in that neighborhood," Bernie added.

"He's not the only one," said Emily.

"There's Gelarean," he admitted.

"And a VP or two."

The computer beeped. The ferret's mission was accomplished. It had found nothing.

"He must keep his notes on paper, or in his head," said Bernie. His voice sounded disappointed.

"Or in the computer in the barn," said Emily.

Sam Dong shook his head. "They're linked. Your ferret would have found anything there. But . . ." He paused. "He does keep a number of loose disks with him."

Bernie grunted. So that was what had been in the case

Chowdhury had carried as he fled the lab. "Perfect security. He leaves no trace in the company's files, no hacker can get into them, *we* can't get into them. Does he always play things so close to his vest?"

Both Emily and Sam nodded. "He likes to pull the curtain aside all at once," said the latter.

"The fait accompli," added Emily. "I'm sure nobody knows of these snakes and jellyfish." Adam nodded, saying, "He insisted we keep them quiet."

"I'll bet that's not what he has in mind this time," said Bernie. The company would not, he was sure, find genimals that injected illegal drugs very compatible with its public image. Nor would it run the risk of an undercover product line. That could backfire much too easily. No, Chowdhury must be developing his little wonders on the side. The nettles had already entered the underworld trade. The snakes, he thought, had not. Not yet. Not quite. And there would be no surprise announcements, no sudden unveilings.

Bernie wanted very badly to talk to Chowdhury, and he thought he knew where to find him. He would check the barn, just in case the man was saying good-bye to his Armadons. But he did not expect to find him there.

He would be at home. Packing.

Chapter
Twenty

THE WINDOWS WERE curtained by strings of wooden beads. A faint odor of curry permeated the air. Wood-block prints of strange, multiarmed deities adorned the walls. Old photographs of a crowded shantytown sat, framed in lacquered bamboo, on a bookcase shelf.

The beads were a tropical affectation, and he knew it. The prints had come from a secondhand shop in San Francisco, in his student days. The curry, like sin, was something that followed the children of Mother India wherever they might wander, unto the seventh generation. The photographs were of his ancestral home, the coloured ghetto in which his parents had once lived and worked. He had never seen it. He never would.

He sat in a padded armchair, his back to the apartment door, positioned so he could see both the prints upon the wall and the photos on the shelf. The chair was an emblem of the land in which he had been born and still lived, but hardly of the land he felt was most truly his. It was a typical American device, a recliner, designed to foster and reward relaxation, a luxury unknown to billions.

His thoughts stuttered. Those billions, many of them, most, had hammocks, didn't they? And hammocks were more comfortable, more relaxing, more portable, cheaper. But they were not luxury, not unless they were made—or sold!—in America of brightly dyed cord, or of canvas and slung from metal frames. Then they might not even be cheaper.

He was not comfortable. He refused to recline in his sumptuous throne. He was *not* relaxed. He sat erect, clutching the chair arms, staring at the walls, the beads, the prints, the photos. The case full of disks was on the dining-room table. He should, he knew, destroy them before the police got here. Those disks held evidence enough to damn him and all his bosses many times over. But . . . It was already far too late for his own salvation. His bosses had forced him to damnation. If he were caught, he would quite happily see them join him in prison. He would feel special glee because they were white, even, really . . .

Should he flee? The police were not here yet. He had time. He could pack a bag and call a taxi and run to the airport and catch a jet to . . . Where? Argentina? Brazil? Paris? Tokyo? God forbid, Johannesburg?

He shuddered. His hands did their best to shred the upholstery covering the arms of his chair. He could not move. The phone call from Gelarean had galvanized him into fleeing the lab for home. But the motive to run was now exhausted.

A lighted aquarium occupied the bookshelf below the photos of his parents' home. It was a saltwater aquarium, and it held a jellyfish, just one, a large one, the size of two fists, full-grown, the very first of his drug-secreting genimals. He stared at it. He was a success. He was. He could make genes, genes of all kinds, stand up and dance at his command. His bosses applauded his skills. His Armadons would within a year or so begin to displace the Buggies that now dominated the highways. His nettles were already spread wide across the land.

Then why was he cowering here? Why was he about to be arrested and jailed and convicted and sentenced to spend the rest of his life among thugs no better or worse than the South African thugs whom his family had already fled?

He should not have sabotaged the Hawk. He had gone too far with that.

But that cop, that Fischer, Bernie Fischer, had been too close. Nick Gilman had told him so at Gelarean's party. They had a suspect for the Sparrow and the Assassin bird, and they were on the verge of an arrest. And then that Bernie had continued to hang around the building. He had pretended his interest was in Emily, but Chowdhury knew—yes! he knew!—

that Fischer had been watching him, *him*. He had overheard the cop bragging to Emily about how close he was! And he had known that if the cops ever got him, he would have no more chances to kill Emily.

No more chances to free his Armadons of competition from her and her *verdammt* Bioblimps. No, that wasn't true. Killing her hadn't even been his own idea in the first place. If he had accepted the idea, it had been mostly to get rid of her and her snide reminders of details he had forgotten. He knew the Bioblimps were here to stay. The company had the patent, and the orders, and it would see to that.

Something else was truer: If the cops got him, he would have no more chances to obey his masters, to free himself of debt and slavery, to grow rich and famous, to avenge his parents in the pages of history.

But they were white. They all were white. The cops, his masters, even Emily. They were the persecutors of his people and of his family. They were no better than the blacks, and they would be sure to see that he got all the blame.

Yes, he had made the cocaine nettle and the drug genimals. He looked again toward the aquarium on the bookshelf. He grunted and levered himself out of the armchair. He crossed the room, moving as cautiously as an old man, feeling that fragile, as if abused by years of illness. He unplugged the cord that powered the aquarium's light and water pump, removed the apparatus, and dropped it on the floor. He ignored the puddle that drained from the pump's tubing.

For a moment he simply stared into the water, at the jellyfish, *his* jellyfish. Its drug-laden tentacles were translucent white, almost invisible in the tank's small portion of the sea. The bell, tinged with pink and blue, pulsed gently, slowly, moving water in and out of its internal chamber. In the sea, that pulsing would be used for propulsion; now it simply aided respiration.

He turned away and paced, his hands clutching jerkily at each other, around the dining table. He paused at the window, pushed aside the curtain of beads, and stared at the street below, so green, so empty. That, he thought, would not last long.

He turned, stared toward the aquarium, took a pace, and
looked down at his box of disks. He took off his glasses,
another affectation, pure window glass in the wire frames,
and threw them to the table. They clattered as he took the
final step to wrap his arms around the tank. He grunted again,
lifted it free, and staggered back to his armchair. It was heavy.
He sat, lurching, water sloshing over his lap and the upholstery. He positioned the tank as comfortably as he could and
stared once more into its depths. He ignored the water spill,
though his nostrils flared at the smell of salt. The cops would
arrive soon, and after that it would not matter.

He had never had anything to do with the Sparrow, though
he knew who had. But yes, he had sent the Assassin bird.
Yes, he had put chips in the Mack, the Tortoise, and the
Hawk. But someone else, his master, had given him the chips.
He had given him his orders too, for all but the Hawk. He
had had to ask for *that* chip.

Could he have discharged his gambling debts some other
way? Could he have refused to plant the chips? Could he have
stopped with the nettle? Or the Assassin? Or the Mack? Had
he succumbed, surrendered, obeyed, too easily? Even too
eagerly?

He remembered his mother. His Mama. For as long as he
could remember, she had been confined to her wheelchair,
unable to walk, dependent on his Papa and himself for the
simplest things. The Boers had broken her legs. They had
raided a small, unlicensed clinic where his parents had been
treating blacks. Blacks injured in the demonstrations that before much longer had turned into open warfare. The Boers'
days had been numbered, and they had known it.

The kaffirs had broken her back. She hadn't been black
enough. And she had been treating others who shared that
handicap in the newly all-black, dead-black People's Repub-
lic of South Africa.

They had it coming. They all had it coming.

He was not sorry.

He was terrified.

But he was not sorry.

They had it coming.

And now the cops were after him. They had figured out who had put the chip in the Hawk. They knew who had done everything. And they were coming for him.

That was what the call from Gelarean had been all about. The cop, Bernie Fischer, had been in Gelarean's office. He had a warrant, and he had said he wanted him, him, Ralph Chowdhury. And he had just left. He was on his way to the lab.

Had Gelarean seemed to wish to keep him chatting on the phone? It did not matter. He had hung up. He had made excuses to his *verdammt* technicians. He had run.

And Fischer had been in the hall. With Emily. He had ducked and twisted and lost his lab coat and, gasping, run. For some reason, they had not pursued him. But they would. The Hawk would land on his street and they would climb the stairs to his apartment and they would knock. And . . .

Fischer had been hanging around all that time, just waiting for him to slip. And he had. He had. He had. They had a warrant, and they were on the way, and . . .

He stared at the aquarium on his lap.

He wished the jellyfish had eyes. Then it might look back at him. Maybe it would recognize him as its creator. It might even be grateful. Would it raise a tentacle then? Offer him its cnidoblasts, full of bliss? Offer him escape?

But there were no eyes, only spots of pigment around the edges of the bell, light-sensitive but inadequate to the task of forming images.

It was his own design. It really was. And it was a success. He had doubted its appeal, but his friends were very interested in it.

No, not friends. They weren't. They couldn't be. Masters. They were masters. They had gotten him in their grip and encouraged him and stroked his ego until he would do whatever they wished. And he had.

He had.

His vision blurred as saltwater brimmed his eyelids and spilled to run down his cheeks. Drops landed in the aquarium, splashed, and marked the front of his shirt with further droplets. His breathing grew deeper and more ragged.

Emily, he thought, had brought that cop, that Fischer, to the lab. They had conspired to spoil his dreams of fame and wealth long before he had done anything himself. He had not known it then, but when his masters told him what to do, they had been giving him the opportunity for justice. He wished he had succeeded. Then the cop would have vanished. He thought of Gelarean's house. And he would now be safe and looking forward to a mansion of his own.

He could, he knew, escape, even at this late moment. Even if his jellyfish had too few brains to offer him a tentacle. He could offer *it* a hand. He could reach into the aquarium, fondle it, let it discharge its cnidoblasts, its stingers full of heroin, into his skin. He was no addict. He wasn't used to the narcotic. There might even be enough, if he just left his hand in the water, to take him far away, forever.

Or he could get up again, and return the aquarium to its shelf, and reassemble its pump and light. He could go into the other room, where the terrarium was, and select a snake or two. Pale and potent, full of heroin and other drugs. Or there was a nettle on the kitchen windowsill. He didn't use it, except by accident, when he was watering it and his skin brushed a leaf, but it was there.

But snakes and nettles were too much trouble. Oblivion was close enough within his reach as he sat there, the aquarium on his lap.

He stiffened and looked up. Was that the sound of a jet close overhead? The rush of air over wings arched to brake? A shadow moving swiftly past his window?

He sighed and returned his gaze to the genimal within the tank. Something had indeed landed outside his building. Not hard by his door, not quite, but a little down the block. He heard the ripping sound made by a bird's—a Hawk's—claws as it walked on turf, the clap of the vehicle's closing door, voices with familiar rings, footsteps on the walk outside.

He raised a hand and stared at it as if he had never seen it before. He turned it back and forth, noting the soft brownness of the skin, the wrinkled folds that let the skin slide and stretch over the knuckles, the nails, the hairs, the lines. In a moment . . .

The voices had stopped. The lobby buzzer sounded. There was silence, and then there were footsteps on the stairs, drawing nearer.

The footsteps stopped. He stared at the aquarium and his jellyfish. He felt for the first time the coolness of the water that had soaked his lap.

His doorbell rang, and his hand, that marvelous structure of sliding tendons and folding bones and stretching skin, his hand began to tremble.

"Ralph?" It was Emily. And with her . . .

He sighed. He lowered his hand into the water.

Chapter
Twenty-One

EMILY HAD NEVER been in a Hawk before, but the layout of the pilot's pod did not surprise her except in one thing. The clear bubble of the pod itself she had been able to see from the outside, and the single pilot's seat within it. The control panel was clearly a control panel, though it had a few knobs and buttons that the Tortoise lacked. But when Bernie had said a Hawk could carry two people, or even more if they were not large, she had expected to find a small seat or bench beside his own.

But there was no room for such a thing. The pod was narrower than she had thought, and the passenger seat was a tiny shelf in the narrow space behind the pilot. "That's it," he said when she saw it for the first time. She was hesitating, wondering whether she really wanted to go with him while he chased down Chowdhury. But the hesitation was only brief. She squeezed into the niche, folded herself as comfortably as possible, and said, "Let's go."

The Hawk was clearly designed to function best with only one aboard. It spread its wings, the engine roared, and it lifted from the Neoform parking lot. But its takeoff was not the elegant, assertive leap into the sky she had watched before. With her aboard, the small jet was slower, struggling, lifting off the pavement and climbing at a shallow angle like some ancient mechanical airplane straining to escape the bonds of gravity.

Like that ancient airplane, once aloft the Hawk had no trouble. She peered through the sides of the pod, past the arch of wing, or she knelt to look over Bernie's shoulder and see ahead. When her breath ruffled his hair, and his scent rose to her nostrils and the tears to her eyes, he took a hand from the control yoke and pointed. "There's the airport." The Hawk banked and swept toward an expanse of foliage and bioform houses subdivided by green roadways. "Greenacres." She settled back on her jumpseat and quietly, hoping that he would not look in his rearview mirror and notice, wiped her eyes. She had made her decision, and it was the right decision, but scent was famous for its power to evoke memories. And it *would* be nice if she could have her cake and eat it too, at least for a while.

Her eyes dry, she peered again out the window. Greenacres was still visible to the left. They were descending toward a nearby neighborhood, older, filled with brick walkups, though its roadways were turfed, not paved. Gaps between the trees that flanked the roadways revealed concrete sidewalks.

"I think this is the block we want." The engine fell quiet. The wings cupped to seize the air and brake. The Hawk plummeted toward the ground, brushing the leaves of oaks and maples and elms and making them fly in swirling gusts. It touched the turf and ran a few steps. "There." Bernie made it walk forward half a block before he pulled it to the curb that still marked the edge of the roadway and pushed at a recessed toggle switch. The bird bent its neck until it could tuck its head beneath the feathers of one wing. The movement hesitated when one great eye was even with them, blinking, staring as if reproachfully. "That will keep it out of trouble."

Bernie held the pod's hatch while Emily squeezed out of her niche and jumped to the ground. Then he slammed it shut, and they looked at the three-story building before them. It was an old building, built of yellow brick and sandblasted until it glowed, though the grime of many decades remained visible in its cracks and pores. Its windows and doorways were framed with limestone; its woodwork had fairly recently been painted a rich, dark brown. The windows themselves were closed to keep out the growing heat of the day and keep in the cool of air-conditioning. Thick draperies concealed the rooms behind the glass wherever they could see.

The mixed aromas of genimal manures wafted from the alleys
that flanked the building to either side. It seemed obvious
that behind the building, in its basement or at least quite
nearby, were stables for the use of the tenants.

"This is not," said Bernie, "a poor neighborhood."

"It's not a rich one either," said Emily. She did not know
why she felt impelled to defend Chowdhury against that hint
of ill-gotten gains. She did not like him, and he had tried to
kill her, after all. Was she really defending Neoform, her
company? Or was it simply truth? The neighborhood was
indeed a middle-class neighborhood, if a little toward the
upper crust of the loaf.

"Let's see if he's home." Bernie led the way into the
building's entry. The inner door, just past a tier of mailboxes,
was glass. Beside it was a speaker and a row of buttons, each
one marked with a resident's name. He pressed the one for
Chowdhury.

There was no answer.

He tried another, and then another and another, until finally the speaker burst scratchily into a "Yes?"

"Police. Buzz us in, please."

"Just a minute." They heard a door close upstairs, and in
a moment a woman—her hair short, grey, and unbrushed; her
face round and wrinkled; her body wrapped in a faded bathrobe—appeared on the stairs inside. Bernie held up his wallet, with its badge exposed, in one hand. In the other, he
displayed the warrant he had brought. The woman nodded
and came the rest of the way to the door. "You can't be too
careful," she said as she unlatched the door. "Who are you
after?"

"Thank you," Bernie said as he pocketed his wallet again.
He ignored the question.

Emily glanced at the name list by the door. The helpful
woman was apparently Mrs. Jasper, she looked retired, and
she was obviously curious. Emily shrugged at her and followed Bernie up two flights of stairs and down a short hall.
The doors she passed were painted in bright primary colors. The
walls and carpets were more subdued in beige and brown.

Emily stopped when she came to a door painted bright

yellow. It bore both a knocker and a peephole, and Bernie
was pressing a button that jutted from the wood of the door's
frame. She could hear the doorbell's buzz within Chowdhury's apartment.

When there was no response, and no sound of movement
from behind the door, Emily called, loudly enough to be
heard within, ''Ralph?'' They waited a moment, and then
Emily was startled by the clearing of a throat close behind
her. She turned, and Mrs. Jasper said, ''He's home. I saw
him come in just a little while ago.''

She backed up abruptly when Bernie motioned for the two
women to get out of his way. Then he drew his gun, stepped
back, raised one leg, and delivered a heavy kick to the door
beside the latch.

The only result was a dark imprint of his shoe sole on the
yellow paint. He might as well have kicked a cement wall.
''Goddam steel doors.'' He tried again, harder, and again.
On the fifth try, the wood of the frame gave way and the door
popped open, only to reveal the chain of a security lock. A
sixth kick tore that loose, left Bernie panting, and let them
in.

Bernie went first, the gun still in his hand. From behind
him, Emily sniffed curry and seawater, saw bead curtains
over the windows and grinning demons on the walls, and
heard . . . nothing. Silence. Broken only by . . .

A heavy armchair faced one corner of the room so that
whoever sat in it could see both the wall on which the demon
prints hung and a bookcase to the left. The bookcase carried
photos, books, a small radio, and knickknacks. Irrelevantly,
Emily thought the veedo must be in the bedroom.

''There they are.'' Bernie's voice held a distinct note of
satisfaction. His gun was pointing at a table to the right. On
that table lay Chowdhury's glasses, one lens fallen from the
frame. He must, thought Emily, have set them down hard.
Beside them was the disk-case Chowdhury had been carrying
when he fled the lab. Presumably, she thought as Bernie took
one long step to seize it, it held evidence.

On the floor at the foot of the bookcase was a tangle of
tubing and apparatus that looked to Emily as if it had come

from an aquarium. From the chair came the only sounds that broke the silence: the intermittent sough of breath, quietly hoarse, growing quieter.

"What has Mr. Chowdhury done?" Mrs. Jasper tapped Emily on the shoulder. Emily looked at her, wrinkled her nose at the stale, sour scent of a bathrobe—or a body—that needed washing, and stepped into the apartment. She said, "Excuse me," and closed the door. Then, remembering the now-broken latch, she leaned back against it. Bernie glanced at her, grinned mirthlessly, and stepped around the chair.

"Shit!"

Emily promptly left her post to see what he had found: Chowdhury, head back against the cushions of the chair, mouth open, breath now losing its struggle for life, an aquarium on his lap, one hand in the aquarium. Bernie lifted the hand from the water. It was clenched on and covered by a gelatinous mass of pastel blue and pink.

There was a shriek behind them. He turned and pointed his gun at Mrs. Jasper, who had seized her opportunity to see what was going on. "Out!"

She fled. Bernie turned back to Chowdhury and used the muzzle of his gun to pry the fingers open and scrape the jellyfish away from the human flesh. "Call the department," he told Emily. He recited the number. "Tell 'em we need medics. A heroin overdose."

"I made them," he was saying. His eyes were shut, and his face was beaded with droplets of sweat. He had to strain to speak, and his voice was hoarse. "Yes, I made them. They're mine. Mine. I made them. I'm a genius. They said so. They're mine!"

Siren wailing, the pair of medics, one male, one female, had arrived before Chowdhury's breath could gutter out. The younger medic had dashed up the stairs, a hypodermic in her hand, checked the signs, heard Bernie's report of what the jellyfish had been designed to produce, and administered the antidote. Then, when Chowdhury had begun to gasp and spasm, she had said, nodding, "He'll make it," and gone to help her partner. Now they stood aside, their equipment—

stretcher, defibrillator, blood dialyser, IV stands and bottles, drugs, all that they might need—stacked in cases beside their feet.

Bernie had read Chowdhury his rights as soon as the dark-skinned man could respond to his name. Emily wondered whether he was in any state of mind to know what was going on, but there were witnesses to say that the formalities had been observed. She forced back tears of automatic, involun-tary sympathy and told herself that, yes, he was a genius, she had said so herself, but . . .

"Why did you make them?" Bernie had produced a small recorder from a pocket as soon as Chowdhury could talk. Now he held the machine close to the man's lips, its micro-phone grill ready to capture whatever might emerge.

"I had to."

"Why?"

"Shoulda know' better." The voice tailed off, and the older, senior medic leaned forward, ready to intervene. But it strengthened again. "Owed 'em money. Lost 'tall."

"How?" Bernie's voice turned sympathetic.

"Gam'ling." His voice slurred, and his chin fell forward onto his chest. Bernie gestured urgently, and the medic promptly slipped a needle into Chowdhury's arm. He gasped as the drug took hold, and Bernie said, "Gambling?"

Chowdhury gasped again. "They said, nettles . . . would pay it all. But then . . . wanted gen'als."

Genimals. Once, Bernie thought, that slurred word would have referred to the threat of agonizing torture. He nodded. "Why were you trying to kill Dr. Gilman?"

There was a long pause. Chowdhury twisted in his seat. His face contorted. Then, "S white. Made funna, Armadons. But . . . wasn't my idea."

"Whose idea was it?"

He opened his eyes. When Emily and Bernie had first seen him that morning, they had been wide with panic. Now the pupils were contracted to pinpoints. The whites showed in a ring all around the brown irises. He stared at Bernie, looked past him to Emily, and then to the medics. He groaned, shiv-ering. "Assassin," he whispered. "Mack. Tortoise." He looked back at Bernie. "Hawk. Wanted get rid of you. 'Fraid you'd get me." He paused. "Not Sparrow. He did that."

"Who?"

"Baas. My boss. Gave me . . . chips." The voice weakened again, and Emily laid a hand on Bernie's arm. "Can't this wait until he's fully conscious? There's no rush, is there?"

He shrugged the shoulder above her hand, as if to shake her off. He turned his head to meet her gaze. "Whoever it is could get away. Or destroy evidence. Or try again, and this time he might be more successful. I wouldn't want that."

He aimed his attention at Chowdhury once more, and Emily felt her skin turn pink with embarrassment, or shame. She had rejected him as too cruel, too hawkish, in favor of her meeker husband. She had not, perhaps, truly realized that there was a place for such personalities. And this was it. Only ruthless determination could possibly pry the truth from her erstwhile colleague, so nearly comatose, so nearly dead. If Bernie failed, then whoever was behind Chowdhury would indeed be free to try again. And next time she, Emily, might not survive. She shuddered at the thought.

"Who is he?"

"Had to ask for Hawk. Rest were . . . his idea."

"Who is your boss?" Bernie's voice was louder, more insistent, as if he hoped to break through whatever resistance might be keeping the name concealed.

Chowdhury's grin was a death's-head rictus. "Knew 'bout debts. Drugs. Gave me orders."

"Who is he?"

The grin faded as Chowdhury's eyes dropped closed. He was still breathing, but when Bernie gestured for another injection, the medic refused. "He's had it, Fischer. Save it for later."

"Shit."

Chapter
Twenty-Two

BERNIE AND EMILY stood on the walk, watching the two medics maneuver Chowdhury, on the stretcher, through the building's doorway and into the Pigeon ambulance. The window of one second-story apartment was open now, its drapes pushed back to let Mrs. Jasper lean out, elbows on the sill, mouth half open in fascination. No one peered from the building's other apartments, presumably because their tenants were at work, but small knots of gawking passersby had clustered near the mouths of the alleys to the stables.

"So who's the boss?" Bernie's expression was a dissatisfied frown. Chowdhury had admitted that he was behind every case of sabotage except that of the Sparrow, though only under the duress of blackmail. Bernie recognized that the technique was classic, and that Chowdhury, if he could be believed, thus had some extenuation, some excuse, for what he had done. Bernie did believe him. Chowdhury had been near death and, once revived, barely able to speak at all. But he had spoken, and with a convincing air of sincerity.

So perhaps Chowdhury had been as much a victim as anyone. That did not, could not, mean that the man would not stand trial. He remained responsible for what he had done, for whatever reason, whatever the consequences of refusing. Though the mystery boss's crimes had been far greater. He—or she—had impelled Chowdhury, and had personally, directly caused all the many deaths of the Sparrow incident. Chowdhury had only destroyed two aircraft, one of them police department property, and killed, with the sabotaged

Mack, far too many bystanders. Bernie snorted. Chowdhury was hardly an innocent. "Florin?"

When Emily asked, "Who's Florin?" he took a moment to explain. "He was at the party. Pink tux. Looked very self-important. And was talking to our man there." He gestured toward Chowdhury, whose feet were now disappearing into the ambulance pod. She nodded, and he added, "Runs a casino. God knows what else. Probably drugs, now."

The medics finished securing the gurney, climbed into the front of the ambulance pod, fired their twin jet engines, and boosted quickly into the air. Their siren was silent, for the emergency was over. Chowdhury was no longer in medical danger, and there was no need to rush to get him to the cell that would hold him until a lawyer could pry him loose, or failing that, until his trial.

When the Pigeon was out of sight, Emily said, "There's another possibility."

"What?"

"He has a real boss, you know. Who was also at the party."

Bernie was still for a moment, thinking of locked doors, another Greenacres address, greenery once glimpsed behind a window, something Emily had told him before, that very morning, and the smell of money. "I'll need another warrant."

"So get one."

Within an hour, the Hawk had landed again at the Neoform lot and Bernie was telling Miss Carol that he needed to see Gelarean. The receptionist looked at Emily, who nodded and said, "Yes, we caught Ralph."

Miss Carol's eyes widened. "And he told you someone else was involved? Was it . . . ?"

"Miss Carol!" Bernie's voice was firm.

"Well!" She pursed her lips. "I *am* sorry. He's not here."

"Where is he?" asked Emily.

"He went home right after you left before. When you were chasing Ralph. He said he didn't feel very good. I offered him an aspirin, but . . ."

She had lost her audience. Bernie had turned and begun to run for the door and the Hawk as soon as she said Gelarean had gone home. Emily was right behind him, and minutes later they were in the air over Greenacres.

"There's his place." Bernie didn't bother to point. The upturned shape of the gengineered squash was unmistakable.

The Hawk swept closer, and the dome of Gelarean's tower study became distinguishable, the broad expanse of glass, the green of the plants he grew there, the brown smudge that must be his desk. Closer yet, and that smudge was indeed a desk, its edges overhung by plants, a chair drawn close to one edge, someone in the chair.

"That must be him." This time he pointed, and Emily, leaning over his shoulder, grunted in agreement. They drew closer, and they could make out small, white-bordered squares upon the desktop. Their centers were dark. They seemed about the size of the hands that lay beside them. "Photos," Bernie guessed. "But of what?"

As the Hawk landed on the lawn, Victoria Gelarean opened the front door to stand on the porch, her hands clasped before her and her birthmark far brighter than it had been at the party. Bernie guessed that its lividity meant that she was worried for her husband. The slacks and blouse she wore neither concealed her lumpy figure nor hid the blotch on her face as had the robe at the party. When they approached her, she said, "He told me to keep you out, but . . ." Bernie could almost read her mind: Her husband had worried her for years, now that was at an end, and locking the door would do no good at all. He wondered whether she knew just what Gelarean had been up to, or cared.

She shrugged and gestured toward the interior of her home. "He's upstairs. In the tower."

Bernie put the badge he had had ready to display back in his pocket. The search warrant he had taken the time to obtain, and now held rolled in his right hand, was less easy to dispose of. He passed it to Emily, said, "Thank you," to Gelarean's wife, and led the way into the house.

He paid no attention to the artworks on the walls or the comfortable furniture or the thick carpets that had impressed him at the party. He headed directly toward where he thought the entrance to the tower and Gelarean's den must be, letting himself be guided by Victoria Gelarean's small gestures. The entrance, when they came to it, was an ordinary-looking door at the end of a short hallway. It was, however, locked, and Victoria Gelarean did not have a key. "He keeps it to himself," she said. "He calls it his castle. This is his drawbridge." After a moment of awkward silence, she added, "It's up now."

When Bernie swore and tried to kick this door down too, as he had the one to Chowdhury's apartment, it shrugged him off. "Steel frame," he panted, drew his gun, and aimed its muzzle at the lock. The roar of the magnum was deafening in the confined space of the hall, but it was effective. As the echoes died, they saw that the door was now ajar, revealing a narrow stairway.

"He always said that was the only way anyone would break that door down."

Gun still in his hand, he peered up the stairs. Green light, the hue of forest shade on a sunny day, spilled down to meet him and announced that there were no further obstacles between him and Gelarean. He turned to look at Victoria, said quietly, "*You* stay here," and went through the door. Emily followed him.

At the head of the stairs, they became part of a tableau of classic simplicity: The room, Gelarean's den, was a ring of green in which they stood like lurking predators. Gelarean's desk sat in full sunlight, the only part of the room so illuminated, like a spotlit stage. A small oriental rug lay on the polished wooden floor to one side. Gelarean himself was a grey-haired, round-faced, beak-nosed figure, arms spread, hands flat on the empty desktop. He might have been a medieval judge at his bench, a priest at the altar, a lord about to receive tribute.

He said, "It's all up then, is it?" and Bernie thought that resignation never sounded quite so final as when it was expressed in a British accent.

He pointed his gun at the man, stepped out of the green shadows, nodded, and said, "You are under arrest." Taking the warrant from Emily, he tossed it onto the desk. Then, drawing a small and tattered card from his shirt pocket, he added, "Anything you say may be used . . ."

Gelarean heard him out expressionlessly, his eyes fixed on the cop. When Bernie was done, he shrugged and said, "So much for tradition."

Emily pointed at the desk. "What happened to the photos?"

Gelarean's eyes shifted to her, and his expression grew dark and threatening. Bernie heard the woman step backward beside him, just far enough to tell him that she felt Gelarean's glare like a blow. "You!" he said. "You must have been born under a bloody lucky star."

He shifted his attention back to Bernie. "Nothing worked, did it? And I only wanted her out of the way."

"You wanted your name on my Bioblimps. You've done that before," said Emily.

"I never had to kill for it."

"The photos?" asked Bernie.

"What photos?" He tried to pull himself closer to the desk, but Bernie was already leaning over him, pushing him back with the muzzle of his magnum, pulling open the desk's central drawer.

The photos were there, face down, scattered as if they had been swept suddenly into hiding. Bernie picked them up and threw them on the desk, face up.

They were dim, shadowed, their colors off as colors can only be in instant photos of the sort taken to commemorate important occasions. But the subject was clear: Each one showed a woman, young and black and nude; the poses varied, as did what had been done to her.

"Jasmine." Bernie's voice was barely above a whisper, hoarse and tortured. In a moment, he looked down at his hand. His knuckles had whitened where he gripped the gun. He looked past his hand, past his gun, to the shadows beneath Gelarean's chair. Gelarean had folded his feet beneath him there, as if to hide them. But Bernie could see them clearly, see how small they were, just the size of a certain bloody footprint that he still bore imprinted on his mind.

"Eee kai vai." He felt like vomiting. Deliberately, he relaxed his grip. He forced himself to put the gun back in its shoulder holster. He took a deep breath. He turned to look at the plants that filled the room and glowed in the sunlight. "Nettles," he said. "Cocaine nettles. You are a son of a bitch. I'll bet you even put that chip in the Sparrow yourself." He paused. "Care to tell us how you did it?"

The first time Bernie had met Gelarean had been when the man had so cheerfully announced that Emily had won her patent. He had struck him then as a man whose joviality was a false front, a man who concealed his true self. Now that true self shone through in a smirk of triumph, and Bernie was not happy to be proven right.

"I am," said Gelarean, "a Palestinian. And my fellows are everywhere." Bernie vaguely remembered the Palestinian diaspora from his childhood. The refugee camps had finally emptied, and their occupants had settled throughout the world. They had not, however, surrendered their hatred of Israel, or of its allies. "It was not hard to gain access to the Sparrow," he added, and his smirk became once more a glare. "I thought I left no traces. But then you appeared, pretending to be sniffing after Dr. Gilman." He shrugged. "I delegated the next attempts."

"To Chowdhury. Why him?"

"He was in debt to my wife's cousin. And he was already making . . ." A gesture indicated the nettles and drew Bernie's attention to a single fish tank on the far side of the room. It held three snakes, larger ones than those in Chowdhury's lab.

"He was . . ." He hesitated as if he were searching for the right word. "Vulnerable. Biddable. He would do what I told him to do."

Emily made a disgusted noise. "And you had already told him to make those drug . . ."

He shook his head. "I was not involved with the nettles. The genimals, yes."

He glanced toward the fish tank and the snakes and began to sidle out from behind the desk. Bernie stopped him with one upraised hand. "But why? And how did the girl come in?"

Gelarean's open hands moved up and out. "It was good business for the family. But . . ." Gelarean's tone remained as reasonable as ever, but now his forehead wrinkled and his eyes widened in the intent stare of the fanatic. "The country deserved it. It's always been the Great Satan, the stronghold of Zionism. If it had virtue, if it knew and followed Allah, there would be no problem. It would not be the enemy of all Palestinians, and there would be no market for the drugs."

"But we're not Moslems," said Emily. "We don't know Allah. We have no virtue. And that makes us fair game."

He nodded earnestly, as if pleased that she understood him so well.

"You're raving."

"Let's go," said Bernie.

Chapter
Twenty-Three

THE CASE WAS not quite closed. Bernie had the villains, one in a hospital bed, the other in a cell, and he had many of the answers. But he did not have them all, and he knew that Gelarean's lawyers would be trying to pry him loose as quickly as possible. The weekend therefore gave him little rest. He had to interrogate his catches more thoroughly, turn his ferrets loose in Gelarean's computers, survey Chowdhury's disks, question Victoria Gelarean, and try to find Greg Florin. Unfortunately, though the disks held clear evidence of his involvement, Florin had dropped out of sight. He was not at his casino, nor at his new project, the "farm," and his employees and associates all claimed that they knew nothing.

Bernie had no time for anything but the investigation until well into the next week. It was then that Lieutenant Napoleon Alexander, the Count, called him into his office, pursed his bright red lips, and said, "Well?" Bernie's preliminary report, its cover sheet only slightly curled, was on the desk in front of him. He looked at it and added, "I've skimmed it, but let's have the gist of it."

Bernie gave his boss his usual sloppy salute. "I remember thinking," he said. "When the call went out about the Sparrow. That it was terrorists." He shrugged. "Gelarean's Palestinian, and his records show that he's been giving them money since before he came to this country."

"You can't hang him for that," the Count said. "Randecker gives to the Irish Republican Army, but he's no terrorist."

"No, sir. But Gelarean may have done a little more. When I confronted him Friday, he bragged about his contacts. And the records say he's had guests from abroad. They may have been more active terrorists."

"So he's aided and abetted."

Bernie nodded. "That changed when Chowdhury piled up his gambling debt with Florin. As it happens, Gelarean's wife is a Campana. So he had a line into the Mob."

"If we had known that . . ."

"We might have suspected his involvement earlier, but that's all. If we could be damned for our relatives, none of us would have any hope of heaven."

He paused while Lieutenant Alexander rummaged in a drawer, found an old pipe, tucked its bit between his teeth, and muttered, "There's a little flavor left."

"Anyway, Florin pushed," Bernie continued. "He wanted something to revive the drug trade, and Chowdhury suggested the cocaine nettle. When he produced it, and it worked, that was when the word reached Gelarean. He thought of asking Chowdhury to come up with drug-producing genimals, and when he realized what a grip he had on the man, he had him install the chips, program the Assassin, and so on."

The Count shook his head. "You've done a good job, Bernie. But what's his motive? Greed for the drug money, I can understand." He patted the report on the desk before him with one hand. "Even that business about attacking the 'Great Satan.' But why did he want to kill Dr. Gilman?"

"He has a nasty habit of stealing credit whenever he can. Once her patent was through, there wasn't much point in continuing to try to kill her, but by then I was on the scene. They both thought I was after them."

"And Chowdhury panicked."

"It only has to happen once."

"And the girl? Jasmine Willison?"

Bernie made a face. He had been telling Connie everything, repeating his report to the Count, and she had asked precisely the question their boss had asked toward the end. He wished

there were a better answer than the one he had: He had had
then to shrug and say, "For a while, I thought that would
turn out to be Chowdhury. But it was Gelarean, though he
won't talk about that. He's guilty, he admits it, and the photos
in his desk are quite enough proof of his guilt. But why? He's
nuts. All fanatics are nuts, and too many of them are nuts
about blood." Now all he could do was repeat the words.

They were in Connie's small living room, side by side on
a couch that was little more than a pad of foam rubber covered with soft, loosely woven fabric. An internal frame let it
be bent to hold various configurations. Its back was a line of
colorful pillows leaned against the wall. A bolster covered in
purple shag served them as a hassock. To one side, a low
table of zebra wood and slate held their empty coffee cups.

The rest of the room was no more elaborate. A ceiling
fixture threw spots of light onto one end of the couch, three
metallic photos upon the wall, a veedo unit with slots for
tapes and disks. A goldfish bush sat by the window, where
light could hit the leaves; two colorful fruit, nearly ripe,
wriggled on their stems above a bowl of water. A third had
already fallen into the bowl, where it swam about as if it had
always been a fish. On the floor near the plant's pot lay the
feather Connie had retrieved from the dead Hawk.

"Or damage, anyway," she said. She flipped a pillow flat
on the end of the couch and stretched out. Her bare foot
poked at his knee. He captured it in a large hand and kneaded
the toes. "Wasn't that why he wanted the drug genimals?
And why he didn't simply take an axe to Emily?"

"Yeah." Bernie sighed. "He liked gore, didn't he? Emily
didn't."

Her toes curled around his thumb. "You do too."

"Even if it makes me throw up?"

"In a way. And so do I. That's why we're cops."

"Two of a kind," he said.

"Predators. Hawks."

"But not wild. Not wolves." He meant, he thought, that
they did not prey upon society. They were domesticated, and
they served society, as dogs did the sheep and shepherd. Perhaps, for all that he liked to compare himself to a Hawk, he

was not a hawk. Yes, hawks were as domesticated as dogs, but they were hunters, fighters, not protectors, guardians. If he were truly a hawk, he would have to join the army. But that did not appeal to him at all. He was a cop.

He sighed. He wished it really mattered to anyone but the girl's family and friends why Gelarean had done to her what he had done. But whatever the reason, the man would spend many years in prison. The Sparrow alone was enough to guarantee that. And when he got out, he would surely be deported. He would be no problem ever again for this society. Sadly, there was no shortage of people like him. There never had been. There never would be.

Some things never changed.

With a wiggle of her toes and a shift in position of her foot, Connie changed the subject. "And now she's done with you?"

He nodded. "You were right. At least, we had our fling. And now she's gone back to her husband."

"I thought that might . . ."

He let his hand slide up her calf. "You going to leave me too?"

"No husband to go back to."

He hesitated, letting his eyes search her face. "We could change that."

Now it was her turn to hesitate, and he thought that she must be as used as he to the single life, perhaps as reluctant to let it change. But . . . "Was that a proposal?" she asked. Her voice had a small crack in it.

He looked away. "I suppose it was."

Later, they mounted the dead Hawk's feather on the wall above the couch.

Chapter
Twenty-Four

WHERE BERNIE HAD spent the weekend in a frenzy of investigation, Emily had spent it feeling frustrated and bored. The threat that had been hanging over her was gone, but so were the suspense and excitement that had accompanied that threat. She felt let down, disappointed. There would be no more Sparrows landing on the freeway to gobble her up, no more Assassins in the trees, no more Mack trucks lunging out of traffic to run her down, no more runaway Tortoises. Nor would there be handsome policemen to sweep her off her feet. The romance was gone from her life.

Truly, she knew it, Nick was the man she wanted. Gentle, supportive, reliable, the father of her child, the cradle of her heart. But, for all that she had told Bernie to keep his distance . . .

He had been efficient, smooth, and capable. She had told him he was cruel, and he had agreed. If she had thought to wonder, she would have expected him to show a grand ferocity when he confronted Chowdhury, and then Gelarean. But there had been none of that. He had only been strong and direct and to the point. He was a defender, not an attacker, not a despoiler. He was less gentle than Nick, but he too was supportive, in his way, and reliable.

Halfway through Saturday afternoon, she found herself wondering how much damage her marriage had sustained. Nick was forgiving, yes, but she *had* briefly foresworn her loyalty to him, if not her love, and he knew it. It had to make a difference, and a difference that she would have to struggle to overcome. Not that Nick would keep reminding her, or that his feelings would be lessened by the memory. He was too forgiving for that. But she, she carried the guilt, and she would have to exorcise that burden.

She was pacing back and forth in the living room, her voice echoing within her skull, when Andy tugged at her jeans and cried, "Mommy!"

She bent to him, suddenly aware that she had been ignoring persistent demands for attention, and said, "Yes, dear?"

"My Warbird went under the couch. Get it for me?"

She obeyed, but when Andy followed up that demand with a request for a story, she said, "I think it's about time I baked us some bread. Want to watch?"

"I wanta help!"

"Just watch, until you're bigger." Nick was assembling the ingredients for a cake, but she chased her husband from the counter of "his" kitchen to the table and dove into her occasional specialty. It was also her therapy, for she had long since learned that pounding bread dough into submission could quiet her mind even when her thoughts churned so vigorously that she could concentrate on nothing else.

But her thoughts refused this time to quiet. Instead, they jumped their track. How much had she contributed to the final roundup? She had identified Chowdhury's "boss," but surely only seconds before Bernie would have seen it himself. She had made a phone call. She had . . . What else? She had given Bernie someone to talk to, and that was all. She hoped she gave Nick something more.

On Sunday, she and Nick took Andy to the zoo to see the unmodified ancestral stock of the genimals he knew so well from the veedo and the airport and the highway. In the reptile house, a python was basking in the sun; on the wall beside its cage, a board displayed the skin it had recently shed. "Look at that," said Emily. "See the scales that covered the eyes?"

"They're like windows!" cried Andy.

"They make me wonder if we could make a house, or a car, or a train, from a snake. The windows would be built in, *grown* in, and . . ."

"Your next project?" asked Nick.

She shrugged and grinned. "Maybe, come to think of it. It would be easy enough to enlarge those scales and make them repeat along the body. It would be trickier to transplant the genes into a pumpkin, or Roachster." Or an Armadon, she thought, and she wondered what would come of that project now that Chowdhury was out of circulation.

She did not get an answer to her question right away. Neoform had lost not only one of its chief researchers and product developers, but also its research director, and on Monday, no one knew what would happen next. She and Alan Bryant were in their domed fabric "barn" that afternoon, checking on the growth of the Bioblimps, when Alan said, "Do you think they'll make you the new chief?"

She shook her head. "I'm not political enough. And I wouldn't want the job if I were." She gestured past the net that closed off most of the dome's interior space, forming a huge cage in which young moving vans rose and fell above a long food trough. Their bells swelled and contracted, propelling them about their space, in and out of the zones of blue and gold illumination defined by the dome's panels, in a way that would not be allowed once they reached full size, when strapped-on control pods would cover their mouths, all except a narrow opening for their breathing. Their tentacles writhed as they plucked chunks of unidentifiable meat from the trough and inserted them into the stomachs within the bells. The sphincters that controlled the openings to their cargo holds alternately gaped and puckered. Each van bore a stylized sailing ship on the side of its gasbag. "They'll be too big for this place soon. We'll have to take them outside and tether them."

"You would if you were political," said her aide. Then he shook his head. "We won't need to tether them. Their nervous systems are so rudimentary that we've had some problems designing the control circuitry, but it's almost ready now."

"Tether them anyway. If the controls have been that tricky,

something's bound to go wrong. And we don't want them wandering off and eating pedestrians.''

Alan began to laugh, looked sidelong at her, and let it die. The image had been a funny one, straight out of ancient monster movies, but it did, he quickly realized, come a little close to home for his boss. "Have you heard anything about Chowdhury's lab?''

''Not a thing. I think they're pretending he's taking a little sabbatical. Business as usual for now.''

The pretense lasted until Wednesday. That morning, when Emily reached her lab, Alan was holding a piece of paper. As she entered the room, he handed it to her. She stopped, leaned against a bench, and read:

TO: All Employees
FROM: T. Gruene, Personnel
RE: Supervisory changes

We have recently lost one of this company's three founders, Director of Research Dr. Sean Gelarean, and a valued employee, Dr. Ralph Chowdhury, Senior Researcher in Product Development.

We will shortly advertise for a new Director of Research. Until the results of our search for a replacement are in, Dr. Gelarean's post will remain vacant. All reports and requests for travel funds, supplies, and project approvals should be routed to Dr. Atkinson.

Dr. Chowdhury's position will be filled by Dr. Adam Chand. Until now, Dr. Chand has been a research assistant in Dr. Chowdhury's lab.

"It doesn't say a word about why we lost those 'two valued employees,' '' said Emily. ''But that's good. In fact, Wilma might make a good replacement for Sean. And Adam . . .''

''He'll do fine,'' said Alan.

Something in his tone made Emily think that he too would like to be a lab chief, but she did not respond. Instead, she handed the memo back to him and said, "Better change that routing in the computer."

A little later, crashing sounds, as of furniture breaking, drew her down the hall toward Chowdhury's—now Chand's—lab. There she joined a number of her colleagues as they watched, bemused, while Sam Dong and Micaela Potonegra expelled Chowdhury's chosen furniture, so obviously high, ungainly, and uncomfortable, from the lab, and Chand told a pair of maintenance men, "Out! Get us some decent furniture. But get this stuff out of here!" He sounded exasperated, but there was a strange smile on his face. Emily thought it must signify a sense of triumph and relief, uncertainty and determination.

"But, Dr. Chand," one of the maintenance crew protested. "It takes weeks for an order to come through."

"Then bring in the furniture from the other lab, in the barn. We'll do all our work in here, until the new things come and you install *them* in the barn."

"Uh, we could shorten the legs on some of these . . ."

"Then do it. In the barn. Get it out of here!"

"Yessir!"

Chand's face did not lose its strained mixture of expressions as he turned his attention on the spectators. "The show's over," he said. "We've got work to do." Then, as he seemed to notice Emily for the first time, he added, "Emily! Come on in!" and jerked his head toward the lab behind him.

She followed him in, to find Sam and Micaela pausing in their labors to stare at her, smiling almost as if she belonged with them. Perhaps, she thought, she did, for though they had borne the daily brunt of Chowdhury's temper, she had been the one he had been trying to kill. "Adam," she said. "Congratulations."

"And now what?" he said. Suddenly the uncertainty was uppermost in his expression.

Emily looked around the room. The equipment—workstations, DNA splicers, and more—was now concentrated on a single workbench and the tops of the lab's freezers and incubators. "You'll do your own thing," she said. She pointed at the puffer fish hanging from the ceiling. "What's that?"

Chand's face lit up. "Well, sure," he said. "I was planning to . . ." Then her question penetrated, and he followed her finger with his gaze. "I've been trying to design a submarine," he added more slowly. He explained the fish and the direction of his thought, while Emily nodded encouragingly.

Micaela Potonegra interrupted: "We will be carrying on, though. The Armadon . . ." She hesitated, as if aware that the Armadons might be a sore point. They were, after all, potential competition for the company funds and energy Emily's Bioblimps would also need. They also stood, in the mind of any Neoform employee, for Chowdhury. They *were* Chowdhury, in a much more solid and positive sense than the cocaine nettle and hedonic genimals. "The Armadon prototypes will be ready for testing soon, and we do want to see them into production. We've already put a lot of work into them, you know."

Emily did know. They had done most of Chowdhury's design work, and all of the donkey work of feeding and cleaning and testing, just as Alan Bryant did for her. In a very real sense, the Armadons were as much their babies as they were Chowdhury's. But they had been Chowdhury's idea, and he would get the credit, even if he must enjoy it in a prison cell.

Micaela pointed toward the back of the room. "We still have those four in here." Emily looked and saw the cage on the floor, crowded with the baby Armadons she had first seen just the week before. "And they can't stay in that cage any longer. They can hardly move."

Nodding that Micaela was speaking for them all, Adam Chand said, "Would you like one? It'll grow, you know, and when it's big enough, we can have the prototype shop fit it out. That won't cost you anything."

Emily looked back at three expectant faces. Did they feel that they owed this to her, as recompense for what Chowdhury had done, or tried to do? Then how could she say no? And besides—the thought came to her mind for the first time in weeks—her family did need a second vehicle. Let this one grow up, and it would be perfect for Nick, though they would have to enlarge the garage. And he would be delighted by its rarity on the road, though surely that would not last. Andy would be delighted by it now, as a novel pet and as a replacement for the Chickadee in his affections.

How could she say no?

She didn't.

She said, "Thank you."